She's Marrying
My Man II

Dominique Lewis

Don't let anyone hold you back! Share your talents.

Enjoy!

CHAPTER 1

"I can't believe this day has finally arrived."

Laila stood in the doorway of the church, Fields of Grace, preparing to make her grand entrance. She wore a long, flowing white strapless wedding gown adorned with beautiful beaded lace and flower embroidery. Her sheer white veil was pulled over her face. She watched as everyone in the sanctuary stood and gazed at her in admiration. She focused her eyes down the aisle and saw the love of her life, Alonzo staring back at her. He was the most handsome man she had ever laid her eyes upon in her life. His smooth tanned skin, chestnut brown eyes, nicely trimmed low cut hair, muscular body, deep dimples, and that million-dollar smile, displaying perfect white teeth. He bit his bottom lip and stood proudly and confidently in his light gray tuxedo. His face brightened, and his grin grew even wider.

Standing next to her groom was the best man, Quinton Harris. Quinton nudged Alonzo, and the two did a quick handshake. Laila shook her head and smiled at them. Just to think two years ago, she

5

walked down the same aisle as the maid of honor at her friend, Melanie's wedding rehearsal with Quinton as the groom and Alonzo as the best man.

She finally reached Alonzo and stood by his side.

"Babe, you look amazing."

"You clean up pretty well yourself."

"All the time." He straightened his black lapel.

He gave her a half-smile.

The maid of honor, Alonzo's sister Aliza took Laila's bouquet. Laila saw her girls Melanie Tyler, Gia Malone, and Kecia Jones standing behind her soon-to-be sister-in-law. They were all smiles. Alonzo and Quinton's new preacher from their home church, Pastor Douglas wore a black and white robe with a gold embroidered cross in the center. He motioned for the wedding guests to be seated, and they did as he directed.

Laila noticed Alonzo gazing into the eyes of his mother, Alice on the front pew. On Laila's side, the spot for her parents was empty. Alice softly told her son, "I love you," and then, she blew a kiss at a beaming Laila.

Holding an open bible in his hand, the pastor looked around the congregation as he began to speak.

"Dearly beloved, we are gathered here today to celebrate the union of Alonzo Tyrell Davis and Laila MeAnn McKee. Now before I go any further, I would like to get this question out of the way. Is there anyone here today that has just cause as to why these two should not be united in holy matrimony?" he paused, "Speak now or forever hold your peace."

Laila's heart began to beat rapidly. They peered around the congregation, and there was silence. Laila let out a sigh of relief, looked calmly into Alonzo's eyes, and displayed a wide grin.

"I object!" A lady popped up.

With a horrified look on her face, Laila quickly turned her head towards the mystery woman.

She was a short brown-skinned, copper-haired woman in her late 20s.

"I object too," a Latino woman popped up, "She's marrying my man."

"No! That's *my* man she's marrying!"

"Your man?" a lady, who resembled Laila, popped up in the back, "No, he was with me last night."

"Alonzo, I thought you loved me," a blonde haired white woman hopped up.

Laila looked angrily at Alonzo as countless women continued to rise from their seats. His eyes grew wide, "I–"

"I have a confession," another lady stood up while holding a baby, "Alonzo is the father of my children, Carlotta, Noella, Consuela, Diego, and Alonzo, Jr." Four kids between the ages of 5 and 12 stood up next to her.

"But I'm pregnant with his baby," a Chinese woman struggled to stand. She looked about eight months pregnant.

Laila stood frozen at the altar. She tried to run out, but she couldn't move.

She heard Gia say, "Laila, say the word, and we'll beat his ass."

Kecia scoffed. "I thought his no good ass had changed."

"Kecia, what I tell you?"

"A ho gon' always be a ho."

"Umm huh," they said simultaneously.

Alonzo was shell shocked. "Laila, I can explain."

All of a sudden, the church doors flew open. A tall slender brown-skinned woman walked in. She wore a short figure fitting black dress and a black hat with an attached veil covering her face. She strutted down the aisle as if she was on a runway.

"Oh no!" Melanie said.

"Is that?" Aliza asked.

"Couldn't be!" Kecia exclaimed.

"It is!" Gia gasped.

The woman, who commanded everyone's attention, pulled off her hat and threw it in the congregation. Three old men struggled to catch it. She swung her hair back as if she was in an Herbal Essences commercial. She stood half-way down the aisle with one hand on her hip and posed. She looked to her right and then to her left.

"Stand down, bitches. He has been and will forever be *my* man." She gave all of the objectors an evil glare, and they all sat down.

"Alexandra!" Alonzo exclaimed. He grabbed the ring box from Quinton, sprinted down the aisle, and got down on one knee.

"I thought I'd never see you again, but you came for me. You've always been the one, girl. None of these women compare to you, not even Laila."

Laila's eyes filled with tears.

"Will you marry me?"

"Of course, I will!"

He grabbed her and kissed her.

Everyone in the congregation started clapping.

"Let's head to Vegas right now," he took her into his arms and carried her down the aisle. Laila was in a state of shock as he walked out of the door with his new bride-to-be in tow.

Someone started laughing maniacally. Laila slowly turned to see Melanie approaching her.

"Karma's a bitch, isn't it?" she gloated.

Everyone looked at Laila. Then, they all started laughing. Quinton and their friend, Tazmon "Taaz" Smith had joined in on the laughter. Her best friends were also killing themselves laughing.

"No, no. I didn't deserve any of this!"

She tried to run down the aisle, but tripped over her train and fell to the floor. People circled around her, pointed at her, and laughed even harder.

"No! Stop! Please Stop…No!"

Suddenly, Laila awoke in a hot sweat. She was in bed. She tried to remember where she was. Her eyes adjusted to the room. She felt someone next to her. Her heart pounded heavily. She was confused. She could not believe what had transpired over the span of 24 hours. What really happened? Did she drink the night away? Did she find solitude in another man? If so, who? Who was the man lying next to her? She slowly turned her head, and it was…

Alonzo?!

She placed her hand to her head, trying to gather her thoughts. Then, she let out a huge sigh of relief. It was only a dream.

Her heart was still pounding profusely. She eased out of the bed and walked to the mini-fridge. She pulled out a bottle of water and drank all the water without pausing. She walked slowly towards the balcony. She pulled back the sheer white curtains and slowly eased back the glass sliding door. She stepped outside. She stared out at a beautiful sunrise on a breathtaking seashore. The cool breeze and sounds of the waves crashing soothed her. She took a deep breath in and out. She closed her eyes. She began to feel cold and folded her arms. She continued to take deep breaths. Soon, she felt warmth from behind.

"Baby, what are you doing up so early?" Alonzo asked as he came close to her and wrapped his arms around her, "Are you okay?"

"Yea, I'm fine. I just…"

She thought, *don't know if you're ready to be with me. I just worry day in and day out about some other woman taking you away from me. I just can't imagine you being faithful to one woman for the rest of your life. I just…*

"…can't sleep," she finally said.

"Everything's going to be fine. You hear me?" He kissed her cheek. "We have everything in place. You saw that yesterday, right?" he asked.

She nodded.

"All we have to do now is wait."

He let her go and gently held her hand.

"Now, please come back to bed before everyone starts coming in today." He led her back into the room. "You know how they are…we might not get to see each other again until the day of our wedding."

They got back in bed.

"Yeah, you're right. This will be interesting," she murmured unenthusiastically.

"It will be great, and soon you'll be Mrs. Alonzo Davis."

She smiled as he caressed her face.

"I love you, Laila."

"I love you too."

He gently kissed her.

"Dang girl, your breath is kicking," he laughed.

She put one hand to her mouth and hit him with

the other. She was about to get up, but he grasped her arm.

"I was just playing."

She frowned.

"Come here girl," he pulled her close, attempting to kiss her.

Her voice muffled, "No, uh uh…I'm about to go brush my teeth. Move."

He tried to take her hand down. "Naw, give me that hand."

"No," Laila murmured with her hand firmly cupping her mouth.

"I'ma bite it." He got on top of her. "Okay, guess I will have to kiss something else."

He eased down her body.

"No!" she quickly pulled both of her hands under the sheets to cover herself, "You promised none of that again until our wedding night."

He grabbed her hands, placed them on either side of her, and pinned her down.

"But you didn't say I couldn't kiss on you or feel on that booty."

"Really, Alonzo?"

He chuckled, bit his bottom lip, and stared at her.

"Just to think it's going to be like this for the rest of our lives. I get to wake up every morning to this beautiful face."

"You're going to make me give in like last time."

"Shh…"

He pressed his lips against hers, then drove his tongue deep in her mouth.

CHAPTER 2

"You're not going!"

Marla said to her husband, Quinton as she tossed Alonzo and Laila's wedding invitation on their king-sized bed. They were in their bedroom at their new two-story home in Dallas.

Quinton rolled his eyes and continued to zip his bag. "Marla, we've already been through this, six months ago."

She plopped down on the bed and folded her arms. "I know, but you're traveling to a luxurious resort for an entire week. You're going to be surrounded by beautiful women, and two women you've slept with only days before our spontaneous union."

"Marla, you know I only want you. That's why you are my wife. You don't have to worry about me jeopardizing that."

"Well, I hope you won't throw us away over the bride or her maid of honor."

"Um, I highly doubt Laila's going to let Melanie be

the maid of honor." Quinton walked to the dresser and opened his top sock drawer. He paused and stared at the framed photo of his mother, Carol. The steel frame read, "If Heaven was a mile away…"

"Humph," she smirked, "Well, it would be funny if they get a déjà vu, and Alonzo ends up running off with Gallena Riley or Alexandra Reid."

She laughed to herself.

With socks in his hands, he quickly turned to her. "That's not funny, Marla," Quinton frowned. "You can't be wishing bad things on the man's wedding."

"Well, if you ask me the last two bitches is a step up from the first two bitches."

Quinton shook his head and tossed his socks in a side pocket of his bag.

"This doesn't even sound like you."

"Well, it is."

"Since you're worried about me going, why don't you come with me?"

"Ta, I don't want to be around those people."

"Shh, Taaz is downstairs."

"He knows how I feel about them." She got up and walked into their bathroom.

"It's about supporting Alonzo, and he would love for you to come. There is still time for you to pack a bag. I can get you a last-minute ticket, and you can head to the airport with us."

"Not interested." She reentered with his deodorant, placed it in his Ziploc bag of items, and stuffed it in a different side pocket.

"Well, see," he said, "you're not that worried."

"I won't be worried at all if you don't go." She turned to him.

"*Those* people, as you call them, are my family, and

I'm the best man. I can't *not* go," he said, "Marla, do you trust me?" He gazed into her eyes.

She sighed. "I do trust you, baby."

"Seriously?"

"Yes, I do."

"Come here, girl," he hugged her.

"It's those tricks I don't trust," she mumbled.

CHAPTER 3

Laila was still in bed with a snoring Alonzo by her side. It was now bright outside. She was restless. She had so many thoughts running through her mind. She picked up her journal and pen from out of her purse. She crossed her legs and began to write.

Dear Journal,

It has been a while since I've written you, and I am pretty sure this is about to be a long entry. I think the last time I wrote to you was two years ago when I was in denial about my feelings for Alonzo and holding onto the past with Quinton. Alonzo and I are still together, but a lot has changed. I was expecting Alonzo to mess things up, but he has been on his best behavior and very respectful. These past two years have been trying, but Alonzo and I have gotten through it together, and we were there as a united front to help our friends.

Quinton lost his mother, Carol. She had congestive heart failure and succumbed at the local hospital with Quinton by her side. I thought it would shatter him, but he was so strong and is still so strong. He is not as lively as he once was. He seems

15

distant at times, which has caused some friction in his relationship with Marla. It seems that they are okay now…well, until my name or Melanie's name is mentioned. Marla barely wants to be around me at any event the guys have. She has to get over it because Alonzo and Quinton are going to be around each other no matter what.

Melanie hasn't been around Quinton and Marla since she was engaged to Quinton. She moved to Atlanta and finally found a real job at a major corporation that specializes in real estate, land development, and property management. Though she is climbing the ladder pretty quickly—which has me thinking she is working another angle—she has been out of my hair for a while, which is good for me. She has been trying relationship after relationship, but none of them ever seem to stick. To avoid being the third wheel, she barely comes around us. Recently, she has been talking about a new guy at her job, and she seems pretty excited about him.

Kecia and Taaz broke up. She wanted to take their relationship further, but Taaz was not ready. He just wanted to go with flow and not worry about their future. Now, Kecia has a new man named Winston. She told me that she hasn't seen Taaz in almost a year. Taaz is always casually asking about her, but I can see it in his eyes…he is not over her. I have been so busy with Alonzo and work that I rarely see the girls anymore.

I see Gia the most, and that's when she is styling my hair or when we're having game night, well playing spades. It's usually her, me, Alonzo, Taaz, Chuck and their other guy friends, and their wives or girlfriends. David does not really come around us anymore. Gia is still single and loving it. She is doing very well for herself. She is focusing on her business, and with the help of Alonzo and Quinton, she revamped her business plan and offerings, and is in the process of renovating her shop…like a boss as she always says. She came over to my house the other day to drop off the items that her and Kecia wouldn't take on the plane. She even helped us pack them in Alonzo's vehicle.

Quinton took a promotion at his job, but wasn't happy with it. Since they did not want to lose him, they opted to move him to any branch of his choosing, and he selected Dallas.

Oh me...I am still working at the bank for Mr. Henderson. Him and his wife have been having a time too. They recently lost their daughter, Meagan to cancer, and now Mrs. Henderson's health is failing too. A few weeks ago, they called us and told us that they had a wedding surprise for us. They said they hoped they were not overstepping, but they had been saving up for Meagan's wedding day. And since their son, Brent is married, they thought it would be a good idea to give us her wedding fund. The balance was $150,000! I was completely shocked, but we had already pretty much paid for the wedding ourselves. Nevertheless, we were both ecstatic that they would do something like that for us, and Alonzo gladly accepted the money before I could come to my senses and say no.

As far as our wedding destination, we thought of going to Paris or the Bahamas, but we knew that many of Alonzo's family members, especially the older family members, would only travel in the states.

Therefore, Alonzo and I decided to just get married at a nice resort on the beach in Florida. Alonzo wanted to get us the Presidential suite, but it won't be available until the night of our wedding so we opted for a regular king room with a beach view. With our gifted money, we decided to pay for everyone's travel and rooms. Most of our confirmed invitees agreed, except for prideful Melanie, of course. However, we still booked an extra room for her in case she changed her mind. If not, one of Alonzo's cousins would take the room.

I am just still taken aback by the Hendersons' kind gesture, considering all that has transpired over the years. His poor wife is still in the dark about his infidelity with my *mother, and now he has no choice but to be by her side. She was released from the hospital three days ago, and she has strict orders to remain on bed rest, so they won't be able to attend the wedding.*

We decided that we wanted to enjoy a long vacation prior to our wedding and honeymoon. We just wanted to enjoy a week with our closest friends, but some of Alonzo's family and college buddies wanted to join in on the festivities too. Our other guests opted for a night or two night stay strictly for the wedding and reception.

I know our group of friends have always kept up trouble, but we haven't been together in so long...a week couldn't possibly hurt anything. We just want to spend time with all of them—Kecia, Gia, Quinton, Melanie, and Taaz—those are the people we care about the most. And, I am so glad that they agreed to join us and could be away from their jobs.

We planned a June wedding, so Kecia would be out of school. I really don't like the conventional June wedding. I'd much rather have a spring wedding, but we had to make sure Kecia would be able to attend. And, summer time was the answer. We had to also plan our date around the two weeks that Taaz was off. We wanted to ensure that as soon as he got on land, he could come straight to our destination and jumpstart his vacation. But he had other plans, he went to Dallas as he visits Quinton and Marla quite often. Now, they all are flying down together.

Melanie was able to take off from work. She has been pretty tight lipped about what she does, but I know that she has major pull with her boss, and a lot of time off hours saved up. Gia, our boss lady of the group, she was able to leave her business in the hands of her trusted stylist, Dedra. Since her renovations are well underway, I'm pretty sure she is going to be calling her family constantly. She even made her dad stay behind to monitor the work. Her mother, Ms. Gina wanted to come to the wedding, but she refused to come without Mr. Clyde. Kecia's mother, Ms. Patsy and her dad, Mr. Kenneth were both mad that I planned my wedding to be at the same time as Patsy's family reunion in Indiana. Gia did not want me to invite any of her brothers. The icing on the cake was Melanie's overbearing Aunt Judy. She had planned a cruise with her social club sisters. They ship out from New Orleans on the day of my wedding. I was so relieved when I heard. She would have definitely tried to take over and control every part of my happy experience. My soon-to-be mother-in-law, Ms. Alice is riding down with Alonzo's sister, Aliza on the evening before the wedding.

Notice I've never really mentioned anyone on my actual side of the family. Let's see… my father is an only child, so I don't have any aunts, uncles, or first cousins. He literally had no one, but us…maybe some family overseas, but he never really mentioned them to me. All my mother had was her baby sister, Sarah, and that's it. Wait…I never thought about it until just now, but Quinton also has an aunt named Sarah, and she's not coming either. Anyway, I invited a few distant cousins on my mother's side, and that's all. I made sure to make a "Pick a Seat, Not a Side" sign because the left side seating would be quite bare. I have some college friends and people from the bank that may come.

Alonzo, on the other hand, has a lot of family members, most of whom told him that they would be there. They want to see him get married for themselves because they all know about his ways… well old ways. His dad definitely won't be coming.

Alonzo asked me who will I get to walk me down the aisle, and I told him I wanted to walk alone and that he better let me walk all the way to the arch/altar this time unlike Melanie and Quinton's endless wedding rehearsals.

But, can you actually believe it? I'm having a wedding!

My very own wedding! I am just floored... I never thought my wedding day would come. I mean I've always dreamed of it since I was a little girl, and now it's almost here. And, I'm marrying the last man that I thought I would ever be with... A man who completes me... A man who makes me smile.

I just hate that the bad dreams and negative thoughts keep creeping in that make me question his loyalty, but I will push through, and the next time you hear from me, I'll be Mrs. Davis! :-)

-Yours truly,

Laila

CHAPTER 4

Laila and Alonzo were standing in the hotel lobby.

"Are you ready?"

"Can't be more ready than I am now," Laila said unconvincingly. He put his arm around her.

"Everything is going to be fine."

The automatic sliding glass doors opened. Laila's eyes grew wide as they waited on their guests to arrive. Her heart began to pang. It was only a couple, and their two kids entering.

Laila felt a sharp pain in her stomach. The last time the entire gang were all in the same room was when they were rehearsing for Quinton and Melanie's wedding. And, they all remembered what disaster that ended up being. Each of them had been through so much since then and are still going through changes, trying to adjust to their new lives. And now added into the mix...Marla Gomillion-Harris. Laila was not looking forward to seeing her.

Okay. Laila, you're overthinking. Everyone will behave. Dang, who I am kidding? They NEVER *behave, not in grade school and definitely not now.*

Alonzo welcomed some of his guests, and Laila greeted and hugged them. He walked with them to the front desk. She stared at him and smiled.

Since they had gotten engaged on Quinton and Marla's wedding day, Alonzo and Laila had been taking out the time to date one another. They wanted to make sure not to hop into marriage too quickly. Throughout the years, their bond strengthened. Once they knew they were ready, they set the wedding date and informed the entire gang.

Carrying her totes and pulling her luggage, Gia entered the glass doors.

"Hey girl." Her hair was in long mini Senegalese twists. She wore a blue jersey dress and brown sandals.

"I'm glad you made it safely."

"Oh, I love your new hairstyle," Gia said. She smoothed Laila's blown out hair.

"Thank you," Laila smiled.

"I am damn good at what I do," Gia said. "You kept it up pretty well. You must ain't made it to the beach yet."

"No, we haven't."

"Ohh, well I'm surprised you ain't sweat it out with Lonzo."

"Really, Gia?"

Gia smirked and looked around, "How y'all gon have a pre-honeymoon, then a vacation with all of us, wedding, reception, and then a honeymoon."

"Because we've got it like that," Laila smiled, "but anyway Alonzo and I came up early to make sure everything was set."

"Set? But y'all are gettin' married in seven days though. Ain't nothing set this early," Gia said,

"Unless they ain't been selling banquet space worth a damn. Cuz my cousin, Lonnie be booking venues like crazy at the casino, and they be flipping rooms for different events quick, fast, and in a hurry."

Laila sighed.

"I'm just saying, but that ain't my business."

"Have you talked to Kecia?"

"Yea, she's gonna catch a later flight. It's hard to tear her away from her new man, Winston."

"Aw, I haven't met him yet. Shoot, it feels like months since I've seen her."

"Oh, it has," Gia smiled.

"What?"

"Oh, nothing."

"You think things are going to be awkward between her and Taaz?"

"Maybe... maybe not. Who knows."

"He seemed okay the last time I saw him."

"Oh, he's more than okay. That fool busted my name out at Wal-Mart week before last. I just kept walking like I didn't hear his country ass."

Laila shook her head.

"Um," she admired some guys walking by. "I see some hot ones already. Oh, I'ma have me some fun this week."

"I'm sure you are."

"I'm single and sholl as hell gon' mingle."

"You'll be able to find someone here that's just your type."

"Too bad I won't be able to take 'em home with me."

"You never know."

Gia pursed her lips.

"Come... let's get you checked in."

They headed towards the front desk.

"So has *Bitch* made it yet?"

"No," Laila smirked, "Melanie and her man are on a flight right now as we speak."

"Uh, I am so glad that bitch moved to Atlanta and got her a real job cuz she got on my nerves the first few months she came back."

"Tell me about it."

"And what pitiful guy has she trapped this time?"

CHAPTER 5

On an airplane, Melanie walked down the aisle and sat next to a handsome guy. She leaned back in her seat and looked at her light brown, bald-headed muscular companion.

"Isn't this going to be a lovely trip, darling?"

He smiled and leaned forward. "So let me get this straight. Your best girlfriend is getting married to your ex-fiancé's friend who is your cousin, but she slept with your ex-fiancé when she was your maid of honor and ruined your wedding. Now she's the bride, you're a bridesmaid, and your ex-fiancé is the best man?"

She took a swig of her soda.

"Yep, that's correct."

"If this isn't the soaps, *Love & Hip Hop,* and *Real Housewives* packed all into one," he shook his head, "And you waited to tell me just now because?"

"I didn't want to risk you not agreeing to come," she said, "I know how much you try to avoid drama."

"Well, why wouldn't I come? You gave me an offer I could not refuse," he bit his lip.

"Well, my offers can be quite enticing," she said.

"Yea, I bet."

"I just want you to be on your best behavior when we get there."

"We'll see about that," he said.

"Julian, I'm serious or you can forget about…" She looked around to see if anyone was listening, then she whispered in his ear.

"Now, why would I do anything to jeopardize getting that," he licked his lips.

She shook her head and smiled.

"But I can't wrap my head around why you're still friends with this woman?"

"See…this is exactly why I didn't tell you to avoid this Q&A session."

"Well, it's a valid question," he said, "We're here now in the friendly skies. There's no escape, and you've gone through a lot of trouble to get here so you must have forgiven her. Haven't you?"

"Well…I'm…uhh."

"Or are you plotting something for this wedding? Do you have some dirty tricks up your sleeve?"

"Why whatever do you mean?"

He smirked, "Come on answer the original question. Have you forgiven Laila?"

"Uhh."

"It's a yes or no answer."

"Uhh…I don't know. Okay? We just all have this weird kind of dysfunctional relationship with one another. I guess you could call it a Love-Hate relationship. People may not understand it, but it has always worked for us. All four of us."

"Four? Who are the other two? You've never mentioned either of them. I'm beginning to think we don't know each other very well."

She smirked at him and then looked down the aisle and called out, "Flight attendant, can you please slip me a glass of Merlot?"

CHAPTER 6

At the hotel, Laila waited in the lobby by herself again. "And there's the woman I've been waiting my entire life for," Alonzo accompanied by his fraternal twin cousins, Damien and Duke came up. She hugged and kissed him.

"Baby, you've been down here for a minute. None of the girls showed up yet?"

"Yea, Gia's here. She's in her room freshening up."

"Oh, Gia's gonna be on the prowl and actin' a fool," he said.

"Yea."

"I was trying to hook her up with one of the twins."

Damien and Duke were Alonzo's favorite cousins from New York. They moved to Georgia to play college basketball a few years ago. Alonzo goes to almost every game.

"She's looking for a soul mate, not jail bait."

"Oh, your lady has jokes," Duke said.

"But it's all good yo," Damien said.

"So who are you waiting for now?"

"Melanie."

"Aw, shit," Duke said.

"She called me from the airport not too long ago. Who are you guys waiting for?"

Alonzo smirked and raised his brows, "Taaz and Quinton."

She took a deep breath and exhaled, "Oh boy."

"It may not be as bad as we think," he said as he tapped two sleeved keycards against his leg.

"Well, they haven't seen each other since they broke off their engagement."

"And that was when? The day before Quinton's wedding?"

"Yep, that sounds about right."

Taaz and Quinton walked through the door.

"Q Dawg and T-Money!"

"ZoZo," Taaz did a call.

Laila shook her head as they did their group handshake and did a half-hug.

"Heyy gurrlll," Taaz said.

Laila shook her head, "Hi Taaz." He hugged her.

"Hi Quinton."

"Hey Laila," he said as he hugged her, "Congratulations girl. You got a good guy right here."

"Indeed I do."

"Ah, two seconds is enough, bro. Don't want you stealing my bride away."

Laila rolled her eyes as they let go of one another.

"Naw, you know I already got the perfect woman."

"Where is Marla?" Laila asked.

He gave her a look, "Um, she decided not to come, but she sends you two and Gia her love."

"Well, at least, she included my name this time.

See. We're making progress."

He chuckled. "I guess."

"Laila's all glowing and shit, you been smashing every since y'all touched down, ain't ya?" Taaz play punched Alonzo.

"Taaz, never stops, man," Quinton said.

"Laila!" Melanie exclaimed as she entered. Most of them turned their heads to see Melanie walking in with her companion, carrying their luggage. She was wearing dark shades, a blue tank, and a white flowing skirt. She rushed and hugged Laila.

"Look at you. You're so beautiful."

"And you…you cut your hair," Laila rubbed her hair.

Taaz's phone buzzed, and he stepped away from the group.

"Yea, I needed a change."

"Mel-Mel," Alonzo said.

"Hi Alonzo," she hugged him while Laila introduced herself to Julian and hugged him.

"Congratulations, you two went through a lot to get here, but hey, you two deserve it," she said as she took off her shades and tossed them in her satchel.

"Thanks, cuz."

"Hey guys. You have gotten so big. Damn, near grown now," She hugged the twins. They grinned at her. There was awkwardness when she looked over at Quinton.

"Oh, hey Quinton, I didn't see you there."

They briefly hugged.

"How have you been?"

"Wonderful," she said, "Um, I would like you guys to meet my very special friend, Julian Williams."

"Hey, man, it's nice to meet you. I'm Alonzo.

These are my boys Quinton and Taaz," he gestured towards Taaz, "and my knucklehead cousins, Damien and Duke Dawson."

He shook their hands.

"Ah, we're about to grab a few drinks at the bar in a little while, you want to come chill?"

"Yea, I'll catch up with you guys after I put our things in our room."

"Alright."

Alonzo kissed Laila and smiled at Melanie, admiring her new haircut. "Ol' Mel all faded up now."

"Shut up," she smiled and hit his shoulder.

"Ah, where Taaz go?" Alonzo gazed across the lobby.

"Around here somewhere. He's been on the phone with ol' girl ever since he met up with me in Texas."

The guys made their way to the elevator.

Laila told Melanie, "Well, let me get you two checked in."

"Oh no, I told you before...we've got it. You just go relax. Have any of the girls made it?"

Laila looked towards the front desk to see Julian already speaking with the front desk agent. "Yea, Gia's here. Kecia hasn't made it yet."

Julian tucked the room keycard in his pocket.

"I'm about to take the luggage to our room," he called.

"Okay, honey,"

He walked towards the elevator.

"He is so gorgeous, Melanie."

"Thank you."

"So how did you tw-"

"Woo, that hot tub felt nice." Gia came up to

them.

"Hi, Gia."

"Melanie? Girl, you don' went and cut your hair."

"Yea, do you like it?"

"Um huh, that pixie cut is perfect for your face."

"Was that a compliment? That must have been one hell of a hot tub."

"It sholl was."

"Divas!" they heard Kecia call. They turned around to see a much thinner Kecia. Their mouths dropped. She wore a white sleeveless top with a high waist purple skirt. Her coal black hair was flowing long in curls. The girls screamed and hugged her.

"Girl, you look good. See I'ma have to pull out my purple dress," Gia said as she admired Kecia's skirt.

"Wow, you've gotten so skinny," Melanie said.

"And each of you bitches changed your hair," Kecia said.

"Um huh, so this is why you've been hiding from me?" Laila asked.

"Yep, I wanted to surprise you."

"Well, I am surprised," Melanie said, "Girl, you've got a shape on you. Look at those thick hips and that thin waist. I am green with envy."

"And you knew all along," Laila tapped Gia's arm.

"Of course," Gia smiled.

"You are just beautiful," Melanie said.

"And radiant," Laila said.

"Thank you. I feel so blessed. I'm healthy. I'm now an English *and* Drama teacher."

"Congratulations!" They said.

"Yes, you are the drama queen," Melanie added.

"I have a good man who will be here in seven days, and I have good friends to share moments like this with."

"Aww," the girls said as they did a group hug.

All of a sudden, Laila felt the hairs on the back of her neck stand and a brush of air as a woman in a bright sundress passed by. She slowly turned her head towards the brown-skinned woman with long curly hair. Her heart began to flutter as if an alarm was going off. Her ears rang, and her eyes grew wide.

Alexandra.

Alexandra stood before a group of ladies, and they all embraced her. Then, she finally locked eyes with Laila and gave her a mischievous grin. She motioned for Laila to come to her, and Laila walked slowly towards her. Then, a man passed by Laila and enveloped the woman with his arms. Two of her friends looked happily at the two while another friend looked on in envy. Laila shook her head and blinked her eyes. She studied the woman's face as she continued to embrace her companion.

"It's –it's not her."

"Not who?"

Her girls walked up to her.

"Laila, are you ok?"

"Oh, yea. I thought those were some girls I went to college with."

"Girl, you know ain't none of those bitches studdin' you, especially that Kayla chick," Gia said.

Kecia and Melanie agreed.

Laila laughed uneasily. "Come on Kecia, let's get you checked in."

"Okay."

"Oh yeah," Laila said, "I think we're all having drinks at the Chateau tonight."

"Ooo, fancy." Gia said.

CHAPTER 7

Julian sat alone at the bar in the hotel's fine dining restaurant, Chateau. He took a sip of his drink and turned around to see a beautiful woman walk through the door. She had a seductive sway in her walk. She sat a few stools away from him. She looked over at him to see him admiring her. She smiled and looked away. He got up and approached her.

"Hi, my name is Julian."

"Gia," she said.

"Gia, that's a beautiful name."

"Thank you."

"Um, can I buy you a drink?"

"Sure."

"What will you have?"

"Um, I honestly don't know. I've never been to a place like this before."

"Okay. Two Shirley Temples on the rocks," he told the bartender.

"So where are you from?"

"Georgia."

"Really? Me too."

She smiled, "That's such a coincidence. I bet you live in the ATL."

"Yes."

"I could tell, but I bet you're originally from out of state, probably up North."

"Yes, Milwaukee."

She smiled.

"And you could tell this all from my demeanor."

"Yes," she smiled.

"So where are you from?"

"A small town 60 miles from Atlanta."

"Ok, that's not too far from me. Maybe we can meet up, and you can show me around."

She smiled, "Maybe."

"So what do you do? If you don't mind me asking."

"No, I don't mind. I own a hair salon."

"Really?" he raised his brows.

She smiled. "So how about you?"

"Aw Gia, I see you've met Julian," Melanie approached them. Gia's eyes grew wide. "Hi honey." Melanie kissed him on the cheek, and he gave Gia a coy look.

In a matter of seconds, Gia dropped her act. "Aw, hell naw," Gia jumped up, grabbing her drink just as the bartender was about to sit it in on a napkin in front of them. He watched her walk off and tilted his head back.

"You just bought her a drink, didn't you?"

Julian sighed, "Yes, and this one is yours, of course." He slid the glass in front of her.

She frowned. "You're *my* man or did you forget that too?"

"Regretting that move more and more by the

minute," he mumbled.

She glared at him. "You don't take me serious. You know what, we can just call this whole relationship off, and you can go home."

"No, I said I was going to be with you, so that's what I'm going to do."

She sighed, "I know men will be men, but I can't have you chasing after my best friends, especially Gia."

"Best friend? You've never even mentioned a Gia to me."

"Well, I am now, and she's off limits. You see that table right there? All of the women who will be sitting at that table are off-limits. I brought you with me because I thought you'd show me a little respect, my goodness."

Julian sighed.

"I can't believe him," Gia said to Laila as she sat at their table.

"Who?"

"Melanie's man. He just tried to get with me," she guzzled her drink.

"Really?" Laila shook her head. "Melanie is like a magnet for cheaters."

"I didn't know he was the guy she was kicking it with. We talked and were connecting and stuff. Then I thought maybe he…" she sighed, "Never mind."

Melanie sat at the table. "The nerve of him trying to get back at me."

"What did you do this time?" Laila asked.

"Oh, he claimed I was vehemently flirting with this guy at the airport."

"Well, you probably were," Gia got up and left the

table.

"Well, I see her bitterness is back," Melanie said.

Julian walked over to Alonzo, Quinton, and a few more of Alonzo's friends. He watched Gia as she made her way back to the bar with her empty glass. Taaz came up.

"What up, man?"

"It's about time. Where have you been?" Quinton said as he picked up his drink.

"Oh, just enjoying the view and shit."

"Yea, right man," Alonzo said, "You've been glued to your phone since you got here." He handed Taaz a drink.

"Somebody misses his girlfriend?"

"I still can't get over how you ended up being with a registered nurse with not one but three degrees."

"A traveling nurse at that, and she is fine as hell too."

Taaz shrugged. "What can I say? I was at the right place at the right time," He sipped his drink, "You and ol' Laila tying the knot is what I can't get over. I didn't think the playboy would ever be tied down."

"Yea, never thought I could commit myself to one woman, but damn, Laila makes me feel ways no other woman can."

"I feel you. Marla makes me feel like that."

Taaz started laughing. "You want me to go get you girls some tissues?"

The guys laughed.

"Man shut up. You just mad cuz Nyema ain't doing it for you in the bedroom," Quinton said.

The guys *ooed*, and some laughed. He looked from Quinton to Alonzo.

"Alonzo, what's up man? Why you spreading my business?"

"Hey, I ain't tell him nothing. You just let that cat out of the bag your damn self."

Kecia entered the restaurant.

"What do we have here?" Alonzo asked.

Taaz followed the guys' gaze.

"It can't be." Taaz dropped his glass.

The guys started howling and whistling at her.

"Hey Kecia," the guys yelled.

"Y'all ain't got no sense. Y'all better calm down before they throw y'all black asses out."

"We ain't doing nothing, but showing you love," Alonzo said.

"Yea, you look good, girl," Quinton said.

"Thank you, thank you," she sat down with her friends.

She managed to avoid eye contact with Taaz, but he was not taking his eyes off her. Julian looked back and forth from Taaz to Kecia.

"Damn man," Quinton snapped his fingers in Taaz's face, "Snap out of it."

"She's even finer now, ain't she?" Alonzo asked.

"Naw man, I was just in shock...you know. She don' lost a lot of weight."

Julian picked up Taaz's empty glass, which happened to miss the tile flooring and roll onto the thin carpet near a table.

"Thanks man," he said still looking at Kecia. He finally looked at Julian. "So um, you're Melanie or Gia's man?"

"I'm Gi- I mean I'm Melanie's," he coughed, "man."

They looked at him strangely. "Oh okay. Hey, I'ma

go make a phone call. I'll catch up with y'all later."

Kecia quickly glanced at Taaz as he walked past.

"There go Taaz, Kecia," Gia blurted.

"*Tsk*, I ain't studdin' him."

"She is on to the next," Melanie said. She leaned forward, turned towards Kecia, rested her elbow on the table and rested her chin in her hand, "So tell me about your perfect man."

"My perfect man? Look at you. You got the nerve to bring a tall sexy bald-headed brother up in here. Now you know how much I used to love some bald-headed men. He looks like a basketball player."

"He ain't that tall," Gia said as she looked at him. Their eyes met, and she rolled her eyes.

"Enough about Julian. I want to hear about Winston," Laila said.

She went through her bag. "I was about to show you girls a picture of him on my phone, but I guess I left it in my room."

"Well, describe him for us."

"Uh, he is so fine. Tall, dark chocolate brown, jet black hair with nicely trimmed facial hair. Beautiful dark brown eyes, built, full lips, and beautiful perfect pearly whites."

"Ooo, sounds dreamy," Laila said.

"I'm surprised y'all ain't seen him yet. She got pictures of him plastered all over Facebook and Instagram."

"Oh, I don't do social media," Laila said.

"Yeah, I closed all of my accounts a long time ago," Melanie said.

"Y'all will get to see his fine self when he gets here." Kecia glowed.

"Ok," Laila and Melanie said.

"Then, on top of his fineness, he's a clean freak, kind, and considerate. He respects me and my family. He absolutely loves kids…he even coaches a little league baseball team."

"Wow, he sounds so perfect for you," Melanie said.

"I couldn't be happier for you," Laila said.

"Thanks girl," Kecia said, "So Melanie, that's it?"

"What do you mean?"

"You're not going to ask me what my man does?"

"Well, that really wasn't on my mind."

"Woo, I got to write this down," Gia said.

"Hey, I've changed. It takes too much energy to worry about status and trying to be bourgeois as you claim I am."

"I know right," Laila said.

"So be happy with the man you have."

"Thanks, but for the record, he's a veterinarian, and he has his own clinic."

"Oh, she had to throw that in there real quick," Laila said, and they started laughing.

"Didn't she though."

"That's what I'm talking about. You are proud of what your man does," Gia said.

They grew quiet.

"You know what I've noticed?" Kecia said.

"What, girl?" Gia asked.

"We've been going on and on about our lives, but we've been neglecting the bride."

"Oh," Laila smiled, realizing Kecia was referring to her.

"How are you doing, girl?"

"I am so good. Everything is going great with

Alonzo. Since he reentered my life, I just..." she paused, "feel so complete. He's sexy, compromising, confident, romantic, and funny. He makes me laugh everyday. When we are mad at one another, we fuss for a little while and talk it out. Then, we go right back to making each other laugh. I'm so ready to be his wife."

"Aw," Melanie's eyes watered.

"That is just wonderful," Kecia said.

"Damn, girl. We didn't ask you to recite your vows."

They all laughed.

"Shut up!"

"So are there any kids in your future?" Melanie asked Laila.

"We hope so. We want a little boy and a little girl."

"Really?"

"Yeah, that's all Alonzo talks about. He's even picked their names already."

"What did he come up with?" Kecia asked.

"Oh, I've got to hear this," Gia said.

"They're not that bad. It's a mixture of our names."

"Yet you haven't revealed the names yet," Kecia said.

"Okay. The boy's name is Larinzo."

"Oh now, I like that," Melanie said.

"And Azaila."

"Hmm, I don't know about the girl's name."

"Yeah, me either."

"Okay, as your bridesmaid, it is my duty to ask you all of the tough questions to make sure you're truly ready for a life with Alonzo," Melanie started.

"Okay."

"Well, as we all know, Alonzo has been around. What if some children pop up and say that Alonzo is their dad? What will you do?"

Laila swallowed as she thought about her dream.

"Well, if they're his, and he had them before we got together, then I will accept them and love that a part of them is Alonzo."

"Wow, you are a good one."

"To Laila and Alonzo," the girls clanged their glasses.

Alonzo came up to the table and stood by Laila. "Hey y'all. Change of plans. We're going to a Mexican bar and grill tonight."

"What's wrong with this place?" Laila asked.

"Oh, you know I think our first night together should be us kicking back having fun in a casual environment."

"In other words, we can't be loud black folks up in here," Kecia said.

"A Mexican bar and grill, now I gotta change into something more comfortable," Gia pouted, "Y'all need to print out a damn itinerary or something and stick to it."

"Don't start, Gia," Alonzo said.

"I'm just saying."

"I saw it when I was jogging on the beach this morning."

She frowned, "Whatever."

CHAPTER 8

At the Comida Caliente Bar & Grill by the beach, almost everyone, including Alonzo's cousins were seated together. When Laila and Alonzo first arrived, they had their hearts set on spending time with their friends and family on the outside. However, all of the tables were filled. So, they decided to dine on the inside of the restaurant and pull tables together to accommodate everyone.

Kecia and Gia were the last ones to enter the restaurant. A band was on the small stage playing music. The delicious aroma of spices and sizzling steak, chicken, chorizo, shrimp, peppers, and onions filled the air. The two ladies slowly made their way to the adjoined tables. Kecia sat in the empty chair beside Laila. Then, there was only one open seat next to Julian.

Gia sighed, "Damn, I can't even pull up an extra seat."

She stooped down and whispered in Taaz's ear.

"Trade seats with me."

"Naw, this one has your name written all over it,"

he pulled out the seat beside him.

She rolled her eyes at Taaz and sat between him and Julian.

"What?"

The waitress came up. Before she could speak, Gia said, "Hey, let me get two margaritas."

"Water for me," Kecia said.

"Well, make that one watermelon margarita. I don't want it frozen."

"Ok," the waitress said, "They ordered party platters for the entire table. Would you two like to order something else?"

Gia and Kecia shook their heads. They admired the bowls of chips, salsa, queso dip, mini shrimp tacos, taquitos, and quesadillas. They both reached for a plate and grabbed some food.

Melanie asked, "So when is the wedding party rehearsing?"

"We're not having a wedding rehearsal," Laila and Alonzo said simultaneously.

"You've got to be kidding me. How will we know what to do?"

"Get this," Alonzo started.

"You walk in with your escort," Laila added.

"He walks you to your spot."

"And that's it!" they both said.

Gia smirked. "But y'all rehearsed that, didn't you?"

"No," Laila pursed her lips.

Melanie looked away. "Well, that's simple enough."

Alonzo shook his head, "Man, Laila and I are just so glad that each of you could vacation with us and celebrate our big day."

"Yeah, this was a long time coming," Kecia said.

"And it doesn't hurt that y'all are footing the bill for all of us," Gia said.

They all agreed and laughed. The waitress handed Gia and Kecia their drinks.

"Even if y'all weren't, we wouldn't miss this for the world, man," Taaz said.

"For nothing at all," Quinton agreed.

"Aw, look at Quinton and Taaz being all soft," Gia said as she sipped her margarita. She noticed Melanie pouring salsa onto Julian's plate and rolled her eyes.

"Ain't nothing soft on me," Taaz said.

Kecia smirked, "Especially that hard head of his."

"And you know about that more than anyone."

"About you being soft? Most definitely do."

Alonzo and Quinton said, "Ooo..."

Kecia got up and walked to the bar. The bartender handed her a red daiquiri, and she sat at a high round table by herself.

"Dang, you don' ran her off, Taaz," Damien said.

He smirked. "She'll be back."

"Can't we have one dinner without y'all janking on each other?" Melanie asked.

"You know that's impossible," Laila said.

"Yeah, where's the fun in that?" Alonzo asked.

"It's been this way since high school," Gia said, "Ain't nothing changed, but those bags under yo' eyes."

"Bags? Please. I do not have any bags under my eyes."

"Julian been keeping you up all night?" Alonzo asked.

Julian chuckled, "I was not the cause."

"Wait, I actually have bags under my eyes?" she picked up a spoon trying to see.

"No, Melanie."

She got up and rushed away.

"Why did you do that?" Laila asked Gia. "She is going to spend at least 20 minutes in the bathroom mirror."

"She's always been too easy to get," Quinton finally said.

"And you should know," Alonzo joked, "No offense, Julian."

"None taken."

"Oh, you had to take it there," Quinton squinted his eyes at Alonzo. "Julian, I don't know if Melanie caught you up on our history, but…"

"Oh no, she brought me up to speed."

"Well, I hope that we don't make you feel uncomfortable with our-"

"Oh, no worries. It's all in the past, right?" he said.

Gia smacked her lips. "Yeah, he's a big boy. If he can't roll with us, he knows how to take his ass on."

He looked at her. "My ass is just fine right here."

Taaz eyed them. Then, peered behind them.

"Umm…I see a beautiful Latino at the bar calling my name."

"Aren't you with somebody?" Gia asked.

"Do you see her?"

Laila studied him as he got up.

"Well, I better check on Kecia," Gia got up and headed to the table.

Kecia was twirling a straw in her drink.

"Hey, you talk to Winston?" Gia asked. She pulled her chair next to Kecia and slowly eased onto it.

"Yeah, he's been busy at the clinic."

"How can you lay with him knowing he's been fooling with nasty dogs and such?"

"He's sterile. It's much better than laying *with* a nasty dog." She looked over at Taaz, who was sitting on a stool, talking to the woman next to him at the bar.

"I am glad you didn't let him keep you from coming on the trip. You could have come just for the wedding, and that's it."

"It's our best friend's wedding. And knowing her and Alonzo, we both gotta be there every step of the way."

"Look at them," they glanced at the table as the happy couple fed each other a salsa drenched chip.

"They look so happy. I've never seen her light up like that over anyone, not even that fool," she gestured towards Quinton.

"Does he seem different to you?" Gia asked.

"Yeah, he is more distant now."

"I would be too...considering everything that has happened," Gia shook her head. "I don't understand why Marla didn't bring her ass down here with him."

"You know why. Laila and Melanie."

"But she got the man. They ain't studdin' him no more."

"Well, Laila isn't. Thank goodness. Can't say the same for Melanie."

"Shoot, she's crazy if she still is...that fine ass man she brought with her."

"Who tried to talk to you."

"Girl, I can't help that I'm all fine. Men can't resist me."

"Yeah, like Taaz...always flirting with you."

"You know he's done that since the eighth grade to make you jealous. He didn't flirt or make any inappropriate comments when y'all were together."

"He knew I'd beat his little ass."

Gia laughed, sipped her drink, and cut her eyes at their friends' table. Kecia followed her gaze.

"Why are you staring at Melanie's man?"

"What? No the hell I'm not."

Melanie sat back down at the table.

Gia took a sip again and cut her eyes towards him.

"See! There you go again."

"Hey, didn't nobody say a thing about you positioning yourself to watch Taaz's every move at the bar."

"Girl, ain't nobody studdin' that boy."

"Umm huh…whatever," Gia got up.

"I'm not." Kecia called after her. She observed Taaz and the lady.

At the bar, Taaz was busy trying to impress the raven haired woman, who was running her hands all over him. "Dang, girl you're rubbing all on me, feeling on my booty. Just fast. El speedo. Girl, I'm doing big things. Gonna get my own company one day. Call me el presidente."

She rolled her eyes, then slipped away.

"*Mami, chica, senorita,*" he said, "Where are you going?"

Kecia jumped out of her seat. As the lady attempted to leave out, she stepped in front of her.

"Give it here, bitch," she held out her hand.

She began speaking in Spanish.

"Bitch, I know you speak English. I heard you talking to the bartender earlier."

"Give you what?"

"Don't play dumb. My friend's wallet."

"I don't have it."

"I saw you swipe it, and if you don't give it to me,

I will knock you down and hold you in position until management comes over, and the police arrives. Give it to me now, and you can go free."

She rolled her eyes and gave it to her.

Gia yelled out, "Kecia, you need back up?"

"Naw, I got this."

Kecia came closer to her, "You see that group of people? They are not to be fucked with. *Comprende?*"

The girl stormed off, fussing in Spanish.

"Yo' *abuelita,* bitch," Kecia called out to her.

Alonzo smiled. "Kecia over there making a scene."

They watched as the lady made it to the lobby, but was stopped by a Mexican man and woman that worked at the establishment. She struggled to get away, and wallets fell out of her bag. They restrained her and took her to the back. The woman rushed to the phone to call the police.

Oblivious to the situation that transpired behind him, Taaz remained at the bar sipping his drink. Then, he felt his pockets.

"Where is my..." his eyes grew wide, "Man, she stole my-"

"Looking for this?" Kecia asked as she handed him his wallet. "You need to watch your back."

"I would've caught her."

"Naw, if I wouldn't have stepped in, she'd be long gone."

"Well, thank you. I know that's what you want to hear."

"Oh Taaz, I don't expect anything in return from you. I've gotten used to you not saying what I want to hear."

A lady of Indian descent sat beside him, and he eyed her. She smiled at him. Kecia rolled her eyes, walked back towards the group table, and sat in Taaz's open seat beside Gia.

"Who's up for Tequila shots?" Alonzo asked as he placed a shot of tequila in Laila's cleavage and drank the shot. Then, Laila grabbed a shot from the table, drank it, and kissed him.

"Y'all nasty!" Gia smirked.

"Look at Laila go," Duke said as she took another shot.

"Uh uh… y'all know Laila is a drunk."

"Gia!" Laila turned her head to her. Taaz came back to the table and sat beside Laila.

"Who's got a whole wine collection at her house?"

"Quinton's not too far behind. He's swiped quite a few bottles out of his aunt's cellar," Alonzo laughed.

"Yes, I have, and I'll do it again," he said as he took a shot.

"Come on, Kecia," Alonzo held up a shot.

"This nonalcoholic daiquiri is just fine."

"Man, that's a damn slushy," Taaz said.

She wrinkled her brows at him.

"Come on Kecia… live a little," Alonzo continued to offer the shot.

"No, as part of my health and wellness plan, I'm staying away from all alcohol, soda, fried foods, chocolate, and white bread."

"While you're over there chomping on those taquitos," Taaz said.

She sneered at him.

"I want in," Melanie said as she took a shot.

"Welp, you gotta catch up," Alonzo said.

"Aw naw, my money's on Laila then," Gia smirked, "Again."

Laila was sucking on a lime slice.

"Don't suck on it too hard baby," He took the lime from her and squeezed the juice in his mouth.

"I bet that's what you told her last night," Taaz and Gia said at the same time. Everyone laughed. Laila's mouth dropped.

"Taaz, you sure your daddy didn't go creeping with Gia's momma too?" Alonzo asked.

"Don't even play," Gia frowned.

"Hey, I've been saying that for years," Quinton said as he took another shot.

Taaz shook his head. "Naw now."

"Yeah, y'all do act alike," Kecia said to Gia.

"Is that why you fell in love with Taaz then?" Gia whispered. She drank her shot.

"Bitch, don't even..."

Gia started laughing. "He's basically me."

Kecia sighed. "Well, I'm going to bed," she stood up, "And when all of y'all drunk asses end up in the bed with each other, don't call me."

She turned away.

"Aw, Kecia come back," Laila called after her.

Alonzo followed her.

"Heyyy Kecia."

"Alonzo."

She stopped and faced him at the entryway. He put his arms around her and kissed her cheek.

"Ew, don't be kissing my jaws. I know exactly where those lips have been," she wiped her face.

"And, with any luck, they gon' be right back down there tonight, if she let me."

She frowned. "What do you want?"

"Where's your man?"

"At home. He has to work. He'll be here in time

51

for the wedding."

"Ok," he said, "You know you and Taaz are supposed to be standing up there with me and Laila, right?"

"Alonzo, what happened between me and Taaz is none of your business."

"But you two are perfect for each other."

"Naw, he's perfect for Gia, but I kind of messed that up."

"You know they are never going to see each other like that. It's you that he wants. Don't let him make you think otherwise."

"So why are you telling me this and not him?"

"He's gonna come around. I know it."

"He's already too late," she searched his eyes, "So is this why you want me and him to perform at the wedding? Are you trying to get us back together?"

"What?" he scoffed, "No, Kecia. We love you, and I've always loved your voice. Do you know how long it's been since I've heard you sing or Taaz play the piano? It's been years, girl. Laila and I just thought that it would be one of our greatest memories for my brother and her sister to serenade us as we step into a new chapter of our lives together. I just hope you're okay with doing it."

"I wasn't at first, but he'll be sitting at his piano, and I'll be standing at the mic so it's not like we are going to be in each other's faces."

"Okay, I set up a rehearsal for you two in one of the banquet rooms. I forgot which day, but I'll let you know."

"Okay."

"You look really good, girl."

"Thank you, and you look happy to be becoming

Mr. Laila McKee," she teased.

He laughed, "To be honest, I am."

She smiled.

"You want me to walk you to the hotel?"

"No, I'll manage."

"You sure?"

"Yeah."

"Ah, Damien!" he called, "Escort her to the hotel."

Kecia shook her head as his younger cousin came to her side.

CHAPTER 9

After their night of drinking, Alonzo was sound asleep in their room. Laila found it hard to sleep through the night. She showered and pulled on her gray and white activewear. Instead of running on the beach or exercising in the first floor fitness center, she decided to just take a morning walk around the hotel to clear her mind. When she reached the lobby, Laila noticed a little girl wearing a pretty white dress and holding a white satin basket. She was the perfect little flower girl.

Laila and Alonzo had opted out of having children at their wedding, so there won't be a ring bearer or flower girl coming down their aisle. She began to regret the decision as she laid eyes upon the adorable beauty. The girl reminded Laila of herself when she was little. She started thinking of when she was six-years-old playing dress up at her first childhood home except she wore an old lace dress. She threw her mother's old white sheer curtains over her head as a veil. She always loved playing dress up and pretending to be a bride. All she needed was a little boy to pose as her groom. She could see herself twirling around in her mother and father's bedroom.

"Mom, look at me."

"That's nice honey," Laila's mother, Margarette said in her plush suede navy chair, still staring at a J.C. Penney catalog. A lit cigarette was resting in the ashtray on the small round stand next to her.

"I can't wait to get married and have kids."

"Trust me, it's not what it's cracked up to be."

"It's not?" she dropped her shoulders.

Her mother looked up.

"Aw Laila, you're such a beautiful bride."

"I am?" her eyes brightened.

"Yes," she got up, "My beautiful baby girl. And you know what? All you're missing is a diamond necklace, and I have just the one for you."

"You do?!"

"Go stand in front of the mirror, and I'll get it for you."

She went into her jewelry box and pulled out a chunky diamond necklace. She stared at Laila, lowered herself, put the necklace around her neck, and fastened it.

"Now you're the perfect bride. And don't mind your mom. I'm sure Prince Charming is going to come and sweep you off your feet. And, you're going to be happy together forever and ever."

"Forever and ever?"

"Yes, he will come," she said, "but for now, you just focus on reading your books and being my sweet little girl."

She hugged her and kissed her cheek.

"Okay...Mom?"

"Yes, honey."

"Will you be there with me on my wedding day?"
"I wouldn't miss it for anything in the world."

"Come here," someone interrupted Laila's moment of nostalgia.

Laila noticed her event coordinator, Rozalyn holding a clipboard and motioning for the little girl to follow her. She looked down the hall and saw a beautiful Latino bride walking with her mother. Laila walked closer for a better view. She leaned against the wall. The mom straightened out her daughter's dress straps. Then, she pinned up a few curls that had fallen. A young teenage girl handed the mother a veil, and the daughter lowered herself so her mother could affix the comb in her hair.

"You are the most beautiful bride that I've seen in my life."

"Thank you, Mom."

"The best thing I've ever done in my life was have you. To get to experience every milestone in your life is such a precious gift that I will always be thankful for. My precious little girl...I love you so much."

"I love you too."

Laila's heart began to ache, and tears fell from her eyes. The bride embraced her mother.

"Mrs. Rodriguez, we are ready for you."

She took a young guy's arm and blew a kiss at her daughter before going through the double doors.

Then, the bridesmaids lined up to go in, and the flower girl stood right behind them. Rozalyn motioned for the attendants to open the door, and the bridal party began their march.

"Wait, where's my father?"

"I'm right here."

He passed by Laila, looked at her, and greeted her. He walked up to his daughter.

"Absolutely breathtaking."

A male hotel guest walked by them.

"I helped make her."

"Dad!"

They all chuckled. He kissed her hand. They reopened the doors, and the two walked in. Laila kept wiping her eyes with her shirt and continued to cry.

"It's gotta be tough for you," someone said from behind her. She was so busy crying that she didn't notice Taaz approaching her.

"Oh, I'm fine, Taaz."

He hugged her, "No, you're not. Come on, let's get you some fresh air." They walked outside to the lounging area.

"They've been out of my life for so long. I thought not having them here wouldn't phase me, but seeing that family, how happy they are and how proud the parents are to be a part of every moment of their daughter's life just cuts deep. Mine could care less."

"I don't really know the whole story, but what they did to you was fucked up. I know you couldn't have done anything that bad to deserve being cut off like that."

"I've been thinking that for years, and it still hurts. No matter how much I try to focus on love, a life with Alonzo, no matter how much wine I sip, it still hurts so bad. The fact that they are still here on this Earth, but don't even want me in their lives."

"Man, I don't know what to say to that. I mean if it was me getting married, of course, I would want my mom there, but my dad better not show his ass up. I love him. I swear I do, but he just has this way of fucking up the whole moment and making everything about his ass. With his flask, cigars, and countless kids that I have to buy diapers for cuz he can't afford to take care of them," Taaz sighed, "We all go through something with our folks. But in high school, your parents seemed solid."

"It was just a façade...a veil. We weren't the picture perfect family that everyone proclaimed us to be."

"Sholl fooled the hell out of me, but I know what you're going through. Man, Ms. Carol leaving us like that got me. I just don't know how Quinton is holding up like he is."

"Yes, that was a tough pill to swallow."

"But you know what is helping him through it?"

Laila waited for his answer.

"Us. You, me, Marla, Lonzo, our boys, Gia," he swallowed, "Kecia. And, you've got us too, and we're gonna help you through this. Okay?"

"Okay."

"We got you. You ain't gotta worry about nothing."

Worry? She thought. *Should I tell him I've also been seeing Alexandra everywhere I go?*

She took a deep breath.

"Taaz, thank you."

They hugged, "You know you're like my little sister."

"I'm older than you."

"Only by a few months."

Alonzo peered out of the door.

"Taaz, you're trying to steal my bride?"

"Steal?" he put his arm around her, "Bitch, I already took her."

"Alright now," Alonzo approached them. They all started laughing.

"But for real though, we're just having a little talk."

"It's all good."

They did their handshake and a half-hug.

"I'll see y'all at the cove." He walked away. "Laila, remember what I said."

"Okay." He opened the door and headed back to the lobby.

"Are you good?"

"Yeah, I'm fine. I almost lost it when I saw a bride with her parents, but Taaz talked me off the ledge."

"Aww, my baby."

"I thought I had made peace with them not being here."

"Baby, it's natural for anyone to feel this way. This is a huge moment in our lives, a moment that should be shared with our families, with our parents. I'm just glad you're no longer holding it in. Let out those emotions, it'll be good for you."

She cried some more, and he rubbed her back.

He continued, "I know it's been a long time, but no matter how many years have passed. There are always reminders of what we lost, and we have to face it. It's the way you handle it that counts the most. Will you become angry and bitter or will you be joyful for others and allow God to comfort you? He will always send people in your life to make it all better. I know I'm one of those people for you."

"Yes, you are, and I'm not going to let the fact that they're not here break me. I want this to be a joyous occasion for what I do have...what we have."

He smiled and hugged her, "Now come on. We gotta get everyone together for our water adventure."

"I wouldn't call it an adventure."

In the distance, Gia walked along the beach and sat quietly in a lounger. She noticed Julian as he approached her.

"Uh, what do you want?"

"I just wanted to apologize."

"Okay, I hear you. Now get the hell on."

"I know you must think of me as some womanizer, but I'm not."

"Ho...gigolo. Call yourself whatever you want to get through the night."

She got up.

"Whoa, wait." He held her arm.

"You got nanoseconds to take your hands off me."

He quickly let go.

"Wow," he said, "I'm seeing a completely different side of you than when we first met at the Chateau."

"Yes, you are. This is me being real. That was a front. I was all sweet, sophisticated and whatever to get a man. So guess you dodged a bullet cuz I am what people call a loud, ghetto, skinny bitch who is always down to beat some ass."

"I've never heard a quote-unquote ghetto girl say nanoseconds."

She glared at him.

"But, I don't see that when I look at you. Well, I can't deny that you'll probably beat somebody's ass, but you are beautiful. I can see that you're mad at me. The fire in your eyes, the way your lips are curled, the wrinkle in your forehead, you couldn't be more beautiful."

"I have had to deal with many players and

Casanovas, mainly the one that's about to marry my best friend. So your words are like dry wall paper...not...gonna...stick," she turned to walk away.

"Unless it's the adhesive kind," he smiled. She rolled her eyes. "Wait."

"Look, I saw you and Melanie going to separate rooms last night, so I know you two are probably going through some things. Me and the bitch have had our trials too, but I'm not about to be your revenge, side, or bogus reason for you two to break up. And even though I am single, Gia Malone will never...and get this through your head...never settle for one of Melanie Tyler's leftovers. I want *nothing* she's had. I am above that. I'm above that bitch, and I am above you."

She finally walked away.

He let out a sigh and said, "Damn."

CHAPTER 10

On the beach, the guys were dressed in colorful trunks. Some were shirtless, and a few had on t-shirts. The ladies wore two piece swimsuits with cover ups and carried huge flowered or straw totes. Each of them wore shades. They made their way to a cove on the far left hand side of the shore. They entered the cove and admired the rock walls. People were in the cove taking pictures. The circular hole at the top allowed the sunrays to illuminate a large section of the water. A few people were getting out of the water as others got in. Laila noticed that there were openings on either side of the cove for easy entry and exit. Alonzo snapped a picture of Laila. While the guys were having their photo sessions, the ladies huddled away from the water.

"Okay, so since Alonzo's thrown-together-overnight itinerary is lame, and your maid of honor ain't gon' be here till darn near the day of the wedding," Gia smirked, "I've already planned some fun activities for us to do."

Laila attempted to speak.

"And you had a fit about having strippers, but I ain't gon' speak on that."

"Sounds like you just did," Melanie pointed out.

"Bitch, be quiet. You better be glad I'm including your shiesty ass in our festivities."

"Gia, don't start," Kecia said.

"You know what," Gia eyed each of them, "I'm tired of everyone telling me 'don't start, don't start' cuz y'all know I ain't gon' listen to anyone, especially yo' ass." She glared at Melanie. Laila turned around and started taking pictures of the guys.

"Well, I know you're not still salty over my wedding debacle or are you salty because that man over there is mine?" She nodded towards Julian.

"Ain't nobody thinking bout him or you. But if I wanted him, I could have him just like that," she snapped her fingers.

"Oh please. You wish."

"So is that a challenge?"

"Girl, bye."

"That's what I thought."

Kecia shook her head. "Can we all act right just once?"

Laila turned back to them with a smile on her face. "It wouldn't be right if you did. I wouldn't change you ladies one bit. I like you just the way you are."

They looked at her strangely, "Alonzo finally gave you that dick last night, didn't he?"

"No, I told you we were waiting."

"Umm huh," they all said.

"Who wanna bet they don't make it?"

"Gia, I'm starting to think you have a gambling problem," Kecia stated.

"I know right! You're always betting on me."

"But I'm in," Kecia said.

Laila scoffed. "A sex bet, really?"

"Okay, I bet they don't make it to the wedding rehearsal dinner or whatever they're calling it," Gia said.

Kecia thought. "I bet they make it pass the dinner and the wedding, but not the reception."

"What are we going to do? Run off to a storage closet?"

"Lonzo, gon' get in where he fit in," Gia gyrated.

"Well, Laila. I'm your only friend who has faith in you," Melanie said, "I bet that you two are going to wait until your wedding night when your honeymoon begins."

Laila smirked, "And I bet I get a new group of bridesmaids."

"You know you love us."

"Just the way we are," Kecia mimicked her.

She shook her head, "Anyway, Gia what do you have planned?"

"Uh uh, first of all, did you do that for me?"

"Yes, I did."

Gia beamed. "We're having a bonfire on the beach just the four of us."

"Aw shoot!"

"That's going to be nice." Melanie smiled.

"Yep, *Waiting to Exhale* style. I can't promise we ain't gon' burn up somebody's shit."

"Or go straight to jail."

"Come on…what else?"

"Jet skiing."

"Jet skiing?"

"Yes, I've always wanted to try that and paragliding."

"Um, I don't know about that."

"Spa massages in cabanas on the beach."

"Ooo, now that's more my speed," Melanie nodded.

"Oh yes, that sounds amazing," Laila said at the same time.

"And a boat ride with champagne," Gia said, "And the fellas can do whatever Alonzo had planned."

"Okay, we will talk about it more later."

Alonzo called, "You ladies ready to hit the beach?"

"Yes we are!" they said.

Soon, the ladies were laying in white lounge chairs on the beach. They noticed how sexy the guys were. The guys walked slowly towards the water. Taaz jumped on Alonzo's back. And they started clowning. Damien and Duke were sitting at a table, and Taaz joined the two and got back on the phone. Alonzo and Quinton grabbed him and dumped him the water. Alonzo threw Taaz's phone towards Laila, and she caught it and placed it in her tote. The guys started play fighting in the water like little boys. Then, they started tossing a beach ball with a group of kids.

"Those guys will never grow up."

"But you've got to give it to 'em, they've always been great with kids."

"Even Julian," Melanie said.

"Yea, and that's a rarity these days."

A little girl grabbed Julian's hand.

"Hey, what's your name?"

"Julian."

"JuJu Bee, you're handsome. Are you a prince?"

"Why yes I am. Where is your mom and dad?"

She shrugged. "Can I stay with you?"

"Sure. Let's play a game of finding mom and dad."

He asked some people next to them if she was with them. They shook their head.

He saw a woman approaching a man with ice cream cones in her hands.

"Where's Bella?"

"I thought she was with you?"

"Hey, is this your little girl?"

"Yes," they let out a sigh of relief.

"She got away from us. Thank you for watching out for her."

"Mom, this is my boyfriend. Can I keep him?"

"Well, honey, you have great taste, but I'm sorry. This nice man has to go be with his friends."

"Aww," she pouted.

"Looks like Bella is already searching for her prince." Her daddy said, "She's just like her mother."

The girl cried and reached out for him.

"No!"

She rushed back and hugged him.

"I'll never forget you, Juju Bee."

Meanwhile, Laila and the girls saw the girl hugging him.

"Aww."

"That's so cute."

Gia looked over and smirked.

The girl's mother handed the ice cream cones to her husband. "Come on, Bella," she picked her up. Then, eyed Julian. "You are gorgeous. Are you a model?"

"Uhh thank you," he smiled, "But no, I'm not."

"Are you on Instagram? Cuz you should definitely be on there."

"Emma, let's leave the man alone," Bella's father said uneasily.

"Oh sorry."

"Women," he shrugged, "Looks like I have to start back hitting the gym. Excuse my family."

"Oh, it's fine," Julian smiled.

"Again, thank you for looking out for Bella."

"You're welcome, and please be more careful."

"We will."

The guys got back together in the water. Gia, Melanie, and Laila were admiring the way each of them came up out of the water. Their mouths dropped at each guy. Then, they got to Taaz, who kept falling in the water, and started laughing at him. He wrung his shirt and slowly pulled it off, revealing his muscles. Their mouths dropped once again, and they pulled their shades down to get a better look.

"Daaaaamn...Taaz has been working out," Melanie said.

"Kecia, you see that?!" Gia asked.

"Umm huh, I saw."

"You *saw*?" Gia whipped her head around towards Kecia.

"I looked up. Now, I'm looking back at my phone. I saw," she pursed her lips.

"I don't mean to be looking at everyone's man

and ex, but damn, they are all packing," Melanie said.

"Mel, by the way you're sounding, you would think you ain't had none in a while," Kecia said.

"Girl please, I get mine," Melanie said.

"I guess," Gia said.

"We've been knowing those boys since high school, them packing ain't nothing new," Kecia said.

"Oh really?" Gia asked.

Laila looked around the beach and spotted Alexandra walking on the sidewalk.

No. No. It can't be. Not her.

She stepped onto the sand. Her eyes were fixated on Alonzo. She turned her head, noticed Laila watching her, and gave her a mischievous smile. Laila frowned. With her sunscreen lotion still in her hand, Laila hopped up out of her lounge chair and marched across the sand to approach her. She turned away from Laila.

"You've got some nerve," Laila grabbed her arm. She turned around. Another woman came up and stood beside her. The second woman wore her hair in dreads, and the left side of her head was shaved.

"Excuse me?"

"Ohhh," Laila's eyes widened, and she gave an uneasy laugh.

Once again, it was not Alexandra.

Laila stammered. "Uhh, you've got some nerve to be looking all beautiful and not have on any sunscreen. Uhh, would you like some of mine?"

The Alexandra look-a-like and her friend looked at each other. "Uh, how can she tell I'm not wearing any?"

"Wait, you don't have any on?"

"No."

"Who cares? Do you see how fine she is?"

"MJ, you have no sense at all, but..." she nodded in agreement.

Laila's eyes grew even wider.

"Um, sure. Would you like to rub it on me?"

"Uhhh..." Laila looked for an escape.

Just say no. That's all you have to do and just walk away.

"Sure."

The lady sat in a nearby beach chair, Laila got behind her. She looked around, and Alonzo looked at her with a confused yet delighted look on his face. She shrugged.

"What is Laila doing?" Gia asked.

"Maybe that's one of those friends from college she was looking for yesterday," Kecia replied.

"Guess the bougie bitches didn't wanna sit with us."

"Well, she could have rubbed my sunscreen on first," Melanie said.

Meanwhile, Laila was steadily placing lotion on her hands and rubbing her *new friend's* back and arms.

"Umm...this feels so good. You're really quiet. What's your name?"

"Uh Lai...Kecia."

"Lakesha?"

"Yes."

"I'm Tricey," she inched back closer to Laila, "It's nice to make your acquaintance. I have to say I like your bold approach. So where are you from?"

"Mississippi," she lied.

"Oh really? I'm from Biloxi. Which city-"

She looked over at her friends who weren't

paying her any attention. "Huh? Y'all bout to do what?!" Laila called out, "Okay, I'll be right over."

Laila hopped up. "I'm sorry. My friends are calling me."

"Oh-"

"Um pleasure…" she held up her bottle, "putting lotion on you."

She turned and rushed away. Tricey looked at her strangely.

"She seems really shy," MJ said.

Kecia and Gia were headed towards the boardwalk. Laila sat down just as Melanie looked up.

"Good. Now you can watch the bags." She laid back and put her ear buds in. Laila noticed Alonzo making his way to her and admired his every move. Then, she stood up to embrace him.

Just as Alonzo was about to reach her, Tricey stood in front of him and handed a piece of paper to Laila.

"You forgot to get my number. Call me before you return home. I'll be here for the next two days. I can't wait to return the favor," she bit her bottom lip, turned and looked at Alonzo, and smiled at him.

"Hi," she said.

With a huge smile on his face, he waved.

She walked towards her friend who was waiting for her.

"That's my dawg, dropped them digits right in front of her brother," MJ said as they made their way back onto the sidewalk. He chuckled.

"Do I even want to know?"

"No, you don't."

"Should I be worried?"

Laila smiled, "You know I only have eyes for

you."

She hugged and kissed him.

He slid the paper out of her hand and balled it up.

"Just in case," He threw it behind him. She smirked at him, and he kissed her again.

CHAPTER 11

Later that night, Gia joined the ladies at their table at the Chateau Restaurant.

"Are we staying in here this time?" she said sarcastically.

"Yes, Alonzo is going to hang with the guys at the bar, and we can kick back here…have a few drinks and order something."

Laila and Alonzo locked eyes, and he smiled at her. He raised his glass at her, and she followed suit. She let out a sigh of relief. It was the first time in a long time that she had felt at ease. She took a sip, then gazed at the entrance from the corner of her eye. Another woman that resembled Alexandra entered the restaurant. She was dark brown with long black hair. She wore a black mini dress and black lace up heels. Her makeup was flawless, and she wore plum lipstick. This lady, however, was curvier than Alexandra's thin frame in high school. This woman had a perfect hourglass figure. Laila turned her head and almost choked on her drink. Kecia and Gia followed her gaze.

"What the hell is that bitch doing here?" Gia asked.

Melanie turned around in her seat and gasped.

Damn. It's really her this time.

Laila took a deep breath.

"It can't be..." Kecia said.

"Shit just got real," Gia said.

"Y'all stay right here, I got this."

"The hell we will!" Gia got up, but Kecia held her arm.

"Laila this is your wedding celebration," Melanie said at the same time. "You don't need to be dealing with this."

"It's okay. I got it."

Gia slowly sat back down in her chair, and Laila made her way to the front.

Alonzo rushed up to Alexandra.

"What are you doing here?"

"You haven't seen me in four years, and that's the greeting I get?"

"I say again what the hell are you doing here?"

"I'm here to make you come to your senses."

Laila stood beside Alonzo. "Alexandra, I've been expecting you."

"Laila McKee, well looks like you finally glowed up...a little."

Alonzo was puzzled. "Wait, you invited her?"

"No, but I figured if she got word of our engagement that she would show up uninvited," she looked towards Alexandra, "and here you are."

"Yes, I am here to claim my man."

"Your man? Okay...well, I'm sure you two have a lot to discuss," she said calmly as Alonzo looked at her strangely, "So you two take a seat, and the waiter will be with you shortly."

Alexandra beamed. "I don't know what you're up to, but this may be even easier than I thought."

Laila pulled out her chair for her. She sat down, and Laila pushed it close to the table. Alonzo pulled Laila to the side.

"What are you doing?"

"I'm letting you and your old friend catch up. She's obviously here to stop us from being together, so I want you to talk to her."

"But I don't want to talk to her, Laila. What I want is for her to leave."

"Why wouldn't you want to talk to her unless you think old feelings are going to come rushing back?"

"No, that's not it. I just don't want her here."

"But do you really? Look at her. She's beautiful. Your first love. Your high school sweetheart. Don't you both owe it to yourselves to make sure nothing's still there?"

"This doesn't sound like you. Where is this coming from?" he asked. Laila remained silent, "Is it because of you and Quinton?"

"No..." she shook her head and winced, "Yes...No, Alonzo. It's about you making sure all former chapters of your life have been closed before starting a new one with me."

He blew his breath.

Laila continued, "If we send her away now, who's to say she won't pop up throughout our marriage? Who's to say you won't give in to temptation?"

"Me."

"Prove it to me. Now. Before we even get married. This is your shot to show me that I will never have to

74

worry about 'Same Old Alonzo' rearing his ugly head in our marriage. Do it for me, Alonzo. Talk to her."

She walked over to the table and pulled out Alonzo's chair and motioned for him to sit.

At the bar, the guys were watching the exchange in shock.

"What the hell? Am I seeing this shit right?" Taaz asked. "Laila has lost her mind."

"It's her way of giving recompense for what happened between me and Melanie," Quinton said.

"Recom what?" Taaz asked.

Alonzo was hesitant, almost frozen where he stood.

Quinton and Taaz cringed as Laila continued to motion for him to sit at the table with Alexandra.

"I wish he would look over here," Quinton said.

His cousins motioned for him to look.

"Don't do it. It's a trick," Julian said.

"Don't fall for it, bruh. She's testing you," Taaz said.

"Come on Alonzo...grab Laila's hand and walk out," Quinton said.

"Whatever you do, do not sit yo ass down," Damien said.

"It's a test man...come on," Duke said.

Alonzo slowly sat down.

"Aww..." all the guys groaned as if Alonzo had made an incomplete pass on a football field. They turned around, hit the bar, and grabbed their drinks.

"Man, I thought we taught that bwoi better than that," Taaz said.

They all watched Laila as she walked out of the restaurant.

"So what the hell do we do now?" Taaz asked Quinton.

"Find some excuse for him to leave the table?" Duke asked.

"Are we really gonna let this go down?" Damien asked.

"Well, Laila looked very adamant about them talking to each other."

"I'm sure you know," Taaz smirked.

"Don't start that."

"I'm saying man...what do we do now?" he repeated.

"We just need to make sure they don't go anywhere else if you get what I'm saying."

At the ladies' table, they were watching Alonzo and Alexandra in disgust.

"So I can't go over there and pull his ass from that table?" Gia asked.

"Nope," Kecia replied.

"Or pull her by her 26 inch Yaki Malaysian?"

"No, Gia."

"It's what Laila wants... I'm about to check on her," Melanie said.

"We're coming with you. Then, we're heading right back in here to monitor this situation," Kecia grabbed her phone and clutch.

"I mean how long are we gonna let this go on?"

"I guess as long as it takes," Kecia said, "But we are not letting them leave out of this restaurant together."

Alonzo looked around and then looked at Alexandra, "Umm...soo?"

"Sooo…"

"Why are you really here?"

"To stop you from making the biggest mistake of your life."

"And that is?"

"Missing out on marrying me."

He laughed. "Come on Alley Cat, you're not the marrying type."

"I'll admit…I wasn't then, but I am now."

"And what changed you?"

"You did."

"It's all been a competition. I have always been a prize for you to win. I am what made you feel dominant over every woman I've been with. If I didn't have anyone right now, I wouldn't even be on your radar."

"That's not true. I've always thought we would cross paths again, and I've always known that we were made for each other, which is the reason why I was so competitive. You're my soul mate, Zo. You know it, and I know it. We've always known it. We're the same."

"I once thought that a time or two, but you kept throwing that ass at me and clouding my judgment. At one point, I didn't know whether I loved you or just fucking you."

"It was both for me, and I can't let you marry her. Not when I know there's still hope for us."

"But is there though?" he asked.

"Laila!" Kecia and Melanie caught up with her down the hall.

"Can you explain what's going on?" Melanie asked.

"Bitch, are you okay?" Gia said approaching them.

"Yes, I'm fine. I just kept having this recurring dream that she showed up among many others. And in those dreams, I have reacted in so many ways except I was never the bigger woman. So I just want them to sit and talk like adults…figure out if something is still there. If there is, we can cancel the wedding or let her step in my place like Marla did."

Melanie dropped her head and looked away. Gia studied her face.

Laila continued, "And I can go on with my life instead of living my entire marriage with her overshadowing us."

"But this is not the same as Quinton's situation," Kecia said.

Gia clicked her tongue. "Lonzo wouldn't go back to that nasty ran through skank."

Laila took a deep breath. "Well, if nothing is there, we can send her on her merry way and move forward into a new life together without any baggage."

Melanie thought for a moment. "Well, that makes sense."

"Yeah, I just knew she was coming. I knew it."

"Is that why the wedding was not at home?" Kecia inquired.

"No…Yes…No…Maybe…I don't know."

"Okay, well you get some rest. We'll keep an eye on them," Melanie said.

"There is no rest for me until she's gone," she walked away.

Melanie sighed and headed towards the restaurant. Kecia looked at Gia, "You sure she didn't have anything to do with this?"

They followed her.

Gia called out, "Melanie, we were thinking, and

78

you know what?" Melanie turned to them. "This has you written all over it."

"Me?"

"Yes, you."

"How could you think that I'm capable of doing something like this?"

"Because you are," they said together.

"You probably found Alexandra and flew her down here."

"I don't have time for this," she attempted to walk away.

"Oh, you finna make time." Gia jumped in front of her and eyed her. Melanie attempted to go left and then to the right, but Gia blocked her every move. They looked as if they were about to fight.

"Melanie, you might as well answer the questions cuz you're not getting away," Kecia pushed them away from one another. Then, stood by Gia to wait for Melanie's answer.

"Did you concoct a scheme to get Alexandra down here?"

"No, I didn't. I can't believe I'm actually defending myself."

"Drop the front. We got you. You really think we believe that you gon' let Laila messing up your wedding and marriage to Quinton fly? She slept with your man."

"Well, damn. Thanks for the constant reminders." Melanie rolled her eyes.

Gia scoffed. "Laila's crazy for letting you come near her wedding."

"And you're trying to make sure they don't get married, aren't you?"

"As clever as that plan would have been, I am not

the mastermind behind this. I forgave her...and yes, the old me would have been vindictive. But, I value our friendship too much to do anything like this. And, think about how Alexandra tortured me in high school, why would I want her anywhere near me now?"

"Well, that's true."

"Maybe you two buried the hatchet and are allies now."

"Allies my ass," Melanie said, "You can believe what you want. I don't care. When you want to talk about ways to get rid of this bitch, you know where to find me."

"Gia, I don't think she's lying."

Gia scoffed again.

Melanie turned around. "I guess I understand why you have your reservations. If I were you, I would be the same way considering how I've behaved over the years. But I'm different now, you'll see."

Meanwhile, Alexandra and Alonzo were still at the table. They were both laughing and drinking champagne.

"Oh no, this is not good," Quinton said to the guys at the bar.

"Waiter, can you bring us Merlot as well?" Alexandra asked.

Alonzo was reflecting on their past. "That was not me. That was Quinton."

"It was you! Mr. McClelland never walked the same again."

"All I did was loosen a few screws in his chair. Quinton was the one that poured that honey on the floor."

"Well, you had me hiding you in the girls' locker room."

"Yeah, I probably would have gotten expelled or suspended and kicked off the football team."

"See, I had your back by giving you that alibi."

"Yeah, you did."

"All you got was detention for being mannish and making out with me," she smiled, "And boy did we have some good times especially in our 20's."

"Yeah, when we weren't arguing and when you weren't fighting girls over me...like Gallena."

"But we eventually tongue kissed and made up."

His eyes brightened. "Yeah, you two started getting along really well."

"Well, she couldn't beat me might as well join us."

Alonzo smiled as he thought about their past times.

"You see with Laila, you'll be stuck with just one woman day in and day out for the rest of your life. But with me, you can savor me, and we can bring in any woman you desire."

"And as good as that sounds, I'm just not that guy anymore."

There was silence. Alonzo spoke again.

"So what have you been doing these days?"

"Well, you know I never rose to Naomi Campbell status with my modeling, but I have a large following on YouTube and Instagram."

"You're on YouTube?" He was surprised.

"Yes, I am. I do makeup tutorials, vlogs, and fashion," she beamed. "I make appearances all over the country, and I see the world, but there's always been something missing."

"And that is?"

"You."

He looked away and sighed. "You thought I was never going to get married, didn't you?"

"Yes, I guess it doesn't matter if you're married as long as I can have you whenever I'd like, but I've always thought if we ever decided to get married, it would be to each other. I'm supposed to be your bride. I was always supposed to be your bride."

"Alley, come on."

"Just remember all of our good times."

"I don't want to think about any of that."

"Because you know something is still there."

"My feelings for you were in the past. We've always been volatile to each other. Hurt after hurt. You really want to bring up our past? Ok, let's go deep. I started messing with you when I was 15 because you were fine as hell, and all the guys were talking about you were fire, so I had to give it a try. Then, you blew my mind. I had never felt that way with any of the girls I was messing with...hell, you're the first girl who ever did all the work while I just sit back and do shit... I mean, I let all my girls go for you at one point. I straightened up for you, and what did you do? You messed around with Rodrick Hall at Dana's party. We broke up, and when we finally got back together, I did my thang. And that's when the whole feud with you and Gallena began. And the fighting, I loved it."

"Alonzo, we were kids."

"Oh, you were focusing on our past good times, now I'm focusing on our bad times. So let's fast forward to 2007, I had this beautiful woman named Abigail Houston. She was a sorority girl studying to become a doctor. I did my thang, but I started to care for someone I was in a relationship with for the first time after you. Then, you showed up. I cheated, she caught us, and she left. You pulled me into your world again, and that's when I got back up with Gallena. You told me you were gonna confront her, and the next thing I know you two were giving me the best birthday present I ever had in my life."

"I am very persuasive."

"You...you fucked my head up. But at that point, I couldn't choose between you two. I wanted the both of you all the time. Then, Gallena stopped coming around, and then you eventually stopped popping up. Your out-of-town fashion projects were your excuses for being away from me. And, I waited anxiously for you to come back after each gig, but you never came. I slept with woman after woman to fill that void. I revisited my past over and over again, and then I knew I had to let you go. Because all we ever really had was the sex. Sex that can fuck with a man's soul. If there was no sex, there would have been nothing between us."

"That's not true, and you know it."

"Alley, be honest with yourself. You are not the marrying type."

"Because of what? I'm just a ho ... a thot?"

"I would never call you that Alley, but you've never been faithful to a man in your entire life. How do you expect to be faithful now?"

"You haven't been faithful the majority of yours either."

"Like I said before, I was faithful to you, and I've been faithful to Laila since we've been together."

"And you really expect me to believe that?"

"I'm not asking you to."

"What makes Laila so special?"

"She's special because I know that she's my wife."

She smirked, "So when you're married, if you meet a beautiful woman, and she throws herself at you, you're not going to give in?"

"Alexandra, I can't say what I'm going to do in the future. Who knows I may slip up, I may not. But, right now, in the present, I am going to do everything in my power not to hurt her."

"Alonzo-"

"Alley, you're a good woman, and any man would be happy to have you as his wife, and one day he will find you, but it's not me."

"How do you know that for sure?"

"Because Alley, I didn't bother to look for you or talk to your family. I didn't stalk your pages or slide in your DMs. I didn't even know you were posting videos. I could have found you online. I could have hired a PI. I could have showed up at your apartment or house, at your hotels, at your shows…hell even at your local grocery store, but I didn't. The thought never crossed my mind."

"So you would run to the ends of the Earth to find your wife, huh?"

"Yes."

She smirked and folded her arms. "And so…where did you find Laila after all of these years?"

"Huh?"

"In Dubai? Was she parlaying in Paris? Was she doing whatever it is that she does in Atlanta? Or, was it right in our hometown?"

He didn't respond.

"Just as I thought. You've never worked for what you want. You've never went out of your way to get any woman…You're a man of convenience. You've always wanted what was right in front of you. Out of sight, out of mind and on to the next you go. So don't sit there and tell me all of this crap when I know it's not true."

Alonzo was at a loss for words. "You're something." He glanced across the restaurant and saw Melanie, Gia, and Kecia sitting back down at their table.

"So tell me where did you meet up with her again? Our grocery store? Wal-Mart? Bank? Bar? Or maybe at Quinton's wedding rehearsal? How convenient."

"I see you've been keeping up with me."

"Facebook is a hell of a mouthpiece. News travel faster than you can ever imagine."

"So what point are you trying to make?"

"I am saying, had I never left…had I never gotten out of your sights," Alexandra said, "then I would be the one with the ring on my finger. If I would have stuck around, there's no way we wouldn't be together. And, you can bet my life on that."

"But the fact remains that you left. I wasn't going to make you stay. You were trying to launch a modeling career. I would have been a fool to make you stay."

"You could have come too."

"And do what? Be a model like you wanted me to be? I was a well-educated black man looking to make his mark in the finance world, not the fashion world."

She rolled her eyes, "But I'm here now, and if we can have a second chance, I promise I won't go anywhere. I'll be faithful, just don't close the door on us."

"You closed it when you left and set me free. I

can't...no I refuse to go there with you again. Look, I'm touched that you came all this way, and I'm glad we got a chance to catch up but we had our time, Alexandra...quite a few times, and it never worked out. So I'm sorry, but I'm still marrying Laila." He got up.

"Well, you can't blame a girl for trying."

"It was good seeing you, but I have to say goodbye, Alexandra," he walked back over to the guys as she left out of the restaurant.

"Alonzo, you good, man?" Taaz asked.

"Yeah," he said, then to the bartender, "Can I get a shot of Patrón and a bottle of Pinot Noir?"

"Dang, I was worrying about you for a second," Quinton said.

"Yeah, I'm fine," he leaned his arm against the bar.

"Laila gon' beat that ass, bwoi."

The bartender tapped him and gave him the shot glass. He chugged the shot.

"Everyone, can I have your attention please?" Alonzo announced, "I'm getting married to a beautiful woman named Laila McKee. Rounds for everyone on me." The people cheered.

"Popping bottles, I see," Gia said, "Come on y'all. Let's go."

"I'm about to go get my free round." Melanie rushed over to the bar.

Gia smirked as she saw Melanie interlock arms with Julian.

CHAPTER 12

As Gia and Kecia crossed the front lobby to meet Laila and Melanie for breakfast, they saw Alexandra checking out. She grabbed the handle of her Gucci luggage and walked out of the hotel. They entered the restaurant and saw Julian standing at Melanie and Laila's table.

"Well, well, well…if it isn't Nicole Ari Parker & Boris Kodjoe," she smirked at Julian and Melanie.

"Be nice, Gia," Laila said.

"I'll take that as a compliment," he grinned.

"Julian, would you like to join us?" Kecia asked.

"No, I'll let you ladies enjoy one another's company. Gia looks like she has some news to share."

He walked away.

"Sooo…"

"Girl, the bitch is gone!"

"Good! Thank y'all for not confronting her."

"It's your wedding. It wasn't our place to intervene."

"But if that B would've jumped stupid, I was rett," Gia said.

"We all were," Melanie said as she sipped her

Mimosa.

"I've got to give it to Alonzo. He handled that situation pretty well," Gia said.

"And kudos to you, Laila. You had such dignity and poise. I couldn't...well, you already know my reaction," Melanie referred to their fight.

"Yeah, yeah, yeah," Laila pursed her lips.

Kecia said, "I'm just glad she's gone cuz we ain't got time for any drama this go round."

"Yeah, well if anything else pops off, we got your back, girl."

"Man, Gia! Why would you even say that?"

"What I was just—"

"Nothing else is going to pop off," Kecia assured Laila.

"Well, like I said, if it do, I got your back."

Kecia frowned.

"Thanks girl," Laila said and let out a big sigh of relief, "Now we can sit back, relax, and prepare for the wedding."

"Exactly."

"Hey, have you tried on your dresses since you've picked them up?"

"I haven't."

"Me either."

Laila's phone started buzzing, and she saw a number she didn't recognize.

"Excuse me." She stepped away from the table.

"Now Kecia, you know your dress gon' be swallowing you. We may have to find a tailor out here."

"It'll be fine, Gia," Kecia shook her head. "Did you, Melanie?"

"Yes. I went to the dress shop, tried it out, and

made sure there were no holes or loose threads. Then, I had her to make a few alterations."

"Of course you did," Kecia said, regretting she even asked the question.

"Hello?" Laila answered her phone.

"Laila, is that you?" she heard an older lady say.

"Yes, who's speaking?"

"Hey, uh uh," she stuttered, "This is your Aunt Sarah, baby."

"Sarah?" she frowned. It was her estranged mom's only sister.

"Now please don't hang up. I know you're still upset about me not returning your calls," she said, "But baby, I'm sorry. I was just following my big sister's orders."

"So it's true that she is up there with you," she said.

"We live in Maryland now, but yes."

"So is this call one of her orders or you're calling on your own?"

"Actually both," she said, "Listen. Your mother... she's not doing too good. We're— we're at the hospital."

"The hospital?"

"Yes, she's been battling lung cancer."

"I'm not surprised."

"Well, we heard about your engagement, and we wanted to congratulate you. I hate that we had to interrupt your festivities, but we don't know how much longer she has, and she wants to see you."

"It's really that bad?"

"Yeah, the doctor told me to call up all her loved ones who wanna come in and see her. And you're her only child. She really wants to make amends before she leaves this Earth. I know this is asking a lot, but can you please just come up for a few hours and see her. We'll pay for your way…any expenses just as long as you get here in time."

"So you're saying if I don't come now, I may not ever get the chance to see my mother again?"

"Yes, that's exactly what I'm saying."

"Laila, please," she heard a faint voice say, but it was distinctly her mother's.

"She is trying to make up for it before it's too late. Now, I can wire some money down so you can travel any way you see fit."

"No, that won't be necessary. Tell my mother she had her time to call, visit me, and make amends. It didn't happen, so I'm not about to run up there on a whim on the week of my wedding."

"I understand. Well, if you change your mind, just call me back at this number."

"Uh huh," she ended the call.

Laila felt a pain in her throat, and her heart began to beat rapidly. Her eyes began to water. She returned to the table with tears pouring down her cheeks.

Her friends were laughing.

"I'm going to take a rain check on breakfast." Her hands shook as she put her phone in her clutch.

"Laila, what's wrong?"

"What happened?"

"Who was that on the phone?"

"That…that was my aunt. She said my mother is in the hospital and wants to see me. The doctors are saying she doesn't have much longer."

She wiped her eyes.

"No."

"I just have to process this," Laila said and walked out.

"She just had to pop her ass back up," Gia rolled her eyes.

"After all these years at this particular time in Laila's life," Melanie shook her head.

"With her wedding right around the corner," Kecia added.

"Fuck!" Gia said.

Kecia leaned forward. "You know I was thinking what's worse than Alexandra? Margarette Sanders McKee. That's who's worse. She could lift one finger and shut down this whole damn wedding."

"We can't let that happen. We've got to help pick up the pieces."

"Oh no, she's not about to shatter her again over my dead body," Kecia said. The two were about to get up to check on Laila.

Melanie said, "I know you've had your reservations about me since high school, and I've given you plenty of reasons not to trust me. I've been selfish and self-absorbed..."

"Like now." Gia smacked her lips.

"Let her finish."

"But all the while Laila stood by my side, and I still managed to hurt her too. And even during that time in her life when her parents left, I was nowhere to be found. I was busy living my own life. Let me help take care of her this time. I got this, okay?"

"If you pull any of that shady shi-"

"I won't. You have my word."

"Okay," Kecia said, and looked at Gia, "Melanie will take this one."

CHAPTER 13

On the fourth floor of the hotel, Alonzo was stretched out across Quinton's king-sized bed. He was fully clothed, wearing what he had on the night before. He noticed his shoes were off his feet as he slowly arose and sat on the side of the bed.

"Uhhh," he placed his hand to his throbbing head.

"Hey man," Quinton said, "I got you some water and an aspirin on the nightstand."

"Man, I had this crazy dream. Alexandra was here and tried to steal me away from Laila."

He sat up, took the aspirin, and sipped the water.

"I hate to break it to you, but it was no dream."

"Really? Where is she? Where's Laila?"

He hopped up and felt a sharp pain in his forehead. He grabbed his head again.

"Easy there."

He sat back down.

"Everything is fine. Laila is with the girls, and Taaz saw Alexandra leaving this morning."

"She spent the night here?"

"Yep."

"I thought there were no vacancies," he said. "But

you're sure she's gone?"

"Yes, she is."

"Oh, thank God. I would hate to think of what would happen if she were to catch me drunk as fuck."

"I know…I know. I wasn't gonna let that happen. We've come too far and went through too much to let her mess up what you and Laila have now."

"But damn, she was sexy as fuck though."

"That she was."

"I'm just hoping and praying there's no more surprises."

"Me too, but we got your back though. Taaz went to get us some breakfast."

"You could've just ordered room service."

"Naw, we found this ma and pop place online that has some great reviews. Hot links, country fried steaks, bacon, thick cuts of ham, homemade butter biscuits, grits, the works man…"

"They got a place like that down here?" he asked, "That's what's up. You talk to Marla?"

"Naw, she's ignoring my calls and texts." Quinton paced around the room, "I tried to convince her that she has nothing to worry about. I mean we started our marriage out wrong…of course, problems like this are expected. It's so hard for her to trust me."

"Well, she shouldn't have rushed and married you so abruptly then."

"I know we should have waited."

"But you wanna know why you didn't?"

"Why, man?" Quinton said expecting a long drawn out explanation about love.

"Because you two have that real love…You are soul mates. You have that connection, and once y'all got back up with one another, all of that bullshit didn't matter. Who you messed with…who she messed with…y'all just wanted to finally be together. You both just took a chance and tied the knot before anyone came to their senses…before anyone tried to talk you out of it. You just did it, and said 'fuck the world,' fuck what anybody had to say because you finally realized who your wife truly was. And though you had a lot of shit going on, you didn't run away. You didn't feel ashamed. You went straight to her like a man and asked her. She could have punched you, cussed you out, laughed in your face, but she didn't. You wanna know why?"

"I'm pretty sure you're about to tell me why."

"Because the man she always wanted came and found her. He was at her door. Quinton, you chose her, and deep down, you both knew she would say yes."

Quinton's phone buzzed. It was Marla. He rushed out of the room. "I'll be back."

"Ah, I'm about to," the door slammed behind Quinton, "take a shower in my room."

CHAPTER 14

Walking down the hall, Quinton nodded at Damien and Duke as they headed to the elevator. He held his phone tightly to his ear. "Why haven't I been calling you? Marla, I have! I've called, texted, and left voicemail messages. I've been waiting for you to respond to me," he paused. "Yes! Marla, listen to me. I'm trying to enjoy being here for my boy's wedding, but you won't let me. I'm not doing anything. You could've came with me so you can see for yourself."

He walked into the stairwell, and the door closed behind him. He saw Laila crying on the steps.

"Hey, I'll call you back," he quickly ended the call without waiting for a response.

"Laila, are you ok?"

"I don't know."

He sat beside her, and she collapsed in his arms.

"Everything is handled. Alexandra is gone, and Alonzo stayed in my room."

"No, it's not that."

"Then what is it?"

"I mean I don't even feel comfortable telling you this since you've already went through this."

"Come on. It's me, remember? You can talk to me about anything… okay?"

She continuously sobbed.

"You want me to go get Alonzo?"

"No, I have to collect my thoughts. That's why I'm here. Please…not yet," her voice cracked, "It's my mother. She had my aunt to contact me. She's…she's dying from lung cancer."

"Oh really? I hate to hear that. So after all this time, she finally gets in touch with you."

"Right, and she wants me to come out there and see her before the wedding. And I don't know what to do…I mean why now? And she's dying?"

"I know you don't understand. I still can't wrap my head around it, but it changes you. Fucks up your world until you don't even see the point of going on with your life. It's like having a piece of your heart just ripped out, and all you feel is emptiness and this throbbing pain that never goes away."

"You two were so close."

"Yes, and I know it is a completely different situation with your mom. And it's fucked up what her and your father did to you, but you only get one mom."

"But why did she wait until now to reach out during what's supposed to be the happiest moment of my life? I just don't want to deal with it. Not now."

"I was mad for a long time too, but life happens… and it is something people will never get used to," Quinton said, "But Laila, she is still here right now, and you might not get another chance to see her. You have to go."

She shook her head.

"If not for her, then for you. You owe it to

yourself and Lonzo to hear her out and ask her anything you want to know. Reconcile. Get closure. Some good will come out of it."

"You don't know her, she's...she's the worst."

"Well, if nothing comes of it, you'll know you did all you could, and you'll have no regrets."

She sighed.

"Laila, if I got a phone call with someone on the other end telling me that I could see my mom, that she was somewhere on this planet, I would do everything in my power just to get to her... to get one more hug, to hear one more laugh from her, to see that beautiful smile. I would move heaven and earth to get to her. Nothing and I mean nothing would keep me from her. Now you think hard and talk things over with Alonzo and make your decision."

He got up and helped her to her feet.

"Thanks Quinton."

"Hey, what are friends for?" he hugged her, "And this conversation never happened."

"Ohhh...yeah. Gotta get in the habit of going to my husband first."

"Right," he chuckled.

"Considering our history and your friendship with Alonzo, I'm glad that I can still talk to you."

"Welp, like it or not, we're family. You're stuck with me."

He opened the door for her, and she went searching for Alonzo.

CHAPTER 15

In her hotel room, Laila sat on the bed and watched as a shirtless Alonzo walked across the room in navy blue shorts, wiping beads of water off his chest with a gray towel.

"I can't believe she wants me to come out there before we get married."

He sat down in a chair and grabbed a bottle of lotion off the night stand. "Aw, I was hoping they would come down, but since she's on her...I mean since she's bed ridden, you have to go see her," he said as he rubbed lotion onto his legs.

"I was not expecting you to be for it."

"Laila, if someone called me about my dad right now, no one would keep me from seeing him no matter where he was. We have a lot of things to work out as do you and your parents, but he's still my family," he said. "Laila, you have a lot of things that you're holding on to. It looks like she's ready to give you the answers."

She blew her breath.

"Laila, you've let go of Quinton, but now your biggest feat is letting go of the anger and resentment you have towards your parents. Baby, you have to do this. Our happiness is at stake."

Laila sighed.

"I'll be with you every step of the way."

"Okay, okay. I'll go and see what she has to say."

"I'm telling you if she couldn't say it in a letter or over the phone, it has to be important for her to want you to come right now nearly 1,000 miles away." Alonzo stood up and put on a gray muscle shirt.

They received a knock on the door and heard Melanie say, "Umm, Taaz that breakfast smells good."

Alonzo opened the door and motioned for her to come in.

Laila and Alonzo continued to talk to one another. Melanie sat beside her friend on the bed and placed her arm around her.

"Yeah, but if I do this, you can't come with me."

"Why not?"

"I have to do this alone. You've got your old college buddies coming in. You need to be here making sure everything is coming along according to plan."

He sighed, "No, you're more important. I want to be there to support you."

"And you will be when we're married. I have to do this myself."

He reluctantly agreed. "You are taking at least one of the girls, right?"

"Yes."

He wrinkled his brows. "Which one?"

"Um...that is a good question," Laila thought, "I don't really know about taking Gia or Kecia cuz they been don' flew across that room and jumped on her bed. They'd put her in a coma or on life support."

"You ain't lying," he rubbed the back of his head.

"They would be cussing her out, and I wouldn't get a word in edgewise."

"Yes, and if you tell them to stay outside, nothing but busting in on that ass."

"Uhhh," Laila groaned.

"I'll go with her," Melanie finally said, "And we can leave the others here."

Alonzo was surprised. "You sure?"

Melanie nodded.

Laila turned to her. "What about Julian? I thought you wanted to stay with him."

"Oh, no. He will be fine."

"Cousin, make sure she's safe. I'll go ahead and book the flight." He grabbed his phone.

"No, I want to drive up the coast. I need time to think."

"I thought you said she didn't have much time left."

"Either way it goes, I'm still taking my time and driving up," she said firmly.

Alonzo bit his bottom lip. He wanted to protest, but he told her, "Okay, I'll get you a car."

CHAPTER 16

Gia sat in a white lounge chair on the beach near a tiki bar. She looked around, then picked up her phone.

"Ain't shit better to do. Guess I'll go live."

She looked at herself on the screen, adjusted her cover up, and smoothed out her twists.

"It's your gurl, *G* outchea live, vacationing... getting ready for this wedding."

She started reading the comments.

"Oh hey Dee girl. Uh uh...you're supposed to be working. Don't say you're taking a break. Yeah, bye..."

She saw her brother joined the live feed.

"Hey Gavin! Hey Keeta. Lady Vee. Dang, y'all are nosey? Well, if you must know, I am here at an undisclosed location. The bride and groom doesn't want anybody to know where we are, so I gotta be tight with my shot. I can't have no signs or special landmarks or nothing cuz some of you Private I motherfuckers will find out. I turned off my location feature, and I ain't checking in at *nan* place. Drika, what you say? Hold up!"

She scrolled back to find her client's comment.

"'They act like they're Beyoncé and Jay-Z or something.' You're so wrong, but yep, and I'm Kelly Rowland," she smirked.

"Aunt Rena, I *am* behaving. Get off here. You know I don't like for you to hear me cussing and shi-" She paused, "See! I warned you."

She scrolled through the comments again. She rolled her eyes, "Uh Michael, get your thirsty ass out my comments and out my DMs. You better hope your baby mama ain't on here. Oops, she is. Hey girl, just let that broke joke go. You can do so much better...Wait."

She leaned forward in her seat. "Vic, what are you talking about? What dude in my background? and Aunt Rena saying the fine dude on the right side of me."

She couldn't see the person on her phone, so she slowly turned around and saw Julian. He waved, and she rolled her eyes.

"It's Melanie's thirsty plus one."

She continued to read the comments. She noticed the comments moving along rapidly.

"He's sexy? Greek god? Wait, I'ma need y'all to chill out with all those hearts and heart eyes emojis. More like the vomit emoji. He gets on my last nerves. Somebody need to come get him...Carly, no you didn't say I need to. Y'all are on one today, for real."

She leaned back in her chair and read another comment aloud, "Laila took Quinton from Melanie passed him to Marla," she scrolled back up to the same comment, "Gia might as well take that hottie for herself. See y'all are so petty."

The comments continued.

"'Will there be drama this time?' When has there ever been no drama at any function I be at? Gavin, don't play with me, talking bout I should have stayed my black ass at home then. Aunt Rena, how you gon' say you concur? That's fu-," she almost cussed but cleared her throat, "funny. Hey, I am not the cause of everyone's drama anymore. I know I've stirred up some shit in the past, but I'm growing. Y'all tell my brother to go somewhere. I am not lying. We've all made mistakes, and at some point, you've just got to let it all go and do better. When you know better, you do better. Just focus on your own shit and stack your paper. That's exactly what I'm doing. So I'ma let y'all get back to y'all boring ass lives and tune back into your regularly scheduled lurking…umm huh," she chuckled, "*Luh* y'all bye."

She ended the live video. She looked behind her back, but Julian was no longer in sight.

CHAPTER 17

The next morning, under the porte-cochère in front of the hotel, Melanie and Laila got into their white rental car. Alonzo, Gia, Kecia, and the twins were outside seeing them off.

"Make sure that you call me and let me know what's going on," Kecia said.

"No, I want you girls to sit back and relax while you're here. I will fill you in on everything once we get back. It's your vacation, and I want you both to enjoy it...take in the surroundings and try out all the amenities here."

Kecia frowned.

"Shoot, you ain't gotta tell me twice," Gia said, "But be careful."

"Yes," Alonzo agreed, "You two look out for one another, and if you notice the slightest sign of trouble, call me and I'll come running," Alonzo said.

"Okay, love you."

"Love you more," he rushed around the car to the driver's side, stuck his head through the lowered window, and made out with her.

"Alright, alright. Break it up," Melanie said,

"We've got a lot of ground to cover."

"Melanie," Gia glared at her, reminding her of the promise she had made them.

"I've got it."

They all waved at Laila and Melanie as the car pulled away. Alonzo watched until the car was no longer in sight. He looked around, "Where's Quinton?"

"I saw him in the hall, but he didn't come down," Kecia said as they entered the lobby.

"Shoot, all I know is that I'm hungry," Gia rubbed her belly.

"Come get me in a little while, and we can get some breakfast."

"Alright cool."

Alonzo opened the door to an outside sitting area on the fourth floor. He spotted Quinton leaning against the rail with his head down. He slowly made his way to his friend. Quinton looked back at him and had tears in his eyes.

"You okay, man?" Alonzo patted his back.

"Yeah," he wiped his face, "Just out here talking to Ma. Man, she always talked about you getting married. She said that she knew you would find that one woman that would make you straighten up and forget about everything else. And, she was right."

"Yeah, she knew it before anybody. Not even my mama had faith that I would let go of my ways. But not sure if Ma Carol approved of who I chose."

"Honestly, she didn't at first. She was afraid that she would come between us, and she didn't want that."

"And that will never happen," Alonzo said, "All

you had to do was say the word, and I would have stopped pursuing her."

"Bruh, stop it."

"I fought for her true enough, but I would have eventually bowed out."

"Naw, I'm glad you put up a fight because she was never supposed to be mine in the first place. I was the one standing in the way of you two in high school. Y'all may have been married by now with some bad ass kids."

Alonzo laughed, "Naw I wasn't ready for her in high school or my 20's. Everything happened just as it should have."

Quinton sighed.

"That's what I keep telling myself about Ma, but man, she should be here with us right now."

"But she is. She's right here," Alonzo placed his fist to his chest, "I know I feel her in mine. With every breeze, I feel her. When you and Marla have kids, you'll see her in them. She's definitely still here looking down on us. Keeping us on the right path and being proud of us for becoming the men she taught us to be. Hardworking, faithful, strong men who aren't afraid to be vulnerable and express our feelings about anything. We have her to thank for that.

"Yes we do," he let out a deep sigh, "I know they say it gets easier with time, but it just never gets easy. Never."

"Well, we're here for you. You don't ever have to worry about going through anything alone. We got you."

"Thanks bruh."

They did their handshake and hugged each other.

"Now let's go get fucked up!"

Quinton chuckled as they walked towards the door.

"And, I need your help with my latest scheme."

CHAPTER 18

Wearing a white robe, Kecia was lying on her bed toward the foot of the bed. She held her phone in her hand as she had a video chat with Winston.

"You okay, babe? You look tired."

"I'm fine, just missing you."

He smiled, "Don't worry. I'll be there in time for the wedding. My plane gets in at five o'clock that morning."

"Okay, I forgot to book the rental."

He chuckled, "Don't worry about it. I already booked it before you left."

"But we may not need it since we're flying back out the very next day. We really don't need it."

"Well, I still want to take my lady sightseeing."

"That's sweet," she smiled, "I just hope we'll have time."

"We will, trust me."

"Yes, you are very time efficient, we'll probably have more than enough time to do everything and then some."

He bit his lip, "I love making time for you."

Kecia tried to hide her smile.

"I see the gang has been keeping you busy."

"Yeah...wait, what do you mean by that?"

"Oh, you didn't respond to a few of my texts."

"Yes, I did."

"The one I sent this morning, but not last night."

"Oh, I'm sorry, baby. What did they say?"

"I asked if you were enjoying yourself, and from that beautiful smile on your face, I know that you are."

"Yes, I am."

"And then, I asked what room are you staying in?"

"Oh, I missed all of that, but it's Room-"

A knock interrupted her.

"Oh Winston, that's Gia. I have to go. Love you," she quickly blew a kiss at him.

He stammered, "Love you too." He smiled warmly at her. Then, she ended the video chat.

She opened the door and looked at her friend. "Well, you're all dressed and ready to go."

"Girl, you know I don't play about my food." Gia walked in and gazed out of the glass door. "They gave you a room with a beach view! I'm jealous."

"Well, at least they put us right across the hall from each other."

"I think it just fell into place like that."

"Well, it worked out."

"Man, I got the courtyard view though... all I can do is look at the sitting areas, a pool, and little sunburned blonde girls throwing themselves at old pasty men."

"That's just you being nosey."

"Like you," Gia's stomach growled, "I'm so damn hungry."

"Well, I ordered room service. Our food is on the

balcony."

"You lying."

"I ordered some turkey sausages, veggie omelets, fresh seasonal fruit, croissants just for you, and Martinelli's apple juice."

"Now, that's what I'm talking about."

They went out onto the balcony and sat down in the chairs. Gia looked at the setting on the small table. She took the silver cover off the food. Her mouth watered. She saw a clear pitcher of cold apple juice. They fixed their plates and poured their drinks into wine glasses. They silently prayed, then started eating. They propped their feet up on the foot stools.

"Girl, we living like queens," Gia said, "All I need now is a butt ass naked man fanning me with those big white feather fans."

Kecia shook her head. She held up her glass of apple juice.

"Here's to sitting back and relaxing for a change."

"Damn right," she clanged glasses with Kecia. Then, she joked, "Who's the bougie bitches now?"

Kecia held out her pinky as she drank, "We are and loving it."

They high-fived and laughed. "Girl, we ain't got no kind of sense."

CHAPTER 19

Laila took a deep breath as she looked in her rear view mirror. She turned on her left signal light and pulled onto the left lane to pass a slow gray Corolla. She rushed and got back into the right lane, so the eager black Tundra behind her could zoom by. She was blasting the air, and the car was as cold as a winter's day.

Melanie, who had been asleep with her cardigan covering her, stretched in her seat and came to.

"Laila, are you okay? You haven't said a word since we left."

"How could I? You've been sleeping most of the time." Laila glanced at her. "You even have drool running all down the seat." She chuckled.

"No, I don't, and I haven't been asleep very long." She flipped the visor and looked at herself in the vanity mirror. She wiped the corners of her mouth and applied lip gloss, "But, are you okay?"

"Yeah, I guess. I just have so much running through my mind. From my mom to Alonzo to Alexandra. Mind's racing back and forth between the three."

"Well, I'm here, and we have a few more hours to go, so share."

Laila blew her breath, "I had finally accepted the fact that my parents were out of my life...that I would probably never see them again. Now, here I am heading to see one of them. I don't know what I'm going to say. Like, what will my first words be when I lay eyes upon her? What questions will I ask her? Will I be angry? Will I be happy to see her? Or, will I freeze and not even step foot in the room?"

"Just breath and relax. You have plenty of time to gather your thoughts. Think of the main questions you want answered, and the rest will flow. And if you need help, you can pull me in from the waiting room."

Laila smiled and nodded.

"So what about Alexandra and Alonzo?"

"That whole situation shocked me even though I knew it was coming. I had a feeling, but I just thought it was all in my head. I expected her to pop up, yet I couldn't believe she actually showed."

"So that's why you've been acting strange," Melanie thought, "Well, the mind and tongue are very powerful instruments. Maybe you made it happen by continually thinking on it. There have been a lot of instances that I manipulated. I knew certain things would happen, so I would intervene to either prevent them from occurring or make sure things resulted in my favor. But, what I tried to prevent happened anyway. Look at how hard I tried to keep you away from Quinton. I just knew if he ever saw you again, you would get together. Never did I imagine that he would still want you even after he got with me."

Laila rolled her eyes as she turned her head to glance in the side view mirror. No matter what, Melanie always seemed to make every conversation about herself.

"Melanie, you've got to let that go."

"But think about it. Had I not sought out Quinton, brought him back home, and got you involved with the wedding, you two would have never reconnected. Then, you and Alonzo would have crossed paths under different circumstances. All the awkwardness would have been prevented, and you two would have been married by now. Alonzo wouldn't even be on Alexandra's radar."

"You can't blame yourself."

Melanie sighed, "I should have listened to our teacher, Mrs. Barlow when she quoted Einstein, 'Every action has an equal and opposite reaction.'"

"Well, your actions did not cause all of this. Everything happened as it was supposed to happen. The best thing for us to do is learn from it and move on."

"You're right."

Laila exhaled.

"But something's still bothering you."

Duh bitch.

"Yes, there's just one past I can't get over, and that is Alonzo's past."

"Well, people are capable of changing. I'm proof of that."

Laila stretched her neck. "I guess so, but Melanie, am I crazy?"

"Crazy?"

"Am I crazy for marrying Alonzo? After all the women he's hurt…after everything I know he's done to them, am I crazy to still want him? They say the definition of insanity is doing the same thing over and over and expecting different results. We know Alonzo and the guys better than anybody, and lately, I'm just finding it hard to believe that I'm the exception. What makes me so special for him to leave Alexandra alone for good—a girl that's his true match. They've kicked it for years, and I'm pretty sure they've been way more adventurous than I could ever be. How can I top that and all the other beautiful women he's been with?"

"Oh, he's had some ugly ones too. Believe you me."

Laila quickly cut her eyes at Melanie. Then, she continued, "Am I just signing up to be the good wife that gets cheated on? Is he secretly mad at the fact I slept with Quinton?"

"He said he had a problem with you and Quinton?"

"No."

"Well, he wouldn't have proposed if that was a problem."

"I know, but any normal guy wouldn't be okay with that."

"Well, we've learned long ago that Alonzo is not normal." Melanie said, "Laila, you have valid concerns. I understand that, but in all the time you've been with Alonzo, you have never thought of any of this. In fact, you've just been going with the flow and were ready to drop him without a thought if he cheated…but he hasn't. You've experienced a side of Alonzo that no woman has, and I'm pretty sure your doubts are just now showing up because you're about to get married. It's wedding jitters. That's all."

"I hope so."

"It makes what you two have even more real. It's proof that this is not just a fling or a way to get over Quinton, but a real relationship. You're about to make a real commitment that will last a lifetime. And that scares you. Not to be cheated on, not the thought of being alone, but you now have feelings that you've never felt before. You're in love with him, and you've finally opened up your heart again. In the past, you've been hurt so many times that you completely shut down."

"That's true."

"I know you built this fairytale in your head that Quinton would be your knight in shining armor to come and bring light back into your world, but you had the wrong guy. It was always the guy standing behind him. But, you couldn't see him for us standing in the way."

Laila remembered when Alonzo was staring at her at Melanie and Quinton's wedding rehearsal.

"And you have to stop selling yourself short. You are a great catch, and Alonzo's lucky to have you."

Laila sighed.

"For the remainder of our trip, no matter what happens here on out, remember that what you have with Alonzo is unbreakable."

CHAPTER 20

Gia stepped off the elevator and spotted Kecia sitting in a chair in the lobby. "I should have known I'd find you down here people watching."

"You know it."

Gia sat next to her. "I'm beginning to see why people bring a plus one with them to weddings and on vacations. They keep you entertained when everyone else is doing their own thing."

"Right, I can't believe you actually came solo."

"Yep."

"You could have invited Rico."

"Girl, that's been over with."

"What happened?"

"Girl, he got Quala Luckett pregnant."

"For real? Lil' short Qua?"

"Yep, I heard the news at the shop, so I called him over to my apartment that night and ended it."

"How did he take it?"

"Not well."

"I know he didn't because he loved him some you."

"Yeah, I guess. He gon' tell me he didn't know if it

was his baby. Now, you know Quala was a grade below us. She's never been out there like that. Then, he started crying like a lil' punk telling me he was in love with me, and he really wanted to be with me."

"Aw...at least he told you he loved you."

"Aw my ass. He just wanted to go back to the way things were, but I couldn't go back," Gia said. "I can't go through messing with another dude with a pregnant girl."

"Huh? Who are you talking about?"

"I never told you, did I?"

"Uh no."

"Well, in the tenth grade, Jamel Myers was-"

"I remember him. He had been going with Nikki Sparkman since junior high, and he got her pregnant their senior year."

"Yep, I was messing around with him."

"For real? And here we thought you weren't doing anything. Well, I knew about Dex, but not Jamel."

"Yeah, I found ways to slip away. I think some folks knew, but they didn't say anything. Somehow, Nikki found out. She came to the house, and luckily, I was alone. She told me she wanted to speak to me, so I told her ass no. Then, she told me she'll wait outside so she could talk to my parents and Shawn when they got home."

"Dang, I bet Shawn would have gone crazy if he found out his classmate was banging his little sister and to make matters worse, he had a baby on the way. Damn. What happened next?"

"Well, I let her in, and she told me she knew all about me and Jamel. She told me to end it with him, so I got in the bitch's face. The next thing I knew, that pregnant bitch had kicked my ass in my own house. She threatened to tell all of my brothers on me and Jamel if I didn't keep my mouth shut and stay away from him."

"Damn."

"The next day, Jamel didn't even look my way like she had scared his ass too, and we never spoke again."

"Damn, he was probably scared of your brothers," Kecia said, "It's hard to believe you held that in."

"Yeah, I have my secrets that I can keep, but that situation made me realize I would never keep a man from his kid and the mother of his child. It also made me realize that I don't want a man with a baby mama."

Kecia laughed.

"What?"

"You finally got your ass kicked, and I wasn't there to see it."

"Whatever. You know you would have pulled that pregnant bitch off of me."

"Yeah, you know I got your back girl," Kecia said, "But you've got to admit, you were wrong for how you treated Rico."

Gia smirked.

"If you would have gotten into a real relationship like he wanted, there is no way he would have started messing with Qua."

"I know, but I just wasn't feeling him like that. That *D* was all I wanted, and even *that* got old."

"Shame," Kecia shook her head, "You a savage just like your brothers."

"I'm just real. I probably should have messed with the countless dogs that didn't mind a deal like what me and Rico had, but he was one of the good ones. I knew he wasn't gonna be out there doing any and everything."

"But you do know if he stays with Qua, he's gonna always be pining over you."

"I know, but I'm done. He can do his pop ups around town to get my attention all he want. It's not going to make me change my mind."

"Poor Rico."

"He got that baby to focus on, he'll be alright."

"If you say so," Kecia said, "Uh, I don't know why Laila and Alonzo got me and Taaz performing at the wedding."

"What kind of performance? You gon' be laying on the piano singing as he play?" she cracked up.

Kecia sighed, "Funny. They picked Luther's *Here and Now*. We have to practice in a little while, and I am dreading it."

She got up.

"Afraid of old feelings?"

"No, I'm-" she paused and looked away.

"Kecia, what's wrong?"

She sighed, "You're not the only one with secrets."

"Uh uh, sit ya ass back down and spill."

"You have to promise to tell no one about this."

"Now, you know I won't."

Kecia sat back down.

"You remember two months ago, I barely saw y'all, and I was busy with school and trying to drop another dress size?"

"Yeah."

"And during this time, Winston was out of town for a conference."

"Yeah. Your ex, Leonard had you so messed up that you made sure Winston's conference was legit."

"No, Leonard had *you* messed up. You looked all

of that up on your own and shared it with me."

"Yeah, and you were relieved."

"Yeah, I was," she paused, "Well, Taaz and I ran into each other outside of my apartment. He told me he was there visiting his sister who had just moved in."

"You believe him?"

"Yeah, I've seen her around."

"Okay, just making sure."

"It started pouring down, so Taaz helped me with my groceries. At first, I wouldn't let him in, but he just invited himself in anyway. He put the bags down on my table. He kept telling me, how good I looked, and how I didn't need to lose any more weight. Then, he grabbed me and kissed me."

"Ooo, for real?"

"Yeah, and I slapped the mess out of him. He apologized and then I apologized and kissed his cheek. Then, we started kissing. Uh, I held him again, and he held me uh," she looked at her friend, "Gia, it was so amazing. We got all rough on the couch, the floor, the dining room table, the kitchen countertop, against the wall."

"Damn, I ain't never had none like that. You and Laila make me sick. So, then what happened?"

"Well, we calmed down, and Taaz led me into my bedroom and made love to me. It was so beautiful. He kept staring in my eyes, telling me how beautiful I was."

"Taaz?"

"Yes Taaz, but you know one thing he never told me not even then?" Kecia asked. Gia waited for the answer, "I love you."

"Um, um, um," Gia shook her head.

"And then I remembered why we broke up in the first place. I want to get married and have children in the near future, and he doesn't. It's probably because he really doesn't love me. You didn't love Rico, and that's why you didn't take it further."

"You're right. I don't love Rico, and now he's about to have a child with someone else."

"And if you really loved him, you would have still been with him even after you heard the news about him and ol' girl."

"Maybe. That's why I'm glad love did not trap me in that situation."

"Um," Kecia groaned, thinking about Taaz.

"So you cheated on Winston."

"I hate to admit it, but I did."

"So you made a mistake. Learn from it, keep your man, and have the life you want. It's Taaz's loss, not yours."

"I needed to hear that. Thanks."

"You know Melanie's man keep on flirting with me?"

"Well, he is fine."

"And he belongs to a banshee."

"What would you say? 'Girl, get with that... That bitch don't need him.'"

Gia crossed her legs and sat back. "Haha...very funny. Well, you know I don't think like that anymore. It's gotta be me and only me at the very beginning. That's the only way to have longevity. Besides, I don't want nothing that Melanie has had. Nothing."

"He sholl ain't acting like her man if he is chasing you."

"Right, I wouldn't be surprised if Melanie paid him

to pretend to be her man."

"Really, Gia?"

"Hey, I put nothing past anyone," Gia looked up, "But I'm about to go charge my phone. I'll catch up with you later, and you can tell me all about your rehearsal."

Gia got on the elevator and pressed the fourth floor button. She noticed Taaz quickly approaching. She pressed the button to reopen the doors, but the elevator was already headed to her designated floor.

As she walked down the hall, she heard the elevator ding and the doors slide open.

"Ah Gia, let me holla at you right quick," Taaz called.

"What do you want?" She turned around.

"What's the deal with that Julian cat?"

"I don't know," Gia rolled her eyes.

"I don't like the way he be lurking around you."

"Aw, look at my little brother looking out for a sister."

"I'm serious I caught him eavesdropping on your conversation."

"Where at?"

"In the lobby just now."

"Aren't you supposed to be meeting Kecia for rehearsal?"

"In a little while. I gotta take a shower first."

"Umm huh," she said, "Could you hear what I was saying when he was eavesdropping?"

"Yeah, something about you wouldn't be surprised if Melanie paid him to pretend to be her man."

"Well, don't that sound like something she would do."

Taaz shook his head. "Mel can be crazy, but I don't think she is scheming this go round. I saw dude's face. It's like a light bulb went off in his head or something. So, I wouldn't be surprised if he tried to use what you said to get some ass."

"Let him try me."

He looked at her, "You sure you don't know that dude?"

"What? No, why?"

"I don't know. It just seems like y'all got history or something."

"Naw, that's you and Kecia," she said, "So how are you doing with all of this?"

"Welp, look at the time. Later," he turned away from her and walked down the hall towards the stairwell. A couple came out of one of the rooms.

"Come on. Don't be like that. Taaz! Taaz!"

He continued walking away.

"Get yo' little ass back here. That's yo' problem. Always running from yo' feelings, but stay in them!" The people looked at her strangely and she said, "What?"

CHAPTER 21

"I need a break from this damn phone," Kecia said aloud to herself as she made her way back to the lobby. She had been in her room swiping back and forth between social media platforms ever since she talked to Gia earlier. She had tried to call Winston and sent multiple texts, but she didn't receive a response. She even called the clinic and his assistant, Ms. Beth Anne told her they were swamped, and he was unable to come to the front. Kecia knew he would call her as soon as he had time. In the meantime, she ended up on Taaz's pages on Facebook and Instagram, staring at his pictures. There were no pictures of his new girlfriend, Nyema, and he had deleted all of the pictures of Kecia.

The spot that she sat in earlier was taken by two blonde haired teenagers who were also busy swiping on their phones. Older hotel guests were sitting across the lobby in different chairs, engaged in conversation. She found an empty section, and sat facing the elevator.

It was time for her to meet Taaz for rehearsal, but she didn't want to wait in the banquet room alone.

Alonzo texted her earlier and told her that he booked the room called Dune Hall.

She couldn't stop thinking about Taaz and Winston. Taaz still looked so young…still skinny, but definitely toned now. She always loved his light brown eyes and thick coal black hair. He still had that peach fuzz above his top lip as if he was about to get a mustache for the first time. She had always loved his skin tone, a sexy mixture of caramel and vanilla. Taaz was slightly taller than Kecia.

Winston, on the other hand, was extremely tall, and muscular with chocolate brown skin and deep brown eyes. They're literally like night and day. Winston was definitely sexier than Taaz. She thought of how they were both well endowed, how Winston was working with more than Taaz, but Taaz knew how to work it just right. Taaz won the physical aspect of the relationship hands down, but Winston satisfied her intellectually and emotionally. Her and Winston basically have the same goals, to settle down and have a family some day. She loved that they barely argued, but sometimes she missed arguing and debating with Taaz. She loved Taaz's silly jokes and how he would make any sad day, a happy one. No man could ever make her laugh like Taaz could.

"Kecia," a voice interrupted her thoughts. She looked up, and it was him.

Oh no! she thought.

"Hi."

"You ready to practice on the song?"

"Um, yeah."

He held out his hand, and she looked at it.

"You know I won't bite."

She placed her hand in his hand, and her body

quivered as she got up. He barked and acted like he was about to bite her.

"Stop," she laughed and hit him.

"It's about time you smiled at me."

"Whatever, Taaz."

Soon, Kecia and Taaz were in the banquet room on the stage practicing. It was a spacious room with rows of black chairs facing the stage with two makeshift aisles in between the sectioned chairs.

Taaz sat at a black grand piano, and Kecia was on the other side of the piano, staring at the red curtains that were pulled back and singing the first verse in a pitchy tone.

"Kecia," Taaz took his fingers off the keys.

"Huh?" she turned around.

"Now, you know you don't sing like that. Come here."

"Huh?"

"Come sit by me, please." He patted the bench.

She walked slowly towards him and sat beside him. He wore her favorite cologne, the cologne that always made her go crazy when they were a couple. Maybe it was a coincidence. She closed her eyes and took a deep breath. He started playing a melody, looked at her, and started singing in a smooth sexy deep tone.

She looked at him in shock.

He laughed. "That expression on your face is priceless."

"Wha...wha... I didn't know you could sing."

"Yeah, I don't want many people to know, so shh, don't tell."

"Whatever."

"We're gonna be in here all day. Come on, baby.

Sing with me."

She glared at him.

"I am not your baby," he said trying to mimic her.

She smiled and playfully nudged him.

"Come on," he said, then started singing the second verse, "When I-"

Kecia joined him, and they harmonized perfectly.

At the end of the song, they held out the note and stared at one another. The room grew quiet. They came closer.

Just as they were about to kiss, Kecia broke away.

"I can't," she jumped up, and Taaz fell on the floor. She walked around the piano while Taaz scrambled to get up.

"Damn girl, why not?"

He stood in front of her.

"I can't do this with you again, Taaz."

"But you know you want to be with me just as much as I want to be with you, Kecia."

"But what about-"

"Forget them, Kecia," he said, "It's about me and you."

She gazed off in the distance.

"Look at me, Kecia," he turned her face to his, "Don't you want me?"

One tear ran down her cheek, and she shook her head. He cupped her face and wiped her tear away.

"Well, I want you."

He pressed his soft lips against hers. He pulled back, eyed her, and bit his lip. They held each other tightly. They came closer and started kissing passionately, running their hands all over one another. Breathing hard, Kecia unbuttoned his shirt. He pulled up her dress and sat her on the piano. They were still kissing as Kecia unbuckled his belt and unzipped his pants. They heard the door slam and quickly looked up.

Standing in the aisle, Quinton looked at them in shock. He held a bottle of wine in one hand and two empty wine glasses in the other. Taaz took a step back, and Kecia jumped off the piano.

"Uh, this is so embarrassing," Kecia said, straightening her dress. She rushed off the stage.

"Kecia wait," Taaz said as he adjusted his pants.

"Um, I didn't see anything," Quinton said as she brushed by him.

"Quinton, what are you doing in here, man?" Taaz asked, dashing down the aisle.

"Alonzo wanted me to bring you some wine to get you two in the mood, but I see I'm too late."

"Yeah, thanks a lot," he said sarcastically and rushed past him.

"Ah, I'm sorry that I interrupted," Quinton called, "Damn."

Taaz rushed down the fourth floor hall and knocked on Kecia's door.

"Kecia, talk to me please."

"No, I'm moving on with my life, Taaz."

"I know, baby."

"I can't keep running back to you. I have a man. You hear me? I can't be hurting him like this. He's a good man."

"I know."

"You know what I need from you?"

"What is it? You can have anything you want."

"I need closure."

He mumbled, "Closure?" He took a deep breath, "Well, open the door, and I'll give you all the closure you need."

There was silence.

"Come on, Kecia."

She opened the door, and he came in closing the door behind him. His shirt was still unbuttoned. She gasped and began panting as she looked at his chest.

"Are you okay?"

"Stay back."

But, he was too close. She held out her hand and ended up touching his chest.

He grasped her arms, "Maybe you need to lay down.

"No, I don't," she started rubbing his chest, "I'm— I'm just confused." Tears ran down her face, and he embraced her. Her face was against his bare chest, and she could feel his heart beating rapidly. She started rubbing his back. She looked up at him.

"One more time, and then we have to both move on."

"Whatever you want, Kecia," he said as he came closer to her.

He pulled her face to his and kissed her, sucking her full lips. He reached under her dress and unlatched her bra as she unzipped and pulled down his pants. He finished taking them off. She pulled his shirt off his shoulders, and he took off her dress. He pulled off her bra and panties. He admired her new figure and appreciated that she still possessed her beautiful full mounds of chocolate. He took each breast in his mouth as he played with her, sliding his fingers in and out. He laid her on the bed and stroked his hard throbbing dick. Then, climbed on top of her.

Still kissing her, he slid inside her.

"Shit," she moaned.

"Damn, I missed this shit," he said as he went deep within her. He started pounding as fast and hard as he could. Then, he cupped her cheeks with his hand, raising her up and thrusting her even more. His thrusts pushed her all over the bed, and he continued to stroke her with each move.

"You love how I give you this dick, don't you?"

"Hell yes, Taaz...Shit," she panted.

"You want me to stop now?"

"No, go harder."

He fulfilled her request. She started grinding against him, matching his rhythm. He groaned and pulled out of her, keeping himself from finishing early.

"Aw hell naw, I need some more of that pussy," he said. Then, he kissed her, driving his tongue deeper and deeper in her mouth. He nibbled and sucked on her breasts once more. She shivered as he traced kisses down to her stomach and to her thighs. He gently pulled her moist lips apart and feasted on her. He moaned in pleasure as he licked her clit and stroked himself. Curling his tongue against her clit as Kecia had always liked, she moaned loudly. He held her legs as he fluttered his tongue over her most delicate spot.

She winced and breathed heavily. "Aw Taaz! Damn! Shit! This feels so good, baby." He worked his tongue even faster. Her body continued to quiver. She arched her back and cried out as her juices exploded all over his mouth and on the bed. He took his hand and wiped his face, then dived his tongue back in.

He arose, gazed at Kecia, and licked the corners of his mouth. "Umm...turn that ass over," he said, just as he would always say to her. She did as he instructed and got in their favorite position. He tried to go in, but kept slipping in all her wetness. He finally eased in and started stroking her...in and out. Kecia started moving back and forth, grinding hard against him. He paused and let her take over. She continued as fast and hard as she could, bouncing her cheeks against him while he smacked her ass. As they grinded heavily, they both let out loud moans in utter pleasure and climaxed at the same time.

Taaz collapsed onto the bed, and Kecia laid next to him. He pulled the covers over them as she rested her head on his shoulder. He stared at her, still panting. He pushed her hair back out of her face, caressed her, and planted endless kisses on her lips. At that moment, he knew Kecia was all his.

CHAPTER 22

Laila and Melanie had still been driving all day, hoping to make it to Maryland by nightfall. With Melanie now on the driver's side, they pulled out of the drive thru of a fast food restaurant. She pulled forward, then stopped. She unfolded the wrapper and bit into a juicy burger.

She closed her eyes and smiled as she chewed.

"Really, Melanie?"

"Child, do you know how long it has been since I've had a burger and fries?" she handed Laila the burger, "That's exactly why I hate road trips because my aunts and uncle would always stop, and I would always get a bacon cheeseburger, large fries, and a diet coke." She pulled onto the street and motioned for Laila to hand her back the burger. She took another bite as Laila's side of the car lowered, and the car started shaking. They heard something that sounded like rubber flapping.

"Oh no, is that a flat?" Laila asked, knowing the answer.

"I'm glad we weren't speeding on the main highway," she pulled into a nearby gas station and parked.

"Right."

"And it conveniently happened near a convenience stop," she added, "Like my Aunt Judy would say, 'that ain't nothing but the Lord.'"

"Yes, God is good."

"And all the time He is good." They chuckled.

Laila sighed in relief, "Yes, thank you, God."

Melanie took one more bite of her burger and stuffed three fries in her mouth. She placed the burger in her lap and meticulously folded the wrapper around it. She carefully placed it in the white bag, folded the top down, and sat it on the floor on Laila's side. Then, they both got out of the car.

The gas station was huge. It looked like a welcome center. Cars were steadily pulling in and out. The pumps were full. There were rows of 18-wheelers parked to the left of the gas station.

They examined the rear tire on Laila's side. It was completely flat on the bottom.

"Looks like a nail."

"Now, we've got to find someone to change the tire or maybe we should get roadside assistance," Laila said.

"Oh pish posh," Melanie scoffed, "We can take care of this ourselves."

"Are you serious?"

"Of course, we are big girls. We can handle it," she popped the trunk with the key fob. She pulled up the floor of the trunk and revealed another tire and a case.

"Great, we have a spare and an emergency car kit."

Laila watched in surprise as Melanie got out the tire. Laila pulled out the emergency kit. She sat the case on the ground, opened it, and stared at the tools. She only recognized the jumper cables and the x looking thing that tightens the bolts.

Melanie had just placed a jack under the car and lifted the car. She squatted down.

"Laila, pass me the cross wrench."

"The what?"

"The lug wrench so I can unscrew the lugs," she pointed.

Oh, the bolt tightener, she thought.

She handed it to Melanie. She looked on in amazement as her "bougie" friend changed tires like a pro. Melanie let the car down and sat the jack down by the emergency car kit.

"That should do it," she wiped her hands.

"Hi, do you ladies need help?" a handsome man with black hair and green eyes approached them.

"No, I think our tire is all fixed up, but you can make sure it's good."

He checked the tire.

"Looks good to me," he said, "Got a torque wrench?"

Laila raised her brows, and Melanie handed the correct tool to him.

He quickly tightened each lug, picked up the flat tire, and placed it in the trunk. Laila placed the tools in the case and closed it. The guy reached for it, and Laila gave it to him. Melanie reached into the car and into her purse and pulled out hand sanitizer. She squirted some on her hands and rubbed them together.

"Melanie, I'm going to grab a snack. Will you be okay out here?"

"Yes, I'm fine. I'll probably get a little more gas to

fill up the tank."

In the store, Laila was still confused by what she had just witnessed. She grabbed a bag of plain potato chips, strawberry gum, and a bottle of peach tea. There was one person at the counter so she went ahead and got in line. Then, more people came up behind her.

"Laila," a voice said behind her. She turned around and saw Alonzo's other ex-girlfriend, Gallena Riley. She had short curly brown hair, mocha brown skin, and light brown eyes. They looked at one another. Laila's mouth dropped.

"You want anything from the store while I'm here?"

Laila tilted her head in even more confusion.

She locked eyes with Laila and chuckled. "I'm on the phone," she pointed to her ear piece.

Laila blinked twice and realized it wasn't Gallena.

"Oh," Laila snapped out of it. The cashier was waiting for Laila. She turned around and placed her items on the counter.

"Okay. Mommy loves you too," she heard the lady say, "Bye."

Laila paid for the items and quickly walked out. She looked in the spot where the car was parked, and it was gone. She surveyed the entire front of the store and spotted the white Nissan Sentra at pump five. Melanie was standing at the pump talking to the guy, who was placing the nozzle back on the hook. He passed her receipt to her. She pulled out her phone and pressed the keys. He pulled out his phone and smiled. Laila came around the car.

"Nice meeting you," he said.

"The pleasure was all mine, Toby."

Melanie stared at him as he walked away. Laila looked back and saw the Gallena look-a-like walking to pump three. She looked at Melanie as if she had seen a ghost.

"Aw, don't look like that. What Julian doesn't know won't hurt him. Besides, it's just friendly conversation."

"No. I just...I think I'm losing it."

"What do you mean?"

"Look at that girl," Laila pointed. She had stopped to talk to someone.

Melanie's eyes grew wide, then she smirked, "Yeah, yeah, yeah...she looks like Gallena. Big deal."

"Okay, it wasn't just in my head."

"Laila, I have seen countless girls that look like Gallena. Heck, I've seen countless girls that look like you. That doesn't mean I've lost it."

"But I-"

"Can we get back on the road?"

Laila dropped her shoulders. "Yes ma'am."

Melanie smiled and shook her head as they got back in the car.

CHAPTER 23

On the beach, Gia was lying face down on a massage table in her own private cabana. A handsome guy was massaging her bare back, and a large white towel enveloped the rest of her body. Julian entered the cabana and paid the guy to take his place.

"Umm, your hands feel amazing," she sniffed, "You smell like this fine ass idiot I met earlier. He had me thinking...naw forget him. Get a little lower."

"What did he...*senor* have you thinking?" he faked a Spanish accent.

"You know what...I don't even want to think about him. They deserve each other," she said. "Ooo *papi*, I might have to take you home with me. Those hands are magic."

"Oh, you like that, huh?"

"Hold on!"

She jumped up, cupping her towel over her chest.

"Julian!" She pick up a towel and smacked him, "What the hell?"

"I'm sorry. I saw you lying here, and I thought it was a great opportunity for us to be alone and chat."

"By posing as my masseur?" She let her towel

drop.

"No wait!" he closed his eyes and turned away.

Then, he turned to see her glaring at him in extremely short yellow shorts and a red, yellow and blue striped halter top. She held the hanging straps to her chest.

"Oh, you're not naked," he said relieved, "You don't fully undress for your massages?"

"Gia gets naked for no one, but we're still talkin' 'bout why you're sneakin' in here, posin' as my masseur."

She hit him again with her towel.

"Well, it seemed like a good idea. It kind of seems a little creepy now that I think about it."

"A stranger sneakin' in my cabana to feel on me."

"I did not touch you inappropriately."

"I know that! Yo' ass would have a black eye and some purple and blue balls," she said as she tied her halter straps around her neck. Then, she turned to him. "You're paying me for this session."

"I would be more than happy to."

She held out her hand.

"What? You want it right now?"

"Did I stutter? Give me my money for this session right now."

He went into his pocket and pulled out his wallet.

"One hundred thirty-five dollars and fifty-two cents."

"Here's a hundred fifty."

She snatched it, "And you ain't getting no change back."

"I wasn't going to ask."

"You gon' have me put out a restraining order."

He followed her down the sidewalk.

"What possessed you to come up in my personal space and pose as my masseur?"

"Well, I just like being around you. And with the girls gone and Kecia preoccupied, I thought I could keep you company."

"By feeling on me against my will?"

"Hey, I only touched your back and shoulders. You know you enjoyed the massage, and don't think I didn't peep how you were thinking about me while receiving it."

"That's because I smelled your stankin' ass."

"So you know my scent now."

"Yes, I do. I can smell an asshole from a mile away."

"Whoa, why do you have to be so cold?"

"Cuz you keep following me around."

"I'm just looking after you."

"That's what I have Alonzo, Quinton, Taaz, and the rest of the rat pack for! Not you, bruh. I don't even know you."

"But you can get to know me."

"You can get to know deez nuts," Gia said and stormed off. He looked surprised. He shook his head and chuckled.

CHAPTER 24

Alonzo met up with Quinton in the lobby.

"So did they like the wine? Did she finally try some? Did it help her unwind?"

Quinton chuckled and shrugged his shoulders, "They were already *unwinding* each other on the grand piano."

"What? You're lying, man," Alonzo smiled.

"Naw, they were tearing their clothes off each other."

"Well, my plan is working better than expected," Alonzo said.

"I don't know. They were real pissed when I barged in on them. Kecia ran out. Taaz ran after her, and I haven't seen them since."

"Well, you know what that means."

Quinton's eyes grew wide. "Her man is here."

"No, they're probably in her room tearing that bed up."

"No, her man is here!" He grabbed Alonzo's shoulders and turned him to look at the guy at the front desk.

"That can't be him. He's supposed to come on the

day of the wedding."

"Kecia posts pics of him on Facebook every damn day, man. That's him!"

"Aw, shit! If he catches them, he might kill Taaz, and that fucks my wedding up. Come on, man." They approached Winston.

The front desk agent was speaking to him, "I'm sorry sir, but there's no one here by that name."

"Hey," Quinton and Alonzo simultaneously said to Winston. He turned around.

"Are you here for the Davis-McKee Wedding?"

"Yes, I am."

"Well, I'm Alonzo, the groom."

"And I'm the best man, Quinton."

"You're here with one of the girls?" they asked.

"Yes, I'm Winston. I'm Kecia's plus one."

"Oh, Kecia, okay. Well, she's with one of the girls right now, and we don't know which one of our reserved rooms is hers."

"Oh, I've been trying to call her since I landed, but I haven't been able to reach her. I was trying to surprise her. I guess that's what I get."

"Well, let's see if we can help you out," Quinton said and looked at Alonzo.

"Um, I'll tell you what, Winston," Alonzo said, "You and I can have drinks at the bar while Quinton looks for the girls and get you a keycard to the room that Kecia's staying in."

"Okay, sounds like a plan to me."

"I'm glad you could make it."

"Oh, yeah…no problem and congratulations."

"Thanks, man."

Quinton walked away as Alonzo and Winston headed to the bar. He spotted Gia and grabbed her.

"What the hell, Quinton?" she started hitting him, "Get away from me."

"Shh," he said, "Gia, listen to me. Kecia's man is here."

"So? What that got to do with me?"

"Well, Kecia won't answer her phone and neither will Taaz."

"And you think they're still together. Their practice been over with for like an hour now."

"Well, the last time I saw them, they were in there, tearing their clothes off each other."

"What? You're lying, ain't you?"

"Gia, hell no," Quinton said, "Alonzo has Winston distracted, but we have to find them before he does."

"Damn, Winston might go crazy if he catches them. Come on."

They rushed down the hall to the elevators.

On the fourth floor, Quinton and Gia rushed to Kecia's room.

"Kecia!" Gia banged on the door.

"Taaz!" Quinton called.

They were both lying naked under the white sheets. Kecia was still snug in his arms. "What the hell?" Taaz frowned.

"Uh, I knew Quinton wouldn't keep quiet," Kecia said as she got up and put on her robe.

"Kecia, if you can hear me…if you're in there, girl, Winston is here."

Kecia cracked the door open. "Are you serious?" She tied her robe.

"Girl, yes."

"Is he out there with y'all now?"

"Girl, naw. We don't have much time. Now let us in."

She opened the door, and Quinton and Gia quickly came in. They frowned as they smelled Kecia and Taaz's musky sex scent. Taaz zipped up his pants.

"Damn!" Gia covered her nose, "Even a nun will know that smell."

"You gotta trade rooms with Gia," Quinton said.

"What?" she looked at Quinton and sighed, "Yeah, he's right."

"Kecia, you ain't gotta do all of that. Just tell him you're with me, and he need to go back to where he came from," Taaz said as he put his shirt back on.

Quinton's phone dinged.

"I don't want him to find out like this."

He read his text. "Ah, Winston is still down there drinking with Alonzo."

"Where does he think I am?"

"With one of the girls," Quinton said.

"Well, Gia obviously since Melanie and Laila are not here."

Taaz paced, "Kecia, let's go down there and tell him what's up."

"Taaz, I gotta figure all of this out, okay? If you care anything about me, please don't say anything."

He groaned.

Gia interjected. "Taaz, I haven't unpacked many of my things. You can get my bags."

The two walked out, and Gia swiped her card and let Taaz into her room. Kecia quickly packed her bags. Quinton got a bag and put all of her supplies in the bathroom in it. Gia rushed back into the room. Taaz was sitting on the bed, staring at the wall. She took her hangers and hung Kecia's bridesmaid dress and another dress in the closet.

"Your bags are by the door," Taaz said.

"Thank you, Taaz," she got her bags and put them in Kecia's room. She brought Kecia's bags out of the room and saw Taaz walking down the hall. She placed Kecia's bags against the wall. She spread Kecia's rollers on the table. Quinton spread Kecia's stuff out in the bathroom.

Gia picked up the hangers and threw her own belongings on the floor of the other room.

"Quinton, did you get all of my stuff out of the bathroom?"

"Yeah."

"Okay." Kecia entered Gia's old room. "Here's my keycard." Kecia gave it to Gia.

"And mine is already on the dresser."

"Okay." Kecia cut on the shower. "Thank you, Quinton."

"No problem."

She closed the bathroom door. He walked out, and Gia closed the room door behind him.

Gia grabbed a white plastic bag. "Give me your clothes." Wrapped in a towel, Kecia opened the door and put her robe in the bag.

"I left my dress, underwear, and shoes in a bag in the room ...they wreak of Taaz's cologne."

"Damn, even your shoes," Gia joked, "I got ya."

"Thank you, sister. I owe you."

"Yes, you do. Now get yo' ass clean," Gia was about to walk out, but quickly turned back to her friend, "Wait, hickey check."

Kecia tilted her head back and forth, revealing her neck.

"Okay, you're good," she said, "Don't forget to

spray that dry shampoo in your hair and put your bonnet on."

"I won't forget."

"Oh yeah, me and you just came back from the beach, and you left your phone in the room."

"Okay."

"I got it sitting by the TV."

Gia left out and went into her new room and frowned. She pulled all of the covers off the bed and called the front desk.

"Hi, I'm in Room 445. I need housekeeping up here pronto. I need new sheets, covers, pillows, towels, Lysol, Pinesol, air fresheners, the works... No, there's no issue. I – I just been fucking real hard, okay?"

Winston knocked on the door, then he swiped his card.

"Kecia," he said as he stepped into the room and placed his bags in a chair.

"Winston?" she called from the bathroom, pretending to be surprised, "Is that you?"

"Surprise! Yes, it's me, so please don't be alarmed."

"Aw, hi honey! What are you doing here so early?"

"I was able to get away from the clinic, so I wanted to surprise you. Ms. Beth Anne was in on it too."

"Aw, that's so sweet," she said, "How did you manage to get a keycard? I don't think I ever told you which room I stayed in."

"Alonzo," he said, "What are you doing in there?"

"Oh, I just came in from being on the beach with Gia and decided to take a quick shower," she cut off

145

her water and stepped out, "I'm finishing up now."

"You sure you don't want me to join you?"

"Oh no, baby. I'm putting on some lotion right now," she said while drying off.

How am I going to face him? She could feel her anxiety building in her body. She felt butterflies in her stomach. Her stomach started cramping, and she felt nauseous.

"You enjoy your walk along the beach?"

"Yes," she managed to say.

She whispered to herself, "Okay, Kecia, you can do this." Her heart began racing, and she took deep breaths. "Calm down."

"Yeah, Quinton told me it was hard to get up with you and Gia."

"Oh, it was?"

"Are you okay?"

She rushed to the toilet and threw up.

"Well, that answered my question. Are you sick, honey?"

"No, it's just anxiety."

"Anxiety from what?"

Cheating on you and rushing to hide it so you won't find out, she thought.

"Uhhh oh, you know, the wed…," she hurled again, "the wedding day is approaching, and it's just making me nervous and anxious. You know I don't want Laila to get hurt. You know…I want her to be happy."

A housekeeper walked out of Gia's room. She placed the soiled sheets in her cart. Julian walked up.

"Honey, you deserve a big tip," she said and placed the money in her hand, "Here boo."

"*Gracias*," she exclaimed, "*Gracias*!"

"You're welcome."

The housekeeper pushed the metal cart down the hall.

Julian and Gia locked eyes. He looked confused.

"I thought you stayed in Room-" she ran up to him and covered his mouth.

"Shh…"

She held his hand, led him into her room, and closed the door.

She whispered, "I traded rooms. Do not tell anyone, and I mean *anyone* about this."

"What's the big deal?"

"None-ya."

"Okay, how about I knock on that door and ask the person inside?" He reached for the door knob.

She grabbed his arm. "Are you crazy?" she whispered.

"Okay, I'll tell you what. I won't say anything to anyone if you'll meet me for dinner tonight."

"What?" she frowned, then smirked, "When the bitch is away, the dogs sholl come out to play."

He shook his head.

"Blackmailing me to talk to you. That's low," Gia looked at him in disgust, "But will it keep your ass quiet?"

He nodded.

She thought for a moment. "I have some leftovers for tonight, so tomorrow night."

"That's perfect," he turned to leave, then turned back to her, "Oh and Gia."

"What?"

"Melanie and I aren't really together."

"Aren't really together?" she folded her arms,

"Either you are together or you aren't together? Which is it?"

"We are not a couple. Never have been and never will be."

"So let me guess, and this is just a wild guess. You are posing as her boyfriend to make her look good in front of Quinton and all of us?"

"Exactly! I knew you would see right through this whole charade."

"Oh, I see right through it alright. You must think I'm a damn fool."

"Huh? No, I'm telling you the truth. I'm not with her."

"Just drop it. My boy caught you eavesdropping on my conversation with Kecia earlier before you were feeling on me in the cabana, so you can try your little games on someone else. Cuz I ain't biting yo' bait. Now bye." She opened the door and pushed him out.

"But-" she closed the door in his face.

CHAPTER 25

Melanie and Laila were back on the road, driving in silence. Melanie glanced over at her.

"You know that Gallena episode back there happened only because you're still thinking heavily about Alexandra even though she's long gone," Melanie blew her breath, "And, we both know Gallena is not still interested in Alonzo, so why are you still stressing over Alexandra?"

"You just don't understand how those two were in high school."

"I remember," Melanie pursed her lips, "And you should remember that she doesn't care about anyone but herself. She hasn't even been thinking about Alonzo. She just doesn't want anyone else to have him."

"She's always been a miserable bitch."

"Because she doesn't know what she wants. Always going after this and that, guy after guy and dropping them when she got bored. She only held on to Alonzo because everyone thought he was the shit, and she acted like she won some trophy."

Laila rolled her eyes.

"She bothered almost every girl at school, but she messed with you more so than anybody."

"Yes, she did," Laila sighed, "In fourth period or even between classes, I would go to the restroom, and she would always come in right behind me talking crap."

"Yeah, she hated how Alonzo used to flirt with you in front of her."

"She would always say, 'I hope you know he's playing with you. People like Alonzo will never be with the likes of you.'"

"She is definitely biting those words," Melanie smiled, "But yeah, she was extremely jealous and insecure." She paused. "I don't know why we didn't see that Alonzo genuinely liked you in high school."

"Because he was for everybody."

"Right," Melanie laughed.

"I just thought that once we graduated, it would be the end of Alexandra Reid bothering me."

"But you got engaged to her ex."

"I know," Laila sighed, "Alexandra and Quinton were the reasons why I almost called off our engagement."

"Really? I didn't know you were thinking of doing that."

"Everything is just complicated. Like when we have get-togethers, there is always going to be this awkwardness between me, Alonzo, Marla, and Quinton. We can't hug or talk for too long. It's like they're thinking, 'Oh, are Laila and Quinton about to go off to a linen closet?' It always feels like their eyes are on us. Then, with future arguments, I don't want him to ever throw anything I did with Quinton in my face."

"You shouldn't think like that, you should not care what they think…still be considerate, but I'm pretty sure you and Quinton aren't going to be groping each other. There is definitely a line not to cross, but don't you dare let them stop you from being free to be you. It has taken so long for you to come out of your shell and unapologetically live. Don't spend your time now walking on egg shells. Say what you want and do what you wish."

"Okay."

"But how did Alexandra make you want to call off your engagement before she even popped up again?"

"You actually."

"Me?"

"Yes you. Marla and I showed up and ruined everything for you. I thought long and hard about who could show up and ruin my day. And, tons of women entered my mind, of course."

"I bet."

"I thought Gallena for a second, but then my mind stayed on Alexandra," Laila said, "They've always had this deep connection that I could feel."

"Lust. That's all that was."

"But if she stayed around, you can't tell me they wouldn't still be together now."

"Maybe…maybe not," she shrugged, "You have to stop thinking of scenarios."

"And if she liked kids, she probably would have trapped him just so he could remain in her life."

"Do you hear me?" Melanie waved her hand, "Stop! These thoughts that you're having should not be what a bride is thinking about just days before her wedding."

"I know."

"Are you going to marry Alonzo?"

"Yes, I love him. He is all I think about, but I just don't want him to still be pining over her."

"Forget her," Melanie said, "He chose you. You have to be confident in his decision. He keeps choosing you. Don't do what I did. I pushed Quinton away. I tried to control different situations, but what I am realizing is what's for you is for you. I still fail at understanding this at times, but we have to stop worrying about things we can't change. And right now Laila, the love you and Alonzo have... no one can get in the way, not Alexandra, Quinton, me, nobody...only you and Alonzo can get in the way of your own happiness. Like I said, he is all about you."

"Yes, you're right," Laila thought, "Wait, how can you get in the way?"

"Oh, I didn't tell you."

"Tell me what?"

"About what your little friends said," she said referring to Kecia and Gia.

"So now they are my little friends."

"You know those bitches don't claim me."

"Well..." Laila shrugged and tilted her head to the side.

"They thought I created a little scheme to get Alexandra to ruin your wedding."

"Well, that sounds like something you would do."

"Hey, I'm turning over a new leaf."

"I know. I never thought for a second that it was you."

"And that's what I love about you. You have always seen the good in me. No matter what I've done, you've always forgiven me."

"You can thank my mom for that. She made me

this way."

Your everyday doormat, Laila thought.

"And I am trying to have that forgiving mentality just like you," Melanie said, "I can't lose your friendship, and I hope you know now that I would never do anything to jeopardize it. Because you are the only true friend that I have. If I didn't have you in my life, I wouldn't have anyone. That's why I'm glad Quinton didn't tear us apart."

"He almost-"

"But we are here, and he's out of the picture...sort of."

Laila smiled. "Yeah, sort of..."

"He's our classmate and Alonzo's best man, he is definitely not going anywhere."

Laila's mind went back to Alexandra. "Well, I've been the bigger woman thus far, but if Alexandra rears her ugly head again, I don't know what my reaction will be."

"Right. Do you remember in the tenth grade when Gia called herself a rapper?"

"Oh Lawd, how could I forget?" Laila laughed, "What was her stage name?"

"Lil' G?"

"No, that's not it."

"The Real G," they said in unison.

They chuckled. "You remember when she did that rap about Alexandra at the talent show?"

"I think everybody remembers that."

"The way Mrs. Hutchinson ran to that stage as soon as she started talking about Alexandra getting on her knees."

"She yanked her offstage so fast."

"With the quickness, girl"

"She got suspended for three days and said it was worth it."

"And then all those fights between them."

"If they would have gotten caught, they probably would have gotten expelled."

"Yes."

"Those were the days," Laila thought, "Alexandra may have had Alonzo back then, but he's all mine now."

"Speak!"

Laila leaned back in her seat. "I cannot wait to get this trip over with, so I can get back and marry my man."

Melanie smiled, "Now that's the spirit."

CHAPTER 26

In her red two-piece swimsuit, Gia sat at the edge of the pool and gazed at the night sky. She smiled in delight that she had the pool all to herself. She eased into the water. She stretched her arms on the cool concrete coping for support and kicked her legs up.

"Do you mind if I join you?" Julian said walking up to the pool.

She looked up and rolled her eyes.

"Why is your lurking ass everywhere I go?"

"Maybe you are everywhere I go. Have you thought about that?"

She rolled her eyes once again. It seemed to be something she did often in his presence.

He continued, "Maybe great minds think alike. Or, maybe it's fate putting us at the right place at the right time."

"Naw, this is neither the time nor the place."

"You didn't object to me joining you."

"Well, I don't own the pool. It's for resort guests only so that means yo' ass can hop in whenever you get ready."

He got in.

155

"Why aren't you swimming?"

"I can't swim."

"Are you serious?"

"See…I don't need to lie like some people."

"I'm not a liar either."

She pursed her lips.

He bit his bottom lip. "Let me teach you."

"Naw, I'm good."

"I won't take no for an answer. Please. Please."

He continued to plead.

She groaned. "Will you leave me alone for the rest of the night?"

"Yes."

"I know I'm going to regret this, but alright."

"So we are going to start with some breathing and floating exercises." He told her to clear her mind and hold her breath for five seconds. Then, he began to show her various swimming techniques. He walked on the side of her. He held her stomach and her back as she began to sink. She finally began to float and did a long stroke. She hopped up out of the water.

"You okay?"

"Oh shit, I did it!"

"You're a fast learner. Come on. Let's do it together."

He held her hand as they went into the deeper end of the pool. Then, he let her hand go, and they swam. She stood up in the same spot she was originally in and leaned against the pool wall. He stood up in front of her.

"I can't believe I can actually swim now."

"With a little more practice, you'll be a pro in no time."

"I might just take a dip in the ocean. Thank you."

"You're welcome." He stared into her eyes, and he pulled a twist back out of her face, "The pleasure was all mine."

He caressed her face, then gently held her face. He came closer and softly pressed his lips against hers. He pulled back and braced for her to hit him, but she looked as if she craved more. He leaned forward and kissed her again. He offered his tongue.

She wrapped her arms and legs around him. She could feel him rise against her pelvis. He cupped the back of her head, and they continued to tongue kiss one another hard without gasping for air.

They heard some people whistling as they walked past to the deep end of the pool.

Gia broke away and pushed him back.

"No, no," she said, "I- I can't do this."

"Gia, wait."

She hopped out of the pool and rushed away.

Meanwhile, Kecia was lying in bed with Winston. She read a text message from Melanie that said, *We made it to Maryland. We just got a room and are turning in for tonight. We will go to the hospital some time tomorrow.*

Kecia turned off her phone and handed it to Winston. He placed it in on the nightstand.

"So anxiety, huh?" he said as he caressed her face.

"Yeah, the wedding is getting closer. I have to juggle being the bridesmaid and the wedding singer, so it's just getting to me."

"Oh," he paused, "so is that girl gone?"

"Yeah, I'm glad that problem is over with. Now, Laila and Melanie are in Maryland to see Laila's estranged mother. I just don't want her big day to be ruined."

"Like Melanie's?"

"Yeah."

"Well, what goes around comes around, Kecia."

She thought about her and Taaz having sex and felt a sharp pain in her stomach.

"Yeah, but Laila has always been the underdog. She's a nice person, who has always gotten the short end of the stick. Gia and I have always protected her, and now we get to pass the torch to Alonzo. I just hope he doesn't mess it up."

"I had a drink with him earlier. I think he's a cool cat."

"Yeah, he's Mr. Popularity everywhere he goes which scares me. I hope he's gotten all of that hoishness out of him."

"He probably has, baby."

She sighed, and Winston licked his lips.

"You feel like-"

"Maybe a little later. I still feel queasy."

"Okay, I'm right here to nurse you back to good health, baby."

She smiled, "You finally get a vacation, and now you have to be held up in here, doctoring on me."

"Trust me, baby. There's no place on Earth I'd rather be." He squeezed her tightly.

CHAPTER 27

The next day, Gia met Quinton in the lobby.

"Hey G. We're about to go riding around. You wanna come?"

"Naw Q. I'm good, but thanks for the invite."

Taaz came up and locked eyes with her. He had a mischievous look on his face. He turned his back to her and wrapped his arms around himself, pretending to kiss someone. Then, he quickly turned to face her.

"What yo' little ass know?"

"I don't know a damn thang."

"Don't play."

"I be trying to look out for you, but you don't wanna listen."

"It ain't what you think."

"Ohh, it's most definitely what I think."

Quinton studied their faces. "Do I even wanna know?"

"Naw."

"But, I do think I have an idea. Gia's being bad while half of her crew is away."

"I know you ain't talking," Gia said referring to his tryst with Laila when he was engaged to Melanie.

Quinton shook his head. "Just like a woman to

159

bring up a man's past."

"Hell, it wasn't that long ago."

The elevator dinged. Kecia and Winston stepped out.

"Hey y'all," he said.

"Hey Winston!" Gia hugged him, "Where you been hiding?"

"Oh, I've been in the room with Kecia."

"Yeah, I wasn't feeling too well after our outing yesterday, so I wanted to relax," Kecia said.

"Gurl, the way you were getting it in, I wouldn't feel good either."

Kecia's eyes grew wide. Quinton tried to keep a straight face and looked up at the raised ceiling. Taaz bit his bottom lip and smiled. Kecia cut her eyes at Gia.

"Oh, you went running on the beach?" Winston looked at Kecia.

She smiled.

Gia blurted, "Yeah, I couldn't keep up with her. That's sort of her and Laila's thing now."

Winston looked at Taaz.

"Oh, I don't think we've met."

Quinton stepped in. "Oh yeah, this is our boy, Taaz. Our third amigo."

Kecia nodded for him to be nice to her man.

"So you're the infamous Taaz. It's nice to meet you."

He offered his hand, and Taaz hesitated. Kecia nodded again, and Taaz reluctantly shook his hand.

He cleared his throat, "Yeah, likewise man."

"Kecia has told me so much about you and your times in high school."

"Oh, in high school." Taaz briefly looked at Kecia

and chuckled. She lowered her head.

Gia intervened. "Yeah, he kept getting us into sticky situations with that mouth of his," Gia said, "Ain't nothing changed."

Kecia glared at her.

"Yep, the clown of the crew…that's me," Taaz said with a solemn face.

"Well, we are about to go sightseeing. If any of you would like to come with us, you're more than welcome," Winston said.

Kecia gave each of them her death stare.

"No, we have some last minute things to do for Alonzo," Quinton said.

"And I have all these guys around here to look good for so…"

"I bet," Taaz said.

Winston grinned. "I understand that…so we will see you all later on."

They walked on. Then, Kecia looked back and mouthed something angrily to Gia.

Gia shrugged.

Quinton shook his head at her.

"You are still messy as hell," Taaz said.

"Ah, I did nothing wrong. What I said just came out the wrong way. If y'all wouldn't have been fucking, you wouldn't have even heard it like that."

"Whatever. Kecia gon' pounce that ass."

CHAPTER 28

Laila and Melanie arrived at Union Memorial Hospital. It took everything in Laila to get out of the car, walk across the parking garage, enter the first floor lobby, and step onto the elevator. As the elevator stopped and its doors slowly opened revealing the sixth floor, Laila hesitated and trembled in fear. Melanie held her hand. She saw a family walking in front of her. A teenage girl with a beautiful full fro held flowers in her hands, and an older gentleman held countless "Get Well Soon" balloons in his hand. She watched as they turned the corner past the nurses' station.

"Are you okay?"

"I'm fine," Laila lied.

"You've got this," Melanie assured her. "If you need me, I'll be right here in the waiting room." She pointed to the open area with countless green chairs.

"Okay."

Melanie took a seat on the first row and picked up a magazine.

Laila's heart pounded heavily, and all she could think about was her last fight with her mother and father. She walked past the nurses' station and looked down the next hall. Her aunt told her that her mother would be in Room 613. She prepared for a long dreadful walk down the hall as if she was walking the green mile. But, the door next to her read, *613 Margarette Sanders.* Her mother had gone back to her maiden name.

She took a deep breath and closed her eyes.

Maybe she will be asleep, Laila thought. She knocked.

"Come on," she heard her aunt say.

She pushed the door open.

"Oh my word, Margarette! It's Laila!" Aunt Sarah exclaimed. Her aunt was short with a brown complexion. She wore a brown jogging suit and a brown curly wig.

"My dear sweet child," Margarette sat up in her seat. The aunt helped raise the bed up. Her mother looked a lot different than when she last saw her. She was thin. Her full cheeks now hollow. Her once smooth brown skin had wrinkles. Her thinning hair was gray with hints of black and pulled back in a ponytail.

"Hey," Laila slowly made her way to the bed.

Aunt Sarah came forward and hugged her. Before Laila could react, her aunt wrapped her arms completely around her.

"Isn't she just beautiful?"

"Very beautiful."

"Looks just like you," she said, then motioned to Laila, "Come on. Pull you a seat up."

Laila obeyed.

"Laila, I'm so happy to see you. You know when I had your aunt to call you, I wasn't sure if you would agree to see me."

"Well, being that you were the one who walked out on me, I probably shouldn't have."

"I know. I realized, a long time ago, that what I did was stupid. I was childish and selfish back then. I just wanted things to go my way and blamed you for the mistakes I've made. Now, as you can see, I'm getting my comeuppance. I just want to let you know face to face how sorry I am for leaving your life like I did. I should have been a better mother to you, and I should have stayed in contact with you. I'm truly sorry, and I know it might not be today, but I hope you will find it in your heart to forgive me."

There was silence.

"Well, you actually apologized," Laila crossed her legs and clasped her knee with her hands. "That's a start for you. You've never apologized to anyone in your life."

"Ain't that the truth," Aunt Sarah mumbled.

Margarette chuckled, "Shut up."

"I just don't understand why you decided to come back into my life now. Is it because you're sick? On your death bed? You want to make amends?"

"Maybe, but we're hoping I recover. But if I don't, I want you to know my truth. I don't want to leave this Earth knowing that I failed my baby girl without even trying to make things right."

"Do you know what I have been through without y'all? I was 18, still a child with no family, and you two walked out on me without a trace?"

"I was just so angry, and I thought Lionel would stay in your life. I didn't know we both had deserted you."

"I don't know why I was surprised that you left.

You…you just never really liked me."

"That's not true!" Her mother leaned forward, "I loved you. Still do. I was just so bitter over not having the life I wanted that I couldn't enjoy the wonderful life that I had. I can't tell you how many times I wished I could have gone back and been with you and Lionel as a family."

Laila shook her head. *She rather had been with my boss than with me and my dad, her own husband.*

Laila sighed. "I get why you left, but I don't understand how my own father could leave me. I didn't hurt him. I only revealed the truth about you. I know I kept your infidelity from him for a long time, but he shouldn't have stayed angry with me too."

Margarette sighed. "When you revealed that truth, it confirmed another truth that he had suspected all along."

"What other truth?"

She took a deep breath and looked at her sister.

"Sarah, give us a minute."

Her sister nodded, got up, and left out of the room.

"I know you hate me, and telling you this is just going to make you have even more hate in your heart for me, but I have hidden this from you long enough."

"Hidden what?"

Her mother took another deep breath. "Lionel McKee is not your biological father."

"What?" Laila's heart sank. "Are you serious?"

"Yes."

"Who…who is my father? Do you even know?" Her eyes began to water as she scowled at her mother.

Margarette frowned as if she wanted to cuss her estranged daughter out. Instead, she sighed and said firmly, "Yes, I know."

"Well, who is he?"

Her mom raised her brows, and her eyes widened as she tilted her head like the answer was obvious. Laila understood her mother's nonverbal cues.

"No! You're telling me that my boss, your lover is my real father?" Laila stood up.

"Yes."

Laila tried to gather her thoughts. She placed her hand to her head as she paced the room.

"How is that even possible? I thought you started sleeping with him when I was in elementary school. You're lying."

"Laila, I had been sleeping with that man on and off ever since I was sixteen-years-old. I lost my virginity to him. In fact, I loved the hell out of that white man, and he loved me. But his parents wouldn't have him dating a black woman, tarnishing their legacy. He would have been disowned, and there would have been no chance of him taking over the bank. He wanted to marry me. Instead, he married Delilah, but he's always loved me. I thought maybe when I was pregnant, we could run off together, but he refused to leave his wife. Turned out she was pregnant too, so I didn't know what to do. I didn't know if you were going to come out with blonde hair and blue eyes, but I decided to wait it out. And here, I had this pretty light skinned baby with brown eyes and black curly hair, so I let your father believe you were his."

Tears poured down Laila's face.

She plopped back in her chair. "How could you do

this to me? Keep something this major from me?" She sobbed.

"I know it's a lot to process, but..."

"I-" Laila paused, "I can't do this!" She got up and rushed out of the room. As she walked past the waiting area, she remembered Melanie was waiting for her.

Melanie looked up at her and gasped. "Is she gone?" she asked as her eyes began to tear.

"No."

"Damn," she said under her breath in disappointment.

"She's so hateful...I just need a moment." Laila's face was red, and tears were pouring uncontrollably down her cheeks. Melanie could feel her friend's pain. She watched as Laila rushed away, completely shaken.

Melanie took a deep breath, closed her eyes, and exhaled.

"What would Gia and Kecia do?" she thought aloud to herself, "Okay."

She hopped up, marched into the room, and slapped the mother.

The sister, who was back in the chair, gasped and attempted to leave the room.

"Call the nurses, and you'll be lying on a gurney beside your sister."

"Sarah, it's okay. I deserved that." Margarette sat up, "Melanie, I see time has made you grow some damn balls instead of hiding behind that fake persona. I never liked that bitch you pretended to be."

"You don't know a thing about me. It's been years, and you still manage to hurt her. She's been through enough, and she's about to embark on the happiest day of her life. But, you couldn't let her make it. Just when she was letting go of the hell that you and Mr. McKee put her through, you had to show up and bring it all back to her. Why couldn't you just die and not even bother her?"

"She had to know the truth."

"Well, it's a little late for the *truth*."

They eyed each other.

"If there was a plug to pull, I'd pull it myself."

She walked out.

Laila was in a small room with two vending machines. She stood in the corner and leaned against the window seal. She continued to cry and sob as she called her fiancé.

He answered as he was talking to his cousin, "Ah Damien, get some hot wings for me too."

"Alonzo."

"Baby, what happened?"

"It's a lie. It's all a lie."

He pressed the video call icon on his phone.

"Laila! Laila, look at me"

"What?"

"Look at your phone." She pulled the phone from her ear and rested it in her lap.

"I'm here, baby. Okay?"

She nodded and wiped away the tears.

"Whatever it is we can get through it. Okay?" he sighed, "This is the last time...I refuse to let you do anything else like this without me. Now, just take a deep breath and tell me what's going on."

She closed her eyes.

"Alonzo, my life has been one big lie. I—I don't even know who I am."

"Laila, what did she tell you?"

"The man that I've loved with all of my heart. The man who treated me like his princess then left me like I was trash tossed in the street is not even my father."

"Whoa. Wait...no! Is it-"

More tears poured down her face. "Yes, it's him. I can't believe this."

"Now it all makes sense."

"They both have deceived me. I work for a man who probably knows I'm his biological child, which is probably why he was so quick to drop six figures for our wedding. My whole identity has shifted from who I thought I was...who I believed I was to who I really am, which is a person I don't know at all."

"Laila, deep down you had to have known."

She shook her head. "I truly didn't. How could she do this to me now? It shouldn't have surprised me, but I was not expecting this...not this."

"Damn, I should be there. No, fuck this. I'm taking the next flight out there."

"No Alonzo, please...I'm getting back on the road as soon as I get out of this place."

"So what now? You're finished talking to her?"

"Yeah."

"So she told you that, and you left out, right?"

She nodded.

"Baby, I know this is a lot to take in, but you have to go back in there. You have to talk this out. If not for you, then for our relationship, for our future kids. The air has to be clear between you two. You have to be at peace with one another, so you can move forward with no regrets."

"I don't have to do anything."

"You're right. It's your choice, but as your other half, I am just giving advice. It's up to you as to whether or not you want to follow it. I can't and I won't ever force you to do anything."

She looked away.

"Laila…"

She sighed, "Go on with your advice."

"Okay, where was I?" he thought for a moment, "Aw yes, you have to find it in your heart to forgive her. I can help you every step of the way. I know it takes time, but please don't leave her on a negative note like she did you all those years ago. You have to be the bigger woman. You have to show your maturity. You have to show her that you are not her. You are Laila… my beautiful strong, courageous, loving, compassionate, and forgiving wife. I know you are confused right now, but I know exactly who you are and no bloodline or gene pool can make me believe otherwise."

Laila relaxed. "You make everything better in my life."

"As do you."

"Now I guess I'll go back in there."

"That's my girl," he smiled, "Oh yeah…I was looking into one-way flights earlier. I am going to make some calls and see if there's a nearby location to drop the rental off, and you ladies can take a first-class flight back."

Laila took a deep breath, "Thank you. I sure was dreading the drive back."

"I'll text you your flight information, okay?"

"Okay. I love you, Alonzo."

"I love you too, and if you need anything, just call me back."

"Okay," she ended the call.

CHAPTER 29

Kecia wandered down the fourth floor hall, and discovered a lounge full of couches, chairs, pool tables, and TVs. There were also large windows overlooking the courtyard. She entered the lounge and walked across the room.

"So it's like that?"

She briefly looked behind her to find Taaz eyeing her down intensely. "Taaz, not now."

"No, I ain't going nowhere. You are going to talk to me!"

She turned to him. "What, Taaz?"

"You gon' fuck me, then be up under him like that shit was nothing to you?"

"Taaz, I already told you that I needed closure and you agreed. What do you expect me to do? Leave him?"

"Fuck yes," he said, "Kecia, you cheated on him with me twice. Twice! You don't want to be with him."

"Yes, I do," Kecia said, "I'm sure as hell not getting back with you for you to be doing the same ol' shit."

"Well, you fucked me so obviously you miss something about me."

"Yeah, the sex, but what is sex?"

She remembered her ex, Leonard telling her that sex was just sex, and now she was feeding the same lines to Taaz. She shook her head.

"Don't even open your mouth to say that. We are about more than sex, and you know it. It ain't never been about straight fucking, so don't even play like that."

"Taaz, okay... you want me to say it? I'm still in love with you, okay? And, I wish we had never broken up. But in the same breath, I wish you wanted more for us and saw a future for us."

"That's just you not being patient enough for me to be the man and do what I gotta do."

"I was patient. You were just not ready, and you're still not ready. And now, I'm with a good man who treats me well."

"A good man, huh? How will your good man feel once he knows we were fucking all the while he was trying to find your room?"

"Taaz don't," she grabbed his arm, and he jerked away from her. They froze in their tracks as they saw Winston glaring angrily at them.

"You were what?"

"Winston, I can explain!"

"You-you cheated on me...with him?"

Kecia tried to speak, but Winston cut her off.

"But you told me there was nothing between you and him."

"There isn't."

He turned away, and Kecia followed him. Taaz was right behind her.

"Kecia, don't be running towards this fool. He don't even deserve you."

Winston turned around and pointed at him. "You stay out of this."

"Oh, I'm very much a part of this, and there is no way in hell that I'm letting her leave this hotel with you."

"Is that right, huh? Well, the last time I checked she is still my woman."

"Not anymore, she isn't," They eyed each other.

Kecia said, "Taaz, I can speak for myself."

He ignored her. "I been all in that thang since y'all been together, so it's obvious you ain't hittin' it right."

Winston chuckled and looked over at Kecia. Then, all of a sudden, he punched Taaz in the face. Blood poured down his right nostril. He wiped the blood, bit his bottom lip, drew back his fist, and punched Winston in the jaw. Then, they started fighting violently.

"No, please stop."

They kept punching each other in the face. Taaz got the best of Winston. They ended up near a window, and Winston tackled Taaz, knocking him through the window. As the glass shattered, Taaz frantically tried to latch onto something. Winston fell to the floor near the window seal as Taaz disappeared from Kecia's line of sight. Kecia's heart sank as she rushed to the window.

"No! Taaz! Please no!" His lifeless body was on the concrete. She screamed, "Taaz!"

Laila stood at her mother's door once again. A nurse, who resembled Gia, had just come out of the room. The nurse, along with many other nurses, stared at her from the nurses' station.

"Why does my life have to be so complicated?" Laila mumbled to herself. She took a deep breath and slowly opened the door.

Aunt Sarah frowned and jumped to the edge of her seat. "What the he-"

"Sarah!" Margarette shook her head, silencing her sister. Laila wondered what her aunt was about to tell her. Margarette sat up and looked warmly at her daughter, "Laila, I thought you had left."

"I wanted to, but I refuse to leave you like you left me. You have complicated my life even more than it already is, and it's quite complicated right now."

"I'm sorry. I should have never done that to the three of you. Lionel and Mitch deserved to know the truth from the beginning, and you should have as well without carrying my burdens."

"What you did was an unforgivable act, and it makes since why my dad left the way he did. But I was so close to him, he should have stayed in my life even after he found out I wasn't his. It's like his love was solely dependent on me being his blood. It's crazy how he could drop me like that once he discovered the truth. I was his little girl for eighteen years, and for him to toss me to the side like that... like the bond was never there...like I was now nothing to him...hurts. If I would have found out the truth back then, I would have still considered him as my dad."

"He was hurt, and I know he probably wanted to come back into your life, but probably thought it was too late and that you'd never forgive him. Me, on the other hand, I was selfish. I figured you were nearly grown, taking care of yourself. Heck, you were always watching out for yourself when you were little. I figured you could make it on your own without me burdening you and resenting you whenever you came around."

"I've never really took care of myself. Kecia and Gia have always been there instead of my own mother."

"I'm sorry."

"I just knew how I would have treated you, and I just rather stayed out of your life than bring you down and have you end up like me. I'm truly sorry, and I love you with all my soul...I do. There is not a day that passed in all these years that I haven't thought of you. Year after year, I've wanted to come back into your life, but as each year came and gone, it made it even harder to face you and admit all the wrong I've done."

Laila sighed. "No matter what you say, I'll never understand how you had it in you to just erase me from your life. All I've ever wanted was to be loved. I've obsessed over being loved, and at the same time, I've been afraid of being hurt. I'm afraid that I may be so desperate for love and for people to stay in my life, that I'll do anything to keep them there...no matter how they have treated me. I just clamor for love...I unhealthily romanticize it. All because love was taken away from my own parents, and I was left with emptiness...that I hoped one day would be filled."

Tears poured down her mother's face. It had taken Laila aback. Her mother had never cried in front of her.

"I honestly thought being out of your life would make your adult life much better. I just wish you would have known how much we loved you and still love you. And, back then, I loved you too much to let my issues ruin you."

Laila finally realized that if her mother wouldn't have left, she would have constantly stressed her out, insulted her every accomplishment, and continued to make any of her problems Laila's. Her life probably would have been ten times worse.

"I guess I get it now, but does he know that I'm his daughter?"

"Mitch? I…I honestly don't know."

"So have you let go of your past or are you still stuck?"

"I have no resentment towards you whatsoever. I don't blame you for my mistakes and how my life turned out. I've let go of Lionel, but I would be lying if I said I let go of Mitch. I still love him and a part of me always will."

"Longing for someone you can never have. Welp, one thing is sure."

"And what's that?"

"You're definitely *my* mother."

Her mother chuckled. "Would it be too much to ask you for a hug?"

Laila exhaled. "No." Laila came up closer to the bed. Aunt Sarah helped to lower the right bed rail. Laila sat on the bed, leaned in, and hugged her. Margarette wrapped her arms around her and squeezed tightly. She remembered hugging her when she was a kid. She smelled the same except for the hint of medicine. Laila felt a throbbing pain run from her chest to her throat. She wept softly. Her mother also began to cry as she kissed Laila's head.

"Momma, I've missed you."

"I've missed you too, my sweet baby."

"Can I stay right here for a little while?"

"Yes, please."

Her aunt had tears in her eyes as she snapped a picture of them with her phone. "I'll give you two a moment," she said. Then, she tipped out of the room.

"Mom?"

"Yes, baby."

"I...I forgive you. I don't even know if you wanted to hear me say it, but I needed to hear those words for myself."

Laila felt a weight being lifted from her chest.

"I'm glad that you came, and I'm glad that you found it in your heart to forgive me. You have grown to become an even greater woman than I could ever be and, for that, I'm grateful. I know you are going to make that young man Alonzo happy as his wife."

"Thank you," she held her tightly, "And please don't die on me."

"I'm fighting, darling," she said, "With all my might, I'm fighting."

CHAPTER 30

"No! Taaz!"

Kecia awoke in a hot sweat. She looked around the room. She had called out Taaz's name in her sleep, but thankfully Winston was still sound asleep. The brutal fight and Taaz plummeting to his death was just a dream! She went into the bathroom and cried.

Her heart pounded heavily. It took everything in her not to run to Taaz's room and jump into his arms. She texted him to meet her in the stairwell. He instantly texted her, *ok*. She slowly walked down the hall and into the stairwell. She leaned against the cold wall. She was still shaken. The dream seemed so real. When Taaz opened the door, tears ran down her face.

"What's up?" he looked worried.

Kecia immediately grabbed him, pushed him against the wall, wrapped her arms around him, and kissed him.

Taaz was concerned. "Kecia, are you okay?"

She nodded, held his arms, and embraced him once more. She was happy to see him still in one piece.

"What happened? What did he do to you? I

promise I'll…"

"No," Kecia's eyes grew wide, and she held his arm, "He didn't do anything."

"Does he know?"

"No, he doesn't," she said, "Taaz, I just want to get this off my chest. Taaz, I love you so much. And, I don't ever want you out of my life, but if you can't accept me moving on then I'm going to have to let you go completely. This is the only time I'm going to talk to you about this, then I'm done, okay?"

"Okay."

"I know I've been weak with you. Being with you and sex with you feels so good, but we are at two different places in our lives, and I refuse to wait. So I have moved on with Winston, and what happened between us can't happen again, okay? I really want to see where this relationship with Winston goes. Can you please respect that without trying to sabotage it?"

"Sabotage? I would never do that to you."

"Well, please respect that I have moved on."

Taaz swallowed. "Okay."

"That's it?"

"Yeah, I'm going to work hard to show you that I *am* on the same level as you now. I am that man that you deserve now. And because I know that you're my queen, I know we will find our way back to each other. And Kecia, I got time to wait."

"Taaz, don't…"

"Kecia, you're mine. There's nothing no one can do to change that. So starting now, I won't bother you. I'll let you be free and explore different relationships, and at the right time, we'll get back together. And when that happens, I'm never going to let you go, girl. Believe that."

She sighed, "But I want you to—"

"Yeah, yeah…I'll keep seeing some women. That ain't no problem for me," he said half joking, "But none of 'em gon' do it for me cuz they not you."

Tears fell down her cheeks, and he rubbed them. He kissed her, and they passionately made out. Then, he held her chin and continually gave her short kisses.

"Damn, I'ma miss these lips," he said, biting his bottom lip, "but I'ma say bye…for now."

He opened the door and walked out. Kecia leaned against the wall.

He peeped his head back in. "That was smooth, wasn't it? You liked how I did that, didn't you? That boy bad, ain't he?" He joked.

Kecia chuckled. "Boy, gon' somewhere."

He kept laughing. "Just remember what I said."

CHAPTER 31

Gia received a knock on her door. She opened it to reveal a dressed up Julian. He wore a black thin button-up shirt and black pants.

"What are you doing here?"

"You agreed to a date remember?"

She rolled her eyes and groaned.

"Is 7:30 okay with you?"

"There are so many women around here who don't even know Melanie. Why are you so desperate to get into my panties?"

"Gia, I'm not trying to have sex with you. I just really want to get to know you."

"You keep saying that, but why?"

"Because I find you fascinating."

"You find me fascinating because you're trying to chase your woman's *alleged* friend."

He laughed, "Alleged?"

She rolled her eyes.

Here we go again, she thought.

"You have that much disdain for her?"

"Wait a minute. You actually understood what I meant?"

"Of course."

"Other guys like you would have been quick to insult my intelligence. They say, 'oh you used that word incorrectly.' They attempt to give me an entire English lesson and then I cuss *they ass* out."

He laughed, "I definitely believe you did. I'm not like that... I know an intelligent woman when I see her. It doesn't matter which terminology she uses. We are unique individuals. Each person has different dialects and-"

"Articulation," Gia finished his statement, and he smiled, "A lot of guys hate when I cut off my words. They be like, 'enunciate.' And, I'm like, 'dude, I ain't given you no damn business presentation. We are on a date.'"

He smiled, "So our date is still on, right?"

She sighed and smirked, "It's not a date. I am being blackmailed, so... yeah, I guess."

"Until then, *mi amor*," he said as he walked down the hall. She closed her door.

"Uh, he's so damn sexy," she walked over to her bed, "Ugh, Melanie gets on my damn nerves."

She fell back onto her bed and covered her face with a pillow.

Quinton entered Alonzo's room.

"I was thinking the best time to have your bachelor party is when Laila is away."

"Yeah, it would have been, but she'll be back tomorrow...well, some time past midnight, so technically tomorrow."

"That's why we have it tonight."

"What? Naw man."

"We got you, me, Taaz, Damien, Duke, Landan,

Julian, and-"

"Do not invite Winston, man. You know how Taaz is when he gets drunk."

"Okay, and we've got Chuck, Al, Lawrence, and our boys from college at the Hilton and the Sheraton. The hotels are right next to each other. Carlo 'nem checked in about an hour ago."

"Oh, okay. We'll roll through there in a little bit."

Quinton's phone rang, and he put it on silent.

"All bullshit aside. Your bachelor party is tonight at 10 at Seymour's Lounge."

He smiled, "Seriously?"

"Yes, it's a strip club about thirty minutes away. I have everything set up. We have our own party room, strippers, shots, beer, sandwiches, wings, chips, all of that."

"Oh hell yes. Now that's how a best man is supposed to do the damn thing." They did their handshake and half-hug. "That's my boy."

"I still can't believe Laila is ok with you having strippers."

"Man please. Who are you talking to? I'm Alonzo, behby."

Quinton gave him a look.

"And I got down on my knees and begged."

Quinton said, "Now that sounds more like a man who is about to slice and dice that player card."

"Aw, player card," Alonzo laughed, "I ain't heard that one in a long time. Remember when Taaz made us all a pitch black player card?"

"Yeah, I still have mine. It's at Momma's house somewhere."

"Well, if I still had mine, I would cut it in half. That would be like a symbolic moment for me. When me and my baby get married, I refuse to be that man again."

"I heard that."

"Yeah, I'll do anything for Laila, man. Not even Alexandra can deter me from that girl."

"Yeah, I was worried there for a minute."

"Well, she's gone now, so no more worries."

"I can drink to that."

Julian was in his room getting dressed when Quinton knocked on his door. He had taken off his black shirt and tried on another. Then, he decided to put the shirt back on since she had already seen him in it. He opened the door.

"Hey, what's up man," Quinton looked behind his shoulders, "Can I come in?"

"Sure," he said as he straightened out his collar.

"Ah, we're having a bachelor party tonight. You wanna come?"

"Oh, I uh… I kind of have plans," he said as he picked up his bottle of Acqua di Gio by Giorgio Armani.

Quinton noticed that Julian was getting dressed to impress a woman who definitely was not Melanie.

"Oh," then Quinton realized that he was getting ready to see Gia, and his eyes widened, "Ohhh."

"Um, I might drop by later on. Where is it going to be?" Julian said as he sprayed the cologne on his chest.

"Seymour's Lounge. We'll probably be there until one or two."

"Oh, okay. Well, I'll stop by. Thanks for inviting me, man."

"No problem," they did a handshake.

"See you catch on quick," Quinton said, "Oh and one more thing. Don't tell Winston because he's not invited."

"And Winston would be?"

"Oh, Kecia's boyfriend."

"They're staying in Room 446, right?"

"Yep, that's them."

"Well, I haven't met him yet, but I won't tell if I see him."

"Alright, cool."

Quinton left out, and Julian had a strange look on his face.

As Laila and Melanie stood in the line at the airport, Melanie received a text message. She read it.

"Aw, hell naw."

"What is it?"

"Oh, nothing just a text from a co-worker."

"Thank you for coming with me. I'm glad I came up here after all."

"Oh, it's no problem. Did you get the closure you were looking for?"

"I did actually," Laila said, "But I still have to deal with the boss paternity issue, but I don't even want to think about it until after the wedding."

"Gotcha," Melanie said as she texted Kecia to give them a heads up not to discuss Laila's family drama with her when she returned to the hotel.

"Now, we can focus on getting Alonzo and I down that aisle."

Melanie grinned as she adjusted her bag strap on her shoulder. "So are you ready to be Mrs. Alonzo Davis?"

"Yes, I am. I can't wait to see him. I hope he'll be

as excited. He texted me earlier and told me they were having the bachelor party tonight."

"Oh, how convenient."

"I'm just glad Alexandra is gone."

"Yes, there's no telling what hooks she would have tried to sink into your man if she would have continued to lurk around."

CHAPTER 32

Gia and Julian were sitting at the dinner table at the Chateau. He had just finished watching Gia devour her plate of food and loved how she didn't try to be all prim and proper.

"You look amazing," he said.

"Thank you," she said as she wiped her mouth with a napkin.

Everything grew quiet, and Gia looked around the room as if she was bored.

"So you still want to act like that kiss didn't happen last night?"

"Ta, your charm worked for a quick minute, so what?"

"More like a beautiful five minutes."

"See...there you go."

"So you didn't feel anything?"

"I felt your lips and yo' tongue."

"You know what I mean."

"No, I didn't feel anything. Okay?"

He laughed to himself. "You're lying."

"Hey, no one calls me a liar."

"Well, you just lied. You want to know how I

know?"

"How?"

"Because you raise your right eyebrow whenever you lie."

She looked at him strangely.

"No, I don't."

"You did it again," he smiled.

"Hmm, that's the same thing Mama always told me," she mumbled under her breath as she stretched her arms.

"Huh?"

"So you learned my mannerisms in just a few days."

"What can I say...I've been admiring you."

"More like stalking me."

"Well, women don't kiss their stalkers."

"Well, did you drug me?"

He smirked and shook his head.

"What is it going to take to break through that wall you have up?"

"You ain't breaking through any of my walls, and I sholl ain't gon' break you off nothing."

He looked at her and groaned. He licked his lips.

"Damn, Gia," he said. "You just don't know."

She liked the way he sounded when he said that. She looked at him.

"I don't know what?"

"That you're just the woman I've been looking for."

His statement caught her off guard.

"Well, too bad you found Melanie first."

"But I told you."

"Yeah, I know what you told me."

"And you still don't believe me?"

"Nope, I'll believe it when it comes out of the ho's mouth," she said referring to Melanie.

"Okay, we'll straighten this out when she gets back."

"Okay," she said as she sipped her wine.

"So I solved the big mystery."

"What mystery?"

"The room switch."

Gia's eyes grew wide as she stared at him.

"I see I have your full attention now."

"What do you know?"

"I know that you switched rooms with your friend, Kecia just before her man, Winston arrived. I know the housekeeper had to scrub the room from top to bottom before you would sleep in there. I also know that Taaz has it bad for Kecia, and I was just informed that Winston is not invited to the bachelor party."

"So?"

"So, I put two and two together. Kecia slept with Taaz when her boyfriend was on the way, so you hid the evidence by trading rooms."

"Damn," she said as she sipped her drink, "Um, your ass needs to be a damn CSI, CIA or something."

He laughed.

"So how can I keep you quiet?"

"I am neither a snitch nor a gossiper. I just wanted a date with you. However, for reassurance, I'll continue to stay quiet if you'll agree to lighten up, forget that I'm connected to Melanie in any form, and enjoy our date."

She sighed. "Okay, I think I can do that," she lied.

He smiled, "Sounds good."

"Julian?"

"Yes?"

"You just don't know. If you wouldn't have known her, I would be all on you right now."

He raised his brows and smiled in delight. "Really?"

"Hell no," she laughed, "I just wanted to see you squirm in your seat."

He shook his head.

"But let me be serious," she looked at him, "So uh...what are your future plans?"

"Well, I have a substantial amount of money saved up, so I want to move out of the city. I'm looking into moving to a small town, determine a need that is not being met, and start a business to service that need."

"That's cool. Is there anything in particular that you have in mind?"

"Yes, an antique car restoration shop."

"That's a good idea, especially with all the car shows that people have across the country. I know Taaz took up auto repair as a trade and worked at a local shop before going offshore. He's always loved antique cars, hardly misses any of our local shows."

"Yes, I love them too. Those shows feature some of the most beautiful antique automobiles. These vehicles today are nothing like they used to be," he said, "So you said you own a salon?"

"Yep. We've been doing good, but I have a bigger vision for us. So right now, we are in the middle of revamping the shop and adding more services. We are going to offer products and services that aren't available at the ten different salons across town."

"Hmm, that is very impressive. I love to hear about black women flourishing in business."

"I bet you do," she said, "Who knows, you might

be interested in moving to my town, and maybe I can show you some hot vacant spots."

"I'd like that," he smiled.

Damn you, Melanie, Gia thought.

"So, um what do you like to do in your spare time?"

"Hmm, I like to play basketball with the guys, cook, and watch football and wrestling. Hopefully, when I find that special someone," He pretended to cough, "hint, hint…we can travel because I love traveling."

"Yeah, I love to travel too." She gulped the rest of her drink, "So how are you in the bedroom?"

He choked a little on his drink. "Whoa, that came from nowhere. I think someone's a little tipsy." He gave an uneasy laugh.

"Answer my question. Are you the 'take it slow, make love' type or do you like to get rough and buck wild?"

"Both. It's all depending on the attraction to the woman…the connection that we both share. You see I feel the stronger the connection, the better the sex because your bodies connect and for a moment-"

"You're one," she finished his statement.

"How did you know I was going to say that?"

"I- I didn't."

There was an awkward silence.

"Gia, I can honestly tell you that I've never felt an attraction like this before."

She looked away.

He went on. "I always thought people were crazy for believing in love at first sight, but I understand it."

She looked at him strangely.

"I'm not saying I'm in love, but I like you a lot,

Gia," he smiled, "I know I sound like a little school boy, but it's true."

Be nice, Gia. Be nice. She silently coaxed herself.

"Well, that's flattering...but um, remember *while-ago*...when you told me I'm the woman you've been looking for, why did you say that?"

"Why wouldn't I? You're beautiful, outspoken, opinionated, and just real. I don't like women who try to be more than what they are. I want a woman who embraces the person she is and accepts me for who I am. On top of that, you're an independent successful entrepreneur. That shows me that you have drive, ambition, and determination."

"Wow, I'm all of that, huh?"

"And if you're faithful, if you're not jealous or try to rule your man, and if you respect yourself and your family, and if you believe in God, you are the perfect woman for me."

She continued to look at him with a cynical expression, "So do you possess everything that you want a woman to possess?"

"Yes, I do."

"Well, that would make you the perfect man for me...except for one gigantic imperfection, Melanie." Gia stood up, "Good night, Julian."

"Gia."

He held her hand. His touch made her tremble, and her heart race. She frowned at him.

And damn you, Kecia and Laila for your little love stories making me weak over a man I barely know, Gia thought.

"Thanks for dinner. That king crab hit the spot."

She pulled her hand away and walked out of the restaurant.

CHAPTER 33

At the bachelor party, scantily clad women were dancing around the room, working the crowd of Alonzo's male friends and family members. Two women were pole dancing on two separate round platforms. The guys' friend, Chuck, who was in Quinton's wedding, sat in a black leather chair with two women in his lap. With a Corona in his hand, Alonzo stood next to Taaz, admiring the ladies' pole dancing techniques. Quinton was at the bar talking on his cell phone. He covered his free ear, so he could hear her over the blasting music.

"Marla, there are no strippers around me. I'm– I'm not, Marla. You've got to learn to trust me," he hung up and cut off his phone.

He walked up to Alonzo and Taaz.

"Trouble in paradise, man?" Alonzo asked.

"Hell naw. I told her to leave me alone. At first, she barely answered my calls. Now, she's been calling me so much until I had to cut my phone off," he said, "She's been arguing with me every since I got here."

A stripper brushed against him, "Come here baby." He held her hand and started dancing with her.

"Man, y'all picked out some fine ones, but none of them are as beautiful as my girl," Alonzo said to Taaz.

Taaz was completely drunk and slurred his words, "Man, fu- get her. Tonight's the night to grab some breasts and titties, man."

Alonzo shook his head and laughed at Taaz's redundancy.

"I like 'em chocolate brown, plump lips with dat long black hair," Taaz said, "Fro or down her back. I don't give a fuck."

He gently pulled the arm of a stripper who matched his description.

"Come on," he pulled her close to him, "You're daddy's."

Alonzo watched them inch through the crowd. "Is it me or does she sort of look like Kecia?" He said aloud to himself and shrugged.

"Are you the bachelor?" a lady with freckles and long curly cinnamon hair approached him. She wore black lace lingerie with pink feathers.

"Yes ma'am," he smiled.

"The name's Cinnamon. Umm, you are fine," she started dancing against him, "You sure you wanna get married and give all of this up," she bent over and bounced her backside against his groin.

"Damn, girl. It looks like you're trying to change my mind."

They started freak-dancing with each other.

Quinton was still dancing with his stripper.

"So what you do, daddy?" she asked.

"Oh, I'm an advertising director."

"Okay, so you make good money." She started slowly dipping down low. She was at his crotch still dropping it and looking at him. She ran her hands up his body and came back up.

"Yea, I do good."

"Ain't nothing wrong with that," she wrapped her leg around him.

Taaz and his stripper had just finished dancing. He grabbed another drink and led her to a leather chair.

"Girl, I ain't never got a dance like that before."

"Well, there's more where that came from."

Alonzo was still dancing with Cinnamon, "How about we finish this in one of the private rooms? I promise to take really good care of you," she grabbed his penis.

"Whoa," He moved her hand.

"I can bring my girls, Caramel, Coco, and Vanilla with me. We can give you a night you'll never forget."

"What? Isn't that illegal?" he inched back from her.

"No, we're not prostitutes. We make our money by strictly dancing and performing. Sex in the private room is just an added bonus at our discretion."

"What?" he raised his brows.

"So, your money is no good in there. All we want is your sexy ass and your big dick," she tried to grab his penis again.

"Um, damn girl," he held her hand and led her through the crowd. He spotted one of his college friends.

"Yo, Donnie. This is Cinnamon. She got an offer you can't refuse."

"For real?"

"Hell yes," he put Cinnamon's hand in Donnie's hand. He looked her in the eye, "Now, do your thang, baby girl."

She was confused. "But I-"

Alonzo rushed through the crowd. He grabbed Quinton's arm and pulled him away from his stripper.

"These damn strippers trying to run a train on my ass."

"Well, you wanted strippers."

"Yeah…strippers, not hookers."

Quinton looked at him and smiled.

"What, man?"

"Damn, I'm proud of you."

"For what?"

"You've changed," Quinton explained, "The old you would be getting your threesome on right now. Hell, you probably would have been getting it on with all of the strippers."

He laughed, "Damn, I hate to say it, but you're right, man. You don't need to be with these strippers either. We have our women."

"Yeah, you're right. Come on, let's find Taaz and get out of here."

Taaz was still sitting in the chair with the stripper sitting on his knee.

"Kecia, don't you know I'm the man for you?"

"Um, my name is Chardonnay, and all I'm trying to do is give you a lap dance."

She inched back and sat in his lap. She put her hands on his knees and started gyrating. He rubbed her hair.

"Kecia, why you with him? He ain't even your type. You know you wanna be with me. I know we broke up and everything, but we've fucked two times since you been with ol' dude. Kecia, you left me, girl. You left me just because I don't want to get married and have kids. Damn, don't you know how bad I wanna have your babies, girl? Damn, I want to be your husband. Just not now. Kecia, I work offshore."

"You do?"

"How do you think that makes me feel that I would be seeing my beautiful wife and kids only um... two months a week?"

"Two what?" she looked confused.

"Two weeks a month," he corrected himself, "I don't want to miss a day of my babies' lives. Why can't you wait for me? Wait till I get another job, and I'll be your everything. Then, you complain about me not saying the 'L' word."

"Lesbian?"

"But that just ain't me. I've shown my feelings over and over, Kecia."

"Oh, love."

"I don't have to say it, you should know. I ain't just hittin' cuz I want pussy. I want you, Kecia," he sighed, "And the reason why I pulled away is...man, losing Ms. Carol fucked me up. She was like a mother...that I tried to marry."

Chardonnay frowned and slowed down her movements.

He continued, "but still she had a piece of my heart. And then, I thought about losing you or mom like that...and I don't know if I could take it so I got from around you both for a while. But, now I know I need you both in my life right now from here on out."

Chardonnay looked concern, "Have you told her any of this?"

He realized she was not Kecia, "Naw."

"Well, you need to tell her."

"Taaz! Taaz," Quinton called. They reached him.

"Ah, we're about to go, man," Alonzo said.

"I'm fine right here with Shenaynay."

He stuck some money in her yellow G-string.

"Chardonnay," she corrected him.

"Come on, let's go," Quinton said. Chardonnay stood up, and Quinton pulled Taaz to his feet. She eyed Alonzo and smiled in delight.

"Sexy," she held his arm, "convince your friend to tell Kecia how he feels. That's the only way she'll leave the other man for him."

She made her way through the crowd, and Alonzo wrinkled his brows as he watched her.

Taaz was passing through the crowd as well.

"I wonder what all he told that girl."

"What happened, man?"

"Chardonnay wants Taaz to tell Kecia how he feels."

"Aw damn," Quinton said, "Yeah, it's time to go."

They pushed through the crowd.

"May I have everyone's attention?" a stripper with long black wavy hair said. She stood at the center of the room beside an empty chair. A spotlight was on her. "Can Bachelor Alonzo please come here?"

"Here he go," some guys said, and they started pushing him to the center.

"Oh naw, I-"

Two strippers pushed him into the chair and handcuffed him to it.

The guys whistled.

"Now, it's time for the main show of the night. Gentlemen, I present to you, Thunder."

Most of the guys started clapping and whistling.

"What the hell kind of stripper name is Thunder?"

Quinton said to Taaz.

"If it's a dude, I'ma laugh my ass off, man," Taaz staggered. A tall woman slowly entered the room with a seductive walk. She wore a black eye mask and red and black lingerie. She sashayed towards Alonzo.

The guys were still going wild and throwing money on the floor.

The girl danced sensually in front of Alonzo. She stripped down to her birthday suit. The guys continued to howl and whistle. She got in Alonzo's lap and gave him a lap dance. She started kissing him. His eyes grew wide. He tried to pull his lips away, but she held his head and continued to kiss him.

Quinton stared at the girl, "Wait a minute, is that?"

"Naw man, couldn't be."

She stuffed her panties in his mouth. Alonzo's eyes grew even wider, and the guys started howling once again.

She took off her mask, and it was Alexandra.

"I knew it!"

"Um, um... that's one crazy bitch."

"Um huh," Quinton agreed, "Fine as hell, but crazy." He rushed through the crowd and found Chardonnay. He noticed concerned looks from guys who knew Alexandra. Quinton shrugged at them.

"Hey, how did that girl get in here? She's not a stripper."

"Yes, she is. She's new."

"No, we went to high school with her. That's the bachelor's ex-girlfriend."

"Really?"

"Yeah, and she came up here to stop his wedding. And, I remember picking out ten specific strippers, and she was not one of them. Now, what is she doing here?"

She sighed, "Um, talk to Cinnamon."

He rushed off and found Cinnamon dancing. He pulled her to the side.

"Ah, how did that girl get in here? That's his ex-girlfriend."

Her eyes widened and she sighed, "Busted, huh? Well, she came into the club right after you guys had left. I thought she was a customer, so since she was fine and all, I started dancing on her to make a lil' change. Next thing I know, she slid $500 in my G-string and told me to get her into this party, so I did."

"Seriously?"

She nodded.

"Damn."

Quinton walked off.

"I'm sorry," she called.

Alonzo was still struggling to get away.

She came close to his ear. "Alonzo, I just want to tell you that we're supposed to be together. You know that. We've been together on and off since our school days. I know you know it, and if you go through with this, I will object at your wedding. So, call it off tonight and meet me in my hotel room."

She slid a card in his shirt pocket.

"I still love you. Let me show you how much." She squatted and pushed his legs wide apart. She twerked each cheek individually. The guys yelled out once again. Then, she got between his legs and started unbuckling his belt and unzipping his pants.

Quinton couldn't believe his eyes. "Is she finna suck his—"

"Oh yes."

Quinton quickly jumped in front of them, and

said, "Ayyye! And that concludes this part of the show." He pulled up Alexandra. Some of the men groaned. Taaz looked around strangely at them.

She grabbed her lingerie and hurried out of the room. The guys were clapping. Quinton cringed as he pulled the panties out of Alonzo's mouth and threw them to the floor. Alonzo was breathing loudly.

"Thank you for getting her off me," Alonzo said sarcastically.

"I'm sorry, man," he said, "I had to find out what was going on first."

Cinnamon took off Alonzo's handcuffs.

"I'm so sorry. Please don't tell my boss."

She hurried away. Alonzo rubbed his wrists, zipped his pants, and stood up. He was panting. "Where the hell did she come from?"

They walked towards Taaz as guys patted Alonzo on his back.

"She followed me and Taaz here earlier today."

"Man, I told you someone was following us."

Alonzo shook his head. "Man, same ol' Alley Cat. Never gives up until she gets what she wants."

"Yep man," Taaz said, "She couldn't appeal to you, so she tried to appeal to your lower half."

Alonzo nodded and held himself, "And I'm about 100% sure it worked."

Quinton shook his head. "That girl's psychotic, man. You gotta put an end to this before she does something sick. She might even hurt Laila."

Alonzo grabbed a wine bottle off the bar and took a huge gulp.

"Naw, she won't do anything like that. She's always resorted to this kind of behavior when she used to fight Gallena over me. This was just a little show. She wanted me to remember how good sex with her was, and I guess she thought this was the only way to show me."

"Wouldn't showing up at your door butt naked make more sense?"

"Uh, like Laila did," Alonzo said remembering the first time he had sex with his wife-to-be. He shivered, "Ah, get me out of here."

"Alright," Quinton said. "Ah, we outta here. Y'all enjoy the rest of the party," he told everyone.

Alonzo took another gulp and held up his bottle to them. They left out and headed towards Alonzo's SUV.

"Man, Alexandra don' fucked up. Alonzo likes to chase it, not get stalked by it," Taaz said. "Ah, stop by the corner store and get Lonzo some mouthwash. Ain't no telling where that ho don' been."

"That's not a bad idea," Quinton said.

"Yeah, and get him some Listerine, hand sanitizer, disinfectant spray...hell some baby wipes...Mean Green."

Alonzo and Quinton started laughing.

CHAPTER 34

Alonzo entered the hotel to see Laila and Melanie heading towards the elevator.

"My baby!" He called out. They turned around. He rushed up to her and kissed her.

She pulled away.

"Have you been drinking?"

"Yes, baby," he kissed her again, and she stepped back. Then, he came even closer and hugged her.

"You guys are back early. Doesn't a bachelor party usually end at two?" Melanie asked.

"Oh, we couldn't take it anymore," Quinton said.

"Really?" Melanie asked in surprise.

"Yeah, we found all that ass to be disgusting," Taaz staggered by.

"Hey, Quinton. Make sure he leaves Kecia alone," Alonzo said.

"Damn, I forgot," he said, "Okay, I will."

He followed Taaz down the hall. "Taaz, where are you going?" They disappeared around the corner.

"What happened between Kecia and Taaz?" Laila asked Alonzo as they stood in front of the elevator. Melanie pressed the up arrow button.

"Baby, I'll tell you everything. Just let me make love to you, baby. All night."

Melanie smiled and shook her head at them.

"Well baby, it's been a long trip. I'm really-"

"I know you're tired, baby. We can take a shower, and I can rub your body with that edible body oil you bought us."

"O-kay. TMI," Melanie said, "I'll just be over here." She stepped away.

Alonzo continued to talk to Laila, "Then, you can lay down and let me love you how you need to be loved."

She looked at him strangely. "Um, maybe you need to get over the excitement of your bachelor party."

"Baby, you heard Taaz. We weren't studdin' them. Please, baby."

He kissed her neck.

"Umm," Laila sighed, "If I can stay awake."

"Aw, that's my girl."

The elevator opened, and three people walked out laughing and talking. Alonzo held Laila's hand as they stepped onto the elevator. Alonzo started kissing and licking Laila's neck while running his hands over her body. She kept moving his hands and pushing him back.

"Melanie, aren't you coming?"

"Um, no. I'll wait for the next one."

Laila smiled at her and said, "Okay girl. Goodnight."

"Goodnight."

Just as the elevator was about to close, Melanie noticed Laila kissing Alonzo back and running her hands all over his body.

"Damn...that means I've got to pay Gia her money," Melanie said aloud to herself, thinking of the sex bet they had made.

With Alonzo's arms wrapped around her, Laila opened the door, and they staggered in the room. Laila got out of his grasp to close the door. She dropped her bag on the floor. He immediately pulled her waist close to him. They started kissing wildly as Alonzo walked backwards. He tripped and fell with Laila toppling over him.

She started laughing. "You are sloppy drunk, and I don't think you'll be able to perform. You're not up for it."

He grabbed her hand and placed it on his dick.

"Does it feel like I'm not up for it?"

Laila bit her lip and squeezed him.

Alonzo groaned, "Damn girl, you gotta be gentle."

She kissed him. "Not tonight." She stood up. "Now assume the position."

Alonzo was delighted. He scrambled to get up and made his way onto the bed. He laid on the pillow at the head of the bed. She slipped out of her shoes and pulled off her top and pants to reveal her soft pink lace panties and bra. He kicked off his shoes. She crawled on the bed and started unbuckling his pants. She pulled down his pants and boxers. She held his penis and started stroking and kissing it. Then, she took him in her mouth. He gasped and winced as she savored him.

"Fuck! Yes, I'm so glad you're about to be my wife," he moaned "Damn girl."

Laila focused on pleasing her man that she missed being away from.

"Put that thang in my face girl. Come on," he said, "I gotta taste you."

She finally obeyed. He slid her panties to the side and drove his tongue in and sucked her clit. They continued to taste one another.

"Dang, here it come. Here it come. Oh..."

She felt his warmth fill her mouth as he shivered. He continued to pant and moan. She made her way back to the head of the bed. She curled up against him and placed her head on his shoulder. He wrapped his arm around her.

"I love you, girl. Just give me about ten minutes, and I'ma tear that thang up. Just ten mo-" He drifted off to sleep.

CHAPTER 35

The next morning, Gia walked up to Julian in the courtyard with a huge smile on her face. "What's up?"

He looked up at her. "You're approaching me? This is a pleasant surprise."

"Oh, I'm full of surprises." She sat next to him and noticed a basketball tattoo on his ankle. "So you actually play basketball?"

"Yes."

"I thought you were lying. You played basketball in high school and college?"

"Just high school. I was a point guard."

"Me too."

"No way."

"I just can't picture you playing ball."

"Actually I've never stopped. I hit my local fitness center and the court every week. I have to maintain my health, physique, and stamina. Once you stop, it goes down as you get older."

"I hear you," Gia said as she gazed at the pool.

"And obviously you are doing something to maintain your amazing physique as well."

"It's effortless."

"I certainly see your effortless beauty. I just don't get why you're single."

"And I don't get why you are si—not married."

"I'm *single* because I haven't found the one that makes everything in me yearn for her. You know this undeniable connection, and this feeling deep down that she is the one. And, I can't let her get away. Some people say that it doesn't exist, but I believe that it does."

"Well good luck with that," Gia smirked, "It looks like I'm terminally single. I really do have walls up. It's just so hard to let anyone in, so I try not to be in my feelings. I mostly treat a man like he's my bitch."

"I can see that," Julian said, "Why do you think that's so?"

Gia sighed, "Roger."

"Who?"

"Lac is what they used to call him. He was a dope boy, and I fell hard for him. Then, I caught him cheating on me. I beat that bitch down and his ass too. He tried everything he could to get back with me, but I wouldn't have it. He said since I wouldn't take him back, there was nothing else down here in the South for him, so he moved back to Chicago. A month later, he was killed at a damn trap house. That fool had sent me messages to my phone and on Facebook every day up until his last day. Now, he's gone. His last message to me was, 'Hey beautiful. I will love you forever.'"

"Wow, that had to be rough."

"Yeah, the girls didn't think it bothered me too much, but it did. And since then, I just haven't taken relationships seriously."

"Do you think that will ever change?"

"Well, seeing Laila and Kecia in relationships, I do want something solid with someone. But, even when I start to think maybe I can give a real relationship a shot, the guy always end up being a fuck boy one way or the other."

"So you're not talking to anyone now?"

"Naw, I let my friend go a few weeks back because he wanted more, and I knew he wasn't the one for me. I just decided to cut him loose, so he can be with the chick that's right for him. One thing I don't ever wanna do is keep a man from the lady he's supposed to be with…just because I don't want to be alone. That will make me miss out on my man. I know his ass is out there, and I know he is going to love me for me. He's going to accept all this craziness, intelligence, realness, sassiness, and beauty that is me."

"You definitely make a lasting impression from the first moment you walk into a room."

Gia pursed her lips, "Umm huh."

"You have this confidence like you own the room and every motherfucker in there. Excuse my language."

"Now you know I don't bite my tongue, and I'm the lady."

"Yeah, but I still desire to respect you."

She bit her bottom lip, and they stared at one another.

She broke the stare. "But anyway," she started, "since you can't keep your ass away from me, you wanna go paragliding today?"

"Um sure."

Then, her eyes grew wide.

"Oh shit!" she looked at her phone.

"What is it?"

"I have to go meet Kecia…uh, meet me on the beach in an hour."

She rushed away.

"Looking forward to it," he called after her.

In her hotel room, Laila stretched in bed next to Alonzo. She kissed him on his cheek and climbed out of bed. She noticed that he had already gotten up earlier, taken a shower, and changed clothes. Then, she slowly eased into the bathroom to take a shower as well.

When she entered the bedroom, Alonzo was gone. Wrapped in a towel, she opened the closet door and picked out a blue crop top and a long black skirt with huge pink roses with traces of blue. She pulled the top over her head and stepped into the skirt. She slid her feet into her black sandals. She stood at the mirror, gazed at herself, and smiled. She put an astringent on her cotton ball and rubbed her face. She leaned against the chair to get a closer look at her face when Alonzo's shirt fell off the back of the chair. She reached down and saw an unfamiliar card. She picked it up and saw that it was a room keycard to a nearby hotel. *Room 369.*

She sat at the table, bouncing her leg and tapping the card.

Alonzo opened the door.

"Baby, we've got more guests," He entered, "What's wrong?

"I found this in your shirt pocket," she said, "A room keycard from another hotel."

He looked at her, "Laila, it's not what it looks like…let me explain."

"Did you get a room with one or two of the strippers or is it hers?"

"I don't remember how-"

"It's hers, isn't it? She never left. She's been up here this whole time, held up in some hotel room waiting to answer your every beck and call," she said, "Did you just come from seeing her?"

"I never went, Laila."

"Yeah, but you knew she was still down here, and you didn't tell me. You've seen her again. If you didn't, how did you get this room key then? Huh?"

"I-I..."

Laila frowned.

"Okay. Hear me out. She's been stalking me. She won't leave me alone. She came here, and I told her, 'no, I don't want you.' So then, I thought it was over, but last night-"

"Last night?"

"She popped up at the strip club and took us all by surprise. She has been following Taaz and Quinton around."

"Alexandra Reid, a stalker? Puh-lease, Alonzo. You're lying to me," Laila said, "Just admit it."

"Admit what?"

"You slept with her. Probably all while I was gone to see my mother. Answer the question."

"What question?"

"Did you cheat on me?

"Laila, I would nev-"

"All it takes is a simple yes or no," she said, "Did you cheat on me?"

"No."

"Well, this keycard tells me otherwise," Laila smirked. "I should have known you would never change. Same old Alonzo. Why did I think I was different? That I had some kind of power to keep you at bay? You've always been a dog, and that's what you'll always be, but you know what? You can do it without me."

"Whoa…whoa. Wait a minute. What are you doing?"

She pulled off her ring and sat it on the table.

"We're finished."

"Laila, I didn't sleep with her. I'm telling you the truth. Baby, I want to marry you," she opened the door and walked down the hall. She held the card in her hand, contemplating on whether or not to pay Alexandra a little visit and kick her ass. "You're the only woman for me. Don't let this misunderstanding ruin our special day. Come on baby, let's talk this out. Let me make you understand." He followed her down the hall.

"Alonzo, you're not about to make me understand anything or make me marry you," she said, "Better yet," she threw the card at him. "Marry that bitch."

CHAPTER 36

"Wait…who told you that?" Gia asked Kecia. They were sitting down in the lobby.

"Melanie. She texted me yesterday, but I didn't see it until this morning. But it's true. Mitch Henderson is her daddy."

"I knew it! I've been telling you for years."

"I know, I know, but Melanie said that Laila doesn't want to talk about it until after the wedding so don't say anything."

"I won't, but that's crazy."

"Tell me about it," Kecia sighed, "so we're going to run to the store real quick and get her a small jug of Cherry Garcia ice cream. They didn't have that flavor here."

"In who's vehicle?"

"Girl, Winston has a rental."

"Okay, Leggo."

They went outside, and Gia saw Laila marching towards the street. Gia nudged Kecia.

"Why didn't we see her walk past us?"

They rushed after her.

"Laila, where are you going?"

"To find Alexandra."

"Alexandra?"

"What happened?"

Laila didn't respond as she continued walking. Gia called Alonzo.

"Your ass better start talking."

In Alexandra's hotel lobby, Laila approached the front desk agent. "Is Alexandra Reid still here?"

"Um," the guy checked on his computer, "Yes, she is. Do you want me to call her down to meet you?"

"No, it's fine. She has been expecting me."

She looked around and saw Alexandra coming out of the hotel's restaurant and heading to the bathroom. Laila took off behind her.

Gia asked the front desk agent, "Did you just see a yellow lady looking for Alexandra Reid?"

"Yes, she went that way."

Alexandra stood at a sink, straightening her hair as she admired herself in the mirror. Laila entered and smirked.

"Well, isn't this déjà vu," Laila said, "So you're still here."

"It's a free country. I can be wherever I want to be."

"Yes, you can be wherever you want to be, but you can't be with whoever you want."

"So I guess you found the keycard."

"Assuming, eh? How do you know he didn't show it me?"

She smirked and laughed to herself.

"Please...so? What? You came here to tell me to leave your man alone and yada yada yada?"

Laila smirked, "I am not you. I don't have to

confront you. I trust him to handle his business."

"Yet you're standing here at my hotel, confronting me now," she rolled her eyes.

"No, I'm just here to have a chat with my classmate who is in town for my wedding that she wasn't invited to."

"Well, I hate to break the news to you, classmate, but your wedding is not going to happen just like Melanie's didn't happen," Alexandra said, "Alonzo has always been mine. Had I not left, he'd still be with me."

"I heard you had your claws deep into him. You cheat on him. He cheats on you. Y'all would break up. Get back together...yada yada yada. Just sad." Laila said, "But you no longer have a hold on him nor can you get it back. What you fail to realize is that you made a big mistake back then."

"I didn't make any-"

"I'm not finished talking," Laila said firmly, "You made the mistake of giving him room to clear his mind instead of confusing him with all of your bedroom tricks. He's over you. You're in his past, and I'm his present and his future. And nothing you can say or do will change his mind about that."

"So you actually believe Alonzo is a changed man? Silly girl."

"He's a man, and I'm his *woman*. He may slip up. He may even decide to give you a go again, but all you'll ever be is a side chick or a thought," she said meaning thot, "But me, Laila McKee-Davis will always be his wife."

"Let's say I don't back down. What are you going to do? Fight me?"

Laila smirked, "I've matured. I have no reason to

fight you."

"Oh because I'm not Melanie…I'll beat your ass."

"Oh really? Beat my ass then," Laila got close to her. "Come on. I'm right here…beat my ass."

Alexandra lunged forward, and Laila pushed her to the floor.

"That's all you've got? Come on, beat my ass."

Alexandra attempted to dig in her purse.

"Naw, you don't need nothing out of your purse," she grabbed the purse and flung it, sending all of its contents across the floor. "Come on."

Alexandra got back up, and they circled each other, "Come on, beat my ass."

Outside of the bathroom, Gia and Kecia stood and listened.

"Somebody's going ham in the bathroom ain't they?" Gia asked, "Can't take black folks nowhere without making a damn scene."

"I know you ain't talking…hold on," Kecia held up her hand, "That sounds like Laila."

"Laila?"

They rushed through the door.

"Laila," Kecia said, "Let's go."

"Kecia Jones?" Alexandra eyed her from her head to her toes, "Well, I guess Taaz wasn't lying when he said milk does a body good," she said referring to Taaz's cow joke he made in high school.

"You need to take your ass on before I call the police on you," Kecia said.

"But you're at *my* hotel."

"Laila, let's go," she grabbed Laila's arm.

"Naw, she said she gon' beat my ass. I'm waiting for her to do it."

"She's not worth it," Kecia pulled Laila out of the

bathroom.

"Hey bitch, remember me?" Gia smiled, "You know I was always down to kick your ass."

"Gia, all I'm trying to do is talk to Alonzo one more time, and I'll be on my way."

"You are one crazy bitch...always have been. Alonzo don't want you. He told you when he talked to you the first time. He showed you at the bachelor party that he does not want you. You won't give up. Like in high school, no matter how many times I beat yo' ass, you would get right back up and do the same damn thang."

Alexandra stared at her in silence.

"I'm just begging you...please give me another reason to put my foot all up in that ass. Please...I beg you," she came closer to her, "All you ever been was a punk ass, ho ass bitch who talks cash money shit. If you know what's best for you, you will leave and stay the hell away from that wedding, if it's even still on."

Alexandra sneered at her.

"Or, do I need to shame you in public again?" Gia started rapping, "Please ho just leave/go do what you do best and get on yo' knees/believe/I will shut you down/and that's only in the first round."

Kecia peeped her head back in.

"Gia, let's go."

Gia continued, "I'm telling you...leave Alonzo and Laila alone or the next time I see you, I'ma lay your ass to the ground."

She walked out of the bathroom and looked around the hotel lobby. "Where's Laila?"

"She was just here a minute ago."

They rushed outside and didn't see her anywhere.

"Man, I'ma start calling her the Runaway Bride,"

Gia said, "And where's Melanie's ass?"

"Probably still asleep. You know that trip to Maryland probably wore her out."

"Ol' weak ass."

Kecia texted Alonzo, "We lost her...looking for her now."

In his room, Alonzo read a text message from Kecia and started pacing back and forth. Quinton entered.

"Damn man, I can't find her anywhere. I can't lose her, not this one. She's the reason I breathe, man. She makes me want to be a better me, you know."

"I know, man."

"It can't be over, not like this."

"Just calm down. Let me talk to her. It's just all a big misunderstanding. She'll be back. She just needs time to think and cool off."

"I've looked everywhere...she's—she's gone."

Quinton sighed, "I think I might know where she is. I'll go check it out."

"Ok, and Quinton, please don't let her—"

"Don't worry. I got you. I'll get her back to you, okay? Just let me take care of it."

CHAPTER 37

Quinton walked along the beach and entered the cove they had visited a few days before. He looked around and didn't see Laila. The wind blew through the cove, and he smelled a hint of her fragrance, Sweet Pea. He looked strangely and walked through the cove and spotted her. She was sitting in the sand with her arms wrapped around her bent knees. Her hair was back curly and unruly, blowing in the wind and over her face as she stared out at the ocean.

She reminded him of when he first saw her as the new kid in junior high school.

Never taking her eyes off the crashing waves, she said, "So he sent you."

"No, I came on my own. You mind if I sit?"

She shook her head, and he sat beside her.

"So this is my karma, Quinton? I slept with you as your wedding was approaching, and Alonzo cheats on me," Laila smirked, "with that bi...*tsk*, I guess what they say is true. Karma is a bitch."

"Laila," he said, "This isn't you talking."

She sighed, "Maybe he'll be like you and marry her the day after tomorrow."

"Don't say that."

"Uh, I should have known. If you're capable of doing what you did, Alonzo's more than capable," she groaned, "How can he let go of all those women? It took me a lifetime just to get over you."

Tears began to pour down her face, "If you're not the one, and he's not the one, then who is? Maybe it's no one. Maybe I'm meant to be alone."

Quinton decided not to interrupt, but let her continue on.

She sighed, "Uhh, Alexandra of all people...I'm just so mad. I wish I could do something crazy. Or, anything to piss him off...kiss you or something. But no, I'm too in love to hurt him. No matter what he does, I won't retaliate or seek revenge because I love him just that much. But one thing I can do, thanks to you, is let him go."

"Whoa...whoa. Let him go? Laila, he hasn't hurt you."

She frowned. "Men will lie for other men till the day they die."

"I'm telling you the truth though," Quinton said, "We thought Alexandra was gone, but she crashed the bachelor party. She had a mask on, so we thought she was just one of the strippers. She slipped that card on him just before we kicked her ass out, but he never went to her hotel room. We thought he had tossed the card."

"Uh huh. To get rid of the proof...maybe he was thinking of going. Him holding onto it must mean something. He must have been considering it."

"Alonzo and Alexandra may have been high school sweethearts or whatever you want to call what that was, but I can assure you that she's far from his type now."

"And what is his type now?"

"You! You've got him whipped bad. Being all soft, talking about true love and shit. He's all about you. He's been this way ever since he was trying to save you from me."

"Save me from you?" Laila thought, and she recollected her past obsession with Quinton. "Yeah, we would have never worked out. You longing for Marla, and me harnessing a hidden desire for Alonzo."

"Yeah, I never thought you two would get together, but it's a good match."

"I guess."

"You know you've always talked about holding on to me and never letting go, but doing so finally opened your eyes to Alonzo. Had you held on, you would have never gotten to know who Alonzo truly is."

"A whore."

Quinton chuckled, "A reformed whore who many women, even exes, find attractive. A man who is deeply in love with you because you fulfill his every need."

"Sooo... he said that?"

"Yes, don't tell him I told you, but he said every woman he's met pales in comparison to you."

"Oh please, you're just layering it on...I'm not all that."

"Little Miss Perfect Laila as you unequivocally hate to be called, in Lonzo's eyes, you are the perfect woman for him, and he's damn sure not going to let Alexandra fuck it up."

She pursed her lips.

He went on. "He loves your imperfections and your quirkiness. It's what sets you apart from everyone else. You're not trying to be all that, which makes you one of the realest women out there."

"Quinton, I honestly want to believe you, but what if he actually cheated with her? What if he's slept with other women since he's proposed?" Laila asked, "I just...I just don't want to be *that girl.*"

"What do you mean by that?"

"Quinton, if he cheated, I would forgive him... Not right now, but eventually...and I would marry him. Then, if two years down the line, he cheats again. I probably would be hurt. Then, after his many romantic gestures and apologies, I would forgive him again. I just love that man with all of my heart and soul, but I can't allow myself to be *that girl* who lets a man cheat on her over and over again."

"Laila, I understand what you're saying, but what if Alonzo really is a changed man. What if Alonzo wants to spend the rest of his life with only you?" He continued, "That girl? What if you're *that woman* who ended up with a faithful husband who loves and adores her because he knows in his heart that she's the one?"

She sighed.

"You just have to take a leap of faith. You can't rely on what ifs. You taught me that."

Laila looked at him and was confused. She could not remember what he was referring to. Quinton knew she had forgotten what she once told him.

"What ifs can't keep you warm at night, but your husband, Alonzo will do a damn good job."

Laila closed her eyes and breathed heavily.

"You're thinking too much, Laila. Get rid of all of

these scenarios that's playing out in your mind. Get rid of all of those negative past memories of Alonzo, even me, and any guy who has ever wronged you. Clear your mind, don't think. Just listen...listen to your heart. In your heart, you know that he didn't sleep with Alexandra nor does he intend on sleeping with her or anyone other than you. In your heart, you know you will walk down that aisle in two days, and you won't let people get in the way of you joining hands with your soul mate. In your heart, you already feel that you are Mrs. Alonzo Davis.

"I never thought I'd see the day that my dream man in high school would convince me to marry his best friend."

"Well, stranger things have happened," Quinton smiled.

"You're right. Hell, I even got in Alexandra's face and told her that no matter what she tried, I am still going to marry Alonzo."

Quinton shook his head. "Well, now all you need to do is talk to Alonzo."

He pulled her to her feet and walked with her to the hotel. When they entered the lobby, Alonzo was waiting for them. Quinton placed Laila's hand in Alonzo's, and they stood down the hall. Quinton folded his arms and waited for them to finish their conversation. Gia and Kecia walked up to Quinton.

"Why you ain't answer my texts?"

He didn't respond.

Gia smacked her lips. "Look, I need to know if I need to get ready or chill out tonight. Are we having this rehearsal dinner or not?"

"Hold on," Quinton said.

"Don't be..."

"She's talking to Alonzo now," he pointed to them.

"Ohhhh."

Alonzo spoke to Laila, "Baby, I'm sorry that I didn't immediately tell you about what happened last night. I was just so happy to have you back."

"Never keep anything like this from me again, okay?"

He nodded, "But I did not do you wrong. I would never-"

"Shh..." Laila kissed him. "I know it was a misunderstanding, and you handled the situation as best as you could in the state that you were in. Can't say the same for me, but we have the rest of our lives to figure out how to properly handle issues together."

His eyes brightened, "Damn, I love you, girl."

He quickly put her ring back on her finger. "I love you too." They hugged.

He let out of sigh of relief. "Now, we can have our uhhh...rehearsal dinner. Are we still calling it that?"

"Well, Kecia and Taaz rehearsed, so I think we can still call it that."

"Okay."

"How did that go?"

"Uhhh, I'll share all of those juicy details later."

"Okay. Let's get some rest before dinner." They headed towards the elevator.

Alonzo gave Quinton, Kecia and Gia a thumbs up and mouthed, "Thank you."

"Thank goodness," Kecia sighed in relief.

Quinton smiled and immediately headed to the restaurant for breakfast.

Gia noticed Julian coming out of the elevator. He waved at Alonzo and Laila as they stepped on. He locked eyes with her. She bobbed her head for him to meet her outside.

"Umm huh," Kecia smirked at Gia.

"Mind your business."

CHAPTER 38

Gia and Julian walked up to a high cliff near the beach. They met with three paraglide instructors. They showed them how to operate their paragliders.

"What have I talked myself into?" he groaned.

"Naw, don't back out now."

"I was afraid of heights as a kid."

"But you can hop in an airplane. You scared, huh?"

He stammered. A lady gave them helmets and helped to secure them to the paragliders. Julian's was yellow and blue, and Gia's was red and white.

"Well, you said you wanted to do it with me, but if you're scared, I'll understand…that you ain't nothing but a little chicken."

"Chicken? I ain't ever scared."

"Aw, that's not convincing. Is you is or is you ain't?"

"I-"

"I can't hear you! Are you scared?" she got louder.

"Ain't ever scared!"

"What? I can't hear you! Say what?" she said as if she was his drill sergeant.

"I ain't ever scared!"

"Are you gon' cry like a little bitch or are you gon' do this shit?"

All of the people around them were laughing.

"I ain't ever scared!"

"Are you a lil' bitch or are you a real man?!"

"I'm a real man!"

"Well, then...do that shit!"

"Oh, I'ma do it. Yeah, I got it."

"Do that shit then!"

He took a running start, and then jumped off the cliff.

Gia yelled, "Go Ju! I'm right behind you!"

She took a running start and leaped. She felt the cool breeze and loved how light she felt gliding in the air.

Julian landed in the sand along the beach, and Gia landed roughly close by. The fabric landed on top of her.

"Gia!" Julian called, but she didn't answer, "Gia! Are you okay?"

He took off his helmet, threw it down, and detached himself from his paraglider.

He rushed and pulled the fabric off her. She was smiling. He helped her to her feet.

"You did that shit," she panted as she took off her helmet. He helped to detach her paraglider.

"I did, didn't I."

"That was such an adrenaline rush. I love it!" She started jumping up and down.

"You are crazy," he smiled.

"I told you!"

She looked up at the cliff.

"You see how high up we came from? We're some

227

bad asses," she said, "Woo…I wanna do it again." She jumped up in excitement again and tripped over the cords. He caught her.

"I got you."

They stared at each other. A twist was in her face. He pushed it back and kept gazing in her eyes. He leaned in and kissed her.

"See, I told you not to do that no more. Just for that, I'ma find you an even higher cliff for your ass to jump off."

"Oh boy, I'm going to be no good at the rehearsal dinner."

CHAPTER 39

Laila and Alonzo stood at the door of a banquet room and greeted their guests as they arrived for the rehearsal dinner. The banquet room had blue and gold carpet. The windows were adorned with gold satin valences and white sheer panels. A long rectangular table covered in a white table cloth was set with chargers and glasses. Two servers dressed in black formal attire stood in the corner, waiting for everyone to be seated. Another server came out with a pitcher of tea and filled each of the glasses on the table.

Instead of sitting at the head, Laila and Alonzo sat near the windows in the middle chairs. Jazz instrumental music played softly. The room filled with chatter as everyone, including Alonzo's two other groomsmen, Al and Lawrence, mingled with one another. Kecia and Winston sat near the happy couple, and Kecia avoided eye contact with Taaz. When Julian entered, he searched the room for Gia. They caught each other's eye at the same time. She smiled at him until Melanie appeared from behind him and held his arm as they approached the table.

She waved at everyone and greeted the servers with a warm smile. Gia turned her nose up at Julian and looked away. The servers placed their dinner plates on their gold chargers. Everyone admired their grilled chicken, scalloped potatoes, green beans, butter roll and pecan pie.

Laila tapped her glass with her fork.

"I would like to thank each of you for showing us love and support throughout the years. Instead of us being two separate entities: the boys and the girls. We've grown into a big family. We help each other when we're in a tight spot. We give each other a shoulder to lean on and cry on. Even though the guys can get rowdy, you have each other's back and keep each other out of trouble. I know the girls have had their share of times in keeping me out of trouble."

"And somehow you always manage to get in it anyway," Kecia said. Many of them laughed.

"Yep, that's why Alonzo and I greatly appreciate each person at this table." Laila looked at Winston, "We have a new face that some of you may not recognize. This is Winston, Kecia's companion," Laila smiled, "Winston, you're going to experience the craziness of our family, and you're going to love every minute of it."

He nodded and smiled at her.

"There is one person missing, my maid of honor and soon-to-be sister-in-law, Aliza. She and the rest of Alonzo's family will be here tomorrow evening."

Laila noticed Melanie glaring at her, "Oh, and where are my manners. We also have Melanie's companion, Julian." He smiled at everyone, and Gia rolled her eyes.

Laila sat down.

Alonzo stood up. "Isn't she beautiful, everyone? I know many of you have admired and despised my player techniques over the years. To be honest, I never thought I would actually give that lifestyle up until I met up with Laila again in the oddest circumstances. Most of you know the story, but when I locked eyes with her at that wedding rehearsal, I just knew she had to be my wife. After all, I had been saying that ever since high school cuz I've loved me some Laila, but my ways turned her off. It just felt like fate when we met up at the very time I was trying to change."

He held her hand.

"And my lady is right. We are family. My boys have been there from day one. My beautiful cousin, Melanie has always shown me how to appreciate the finer things in life. And Gia, thank you for kicking my ass and teaching Laila how to kick my ass." Everyone laughed again.

"And we'll tag team that ass if you mess up," Gia said.

He smiled, "Your husband gon' have something on his hands. And, our beautiful, strong Kecia who has always joked and wrestled with us. We've witnessed you transform right before our very eyes. You're beautiful, girl...always have been, and no matter where life takes you, we hope you find happiness in the right place."

She squeezed Winston's hands. "Aw Alonzo, you're going to make me cry."

She got up and hugged him. Winston stood up as well.

"Speaking of finding happiness in the right place, I would like to take this time to make an announcement." Winston looked at Alonzo, "Do you mind?"

"No…by all means."

Alonzo sat down, giving him the floor. Kecia stared at him and wondered what he was up to.

"What are you doing?" she asked.

"Kecia, I love you, and when I picture my future, I see you in it. You brighten my entire world, and I want to spend the rest of my life making you happy."

He reached in his pocket and pulled out a blue jewelry box. Tears ran down her face as he got down on one knee.

The ladies gasped, and Taaz frowned.

He opened the box to reveal a rose gold diamond ring. "Kecia Lashay Jones, will you marry me?"

She started breathing hard and looked at Taaz.

Everyone looked on in utter surprise.

"Say yes, girl," Melanie said.

She breathed heavily, "I…I-" She fainted.

Alonzo rushed out of his seat and caught her as Winston tried to grab her arms.

"Kecia!" Gia jumped up.

"Oh my God! Someone call 911," Melanie said.

Everyone scrambled out of their chairs, but Taaz froze at the table.

"She still has a pulse. Kecia, do you hear me? Kecia," Winston tried to wake her.

"Come on…let's get her to the hospital," Quinton said. They carried her out.

CHAPTER 40

In the emergency room, everyone in the wedding party as well as Winston and Julian were waiting to hear any news about Kecia. Melanie and Winston were pacing. Laila was sobbing, leaning against Alonzo.

"She's going to be fine, baby."

Taaz sat in a corner. Gia came from the front desk.

"Those bitches can't tell me nothing," she sat down by Julian. She started bouncing her knee. "Can't nothing happen to Kecia. She's my sister."

A tear fell from her eye.

Julian held her hand, "She's going to be okay."

Gia moved her hand away from his. "Look, I think it's best we keep our distance.

"But-"

"But nothing. I want someone that I can build a life with. I'm not tryna start up with you like this. You'll do me like you're doing Melanie, and that ain't right."

"I told you. We're not-"

"And, Melanie still ain't cleared up shit so again I

say, bullshit," she said, "Her silence tells me all I need to so bye Julian." She got up and sat beside Quinton and Taaz.

Winston spotted a nurse, "Any news on Kecia Jones?"

She shook her head.

"God, I hope she's okay," Melanie said as she sat next to Laila and Alonzo.

A doctor came up.

"Anyone here for Kecia Jones?"

"We are," Quinton said. Everyone jumped to their feet and crowded around the doctor.

"Whoa, she has a big group," she said.

"How's Kecia?" Laila asked.

"Oh, she's fine."

"Her vitals?" Winston asked.

"Looks good."

They let out a huge sigh of relief.

"She was just dehydrated."

"So she'll be able to go home tonight?" Gia asked.

"Oh, yes. We're getting ready to release her in just a little while."

"You're sure everything's okay?" Winston asked.

"Oh yes, you have nothing to worry about. Her and the baby are fine."

"Baby?" they all exclaimed.

"She's pregnant?" Taaz asked.

She nodded, "I take it that you all didn't know."

"Hell naw, we didn't know," Gia said.

"I'm- I'm going to be a father?" Winston looked confused, then his eyes brightened. "I'm going to be a father!" He grinned. Quinton and Alonzo patted and squeezed his shoulders to congratulate him. Laila, Gia, and Melanie hugged him. Julian shook his hand.

"Congratulations," Julian said.

"Thanks," Winston looked at the doctor again, "Can I see her?"

"Sure. Right this way."

Taaz looked disappointed and stepped outside.

"Hey, I'm about to go see about Taaz," Quinton said.

"I'm coming too." Alonzo said, then turned to Laila, "You're okay?"

"Yes, I'm perfectly fine now."

On the outside of the emergency entrance, Taaz leaned his arm against the column.

"Man, that's fucked up."

Quinton tried to touch his shoulder, but Taaz jerked away, "Get off me, man."

"Taaz, you can't let this get to you, man."

"He don' swooped in and gave her everything that I refused to."

There was silence.

"Ain't no way she gon' leave that nigga now."

Quinton and Alonzo looked at each other.

Melanie and Gia came up to Laila.

"A baby," Laila smiled.

Melanie said, "I didn't see that one coming."

"I don't think any of us saw that coming," Gia thought, "Damn, I just remembered my dream. Those damn fish...um, um...I should have known."

"We're gonna be aunties." Melanie hugged them.

"Ooo...I'm going to spoil the mess out of that baby," Gia said.

Melanie beamed, "I hope it's a girl."

"Well, I want a boy," Gia said.

"Well, whoever he or she may be, we are going to love 'em just the same." Laila smiled.

"I'm just glad she's ok," Gia said, "I was about to blame those weight loss products. Thought we were about to have us a good ass lawsuit."

Melanie shook her head at Gia.

Laila blew her breath. "Well, at least there's a silver lining in these confusing pre-wedding festivities."

"I know right."

"Well, all I know is that I'm going to be the godmother."

"I'm going to be the godmother too."

"And me too."

"No, there can only be one godmother." They went back and forth arguing. Alonzo came back in and stood by Julian. He listened to their argument and shook his head.

"Where's Taaz?"

"Oh, Quinton took him back to the hotel."

Winston came back in with a big grin on his face.

"They're getting ready to release her right now," he looked over at the ladies, "What are they arguing about?"

"Who's going to be the baby's godmother," Julian said. Julian and Winston chuckled.

"Welcome to my world," Alonzo said.

CHAPTER 41

After the ladies fawned all over Kecia at the hospital, they all went back to the hotel. Everyone went to their separate rooms to get some rest. However, Melanie was fully energetic from the rest she had gotten earlier that day when the ladies were out confronting Alexandra. Melanie decided that she wanted to exercise in the fitness center for an hour.

When her hour was complete, her phone alarm sounded. Glistening with sweat, Melanie wiped her face and chest with her white towel, then slung it over her right shoulder. She walked down the first floor hall. She glanced into the restaurant as she passed by. Then, she stopped and thought for a moment. She stepped back and stood at the door. She noticed Quinton at the bar, steadily drinking shots while holding a full glass of scotch in one hand. She folded her arms and started to walk away. However, she couldn't bring herself to leave him at the bar alone.

She groaned, then walked in.

"Hey Quinton."

He looked up at her and was surprised to see her. "Oh, hey Mel." Then, he told the bartender, "This is my ex-fiancé. She probably already had her sip of Merlot, so she'll have a Cosmopolitan."

"No, I'm fine," she told them.

"Quinton, don't you think you've had enough?"

She took his glass just as he was about to take a sip.

"Mel, can you sit with me for a minute?"

She sighed and sat next to him.

"I just want to apologize for everything I did to you. I never got the chance to tell you how sorry I am for how I treated you and how everything went down."

"I'm known to hold grudges, but I've already forgiven you."

"Oh, you have? Then, why is this the first time you're actually talking to me?"

I have spoken with you, she thought.

"Well, it looks like you need a friend right now. So here I am."

"Even if you secretly hate me."

"I don't hate you."

He smirked.

"Everything that happened with us was crazy...from my actions to your actions. We went from being with one another every day for two years so deeply in love to complete strangers once we returned to our hometown. The whole time we were together, I didn't really know you, and you didn't really know me. It was for the best that we didn't take it any further because we would have been unhappy together."

"I wouldn't be so sure about that. It's my karma. Now, I've lost Ma, and Marla hates me," he sighed, "Melanie, I should have married you. I shouldn't have cared about Laila or Marla. I should have been with you. Maybe I wouldn't be getting punished like I am now."

"Oh, I know that's the alcohol talking," she said, "There's nothing you could have done to prevent what was meant to happen. And you suffering like this is all your fault."

"Yeah, it's all my fault because of the actions I've taken in the past."

"That's not what I meant, Quinton. You have to learn to move past this like I did as a child when I lost both of my parents, and you've got to stop drowning your sorrows in booze. You're only making the suffering worse."

"I can move past this with you."

Melanie rolled her eyes.

"Let's get you out of here," she stood up, "Where's your phone?"

"I turned it off and left it in my room."

She shook her head, "Of course you did. Come on...up we go."

He placed money on the bar and waved at the bartender. "Taaz was supposed to be down here drinking his sorrows away with me, but he ran upstairs for some reason." He staggered and placed his arm around her neck. Her towel fell to the floor, and she didn't bother to pick it up.

Melanie and Quinton made their way up to his room. When they finally made it to his door, Melanie said, "Okay, you lean back right here."

He leaned against the wall, next to his door.

"So you really don't think we should've married each other?" He stared at her, "Mel, you and I had some good times."

"Yeah, but I did some soul searching and trust me, I'm good."

"Oh, so you don't still think I look good?"

"I am not about to answer that," she said, "Give me your keycard."

"Uhh," he patted himself.

"Don't tell me you left it in your room."

She stood in front of him and patted his pockets. She reached in his jacket pocket.

"Here it is," she held up his white card.

He grabbed her arms. "After all I put you through, you're still taking care of me."

"Quinton," she warned him.

He grabbed her face and kissed her.

"What the hell?!" they heard an angry voice yell.

They quickly looked down the hall to see an angry Marla with her purse in one hand and holding the handle of her roll-on luggage in the other.

"Oh shit, Marla!"

"I knew it!"

"Marla, it's not what it looks like!" Melanie held up her hands.

Marla turned and rushed back down the hall.

"What the fuck is wrong with me? Marla, wait!" he tried to chase after her, but fell to the floor.

"Quinton! You're not in the shape to be chasing anybody. I'll go get her."

Taaz opened his door and came out of his room.

"What the hell is going on? A brother can't even

go off and take a shit, man!" He saw Melanie at Quinton's door, Quinton on the floor, and Marla turning the corner. "Marla? No."

Melanie heard the elevator bell ding. Taaz frowned at her as she spoke, "Taaz make sure Quinton gets to bed. I have to find Marla." She handed him the keycard.

"Fix this shit, Mel."

"I will. Trust me," she rushed down the hall. He shook his head.

"I gotta get to her." Quinton scrambled to get up.

"No man," Taaz helped him up, opened the door, and struggled to push him in his room.

"She came, man...she actually came. How could I be so stupid?" Quinton collapsed on his bed and sobbed, "I lost Ma. I can't lose her too, Taaz. I can't..."

"Ah, I'm here for you, man, but you're drunk as fuck right now. I've been drinking pretty heavy my damn self, but Marla ain't gon' listen to you till you sober up. Okay?"

"I don't wanna be alone, man. Marla's all I got."

"You got us, man...you got ya boys, and we ain't going nowhere. You hear me?"

"Yeah."

"We ain't going nowhere," Taaz repeated as he sat with Quinton.

Melanie ran out of the hotel sliding doors as Marla jumped into a taxi held by a family preparing to leave. The family looked confused.

"Excuse me. I'm sorry," she squeezed past them, trying not to knock over their luggage.

She was surprised to see Kecia and Winston in the

parking lot. He was helping Kecia walk to the car as she sipped a huge cup of water. The cup read, *Life's a Beach.*

"Kecia!" Melanie called, "I'm glad to see that you're okay. I need your help."

"Well, it can wait because Winston and I are making a quick run."

"Is this his rental?"

"Yes," he said.

"Can you please drive me to the airport?"

"Bitch, you better call an Uber."

"Kecia, it's a matter of life and death. I have to talk to Marla."

Kecia smirked, "What did you do now?"

"I'll explain in the car, please?"

"I didn't say yes," Kecia said, "So you will explain now."

"Marla saw Quinton kiss me, but he was drunk, and I was only trying to help him to his room. I want to clear the air before she flies back."

"Well, I'm pretty sure she can't just hop on the next flight."

"Well, do you want poor little Marla stuck at the airport for God knows how long?"

"If that's where she's going," Kecia mumbled under her breath.

"We'll take you," Winston said.

Kecia glared at him, and he glared back.

"Thank you."

Winston helped Kecia into the car and closed her door. Then, they rushed to find Marla.

CHAPTER 42

Unaware of what had transpired between her friends, Gia leaned against the railed walkway with a bonfire in the distance. She saw Julian walking up.

She sighed. "You never listen, do you?"

He shook his head and bit his bottom lip.

"You're out here all by yourself?"

"Yep," she sighed, "The girls and I were supposed to have our bonfire tonight."

"Oh, recreating the scene from *Waiting to Exhale?*"

"I guess so."

"And let me guess, you're Angela Bassett."

She snickered, "Why cuz it looks like I'll burn some shit up?"

"Well, that's stating the obvious."

"Whatever. Based on my experience with men, I'm more like Lela Rochon's character, Robin."

"So where are they?"

"Well, you know Whitney's gone on, and Loretta Div-"

"Not them," he said, "Your friends."

"Oh, Melanie's around here somewhere. Why aren't you with her?"

"I haven't seen her since we left the hospital nor do I care to see her."

She pursed her lips.

"In the past, I would have stolen Melanie's man or tried to make someone else take him. Now, stuff like that seems so immature to me. I'm just done with the games... with her and these no good men."

"You'll see soon enough that I am one of the good ones."

She pursed her lips again.

"So where's Laila and Kecia?"

"Laila is probably with Alonzo, and Kecia's had her head stuck so far up Winston's ass since he touched down."

"Well, do you blame her considering the circumstances?"

"I guess. Her pregnant ass is supposed to be resting, but knowing her, she's not," she sighed, "I was just looking forward to some quality girl time. Lately, I've been so busy with my business. And now, Laila is going to be the first one out of the group to get married." She started rambling. "Since the engagement, it just hasn't been the same, and I don't think it will be. I have a big family true enough, but what I have with my girls is different. I have five brothers, so Laila and Kecia have been like sisters to me...No, they *are* my sisters. And Melanie, she's like the wicked step-sister that don't nobody like."

He shook his head.

"You're afraid of losing them, aren't you?"

She sighed, "Yeah. When Kecia was with her ex, Leonard, she would be all under him. But, whenever they weren't together, she was with us. Then, she got with Taaz, and we would hang out together, play cards, barbeque, and go out. Now that she's with Winston, I barely see her... And I know I have my own thing going as well, but pretty soon my shop will be complete, and I'll just have an empty apartment to come home too. Everybody keeps telling me to get a house...damn a house. It's just me right now. My sleeping space is all I need at this point in my life."

"That's not really a home if all you see is a sleeping space."

"My shop is my home. My parent's house is my home. Hell, even Laila's house is my home."

She walked down to the bonfire, and he followed.

"I understand where you are coming from, but you've got to understand that change is a part of life. Change can be good. You lose friends. You make new friends. You lose love. You find love. You can't let it get you down. You just have to roll with the punches and embrace it."

Gia sighed again.

"So you're just going to sit out here by yourself."

"Looks that way."

She straightened out her towel, picked up her blanket, and placed it on her legs.

"Aw, there's no fun in that. You mind if I join you?"

She shrugged. "Why even ask at this point? You're just going to sit your happy ass down anyway."

"You know me too well."

She rolled her eyes. Then, she blew her breath as she admired her surroundings.

"Uh, it's so beautiful out here. Beautiful stars, waves crashing, cool breeze...this fine white sand," She picked up a pile of sand and let it fall through her fingers. "I can't even tell you the last time I've been anywhere."

"I've been the same way lately. I've just kind of gotten used to coming home from work, having dinner, working on one of my cars, watching a game or sports highlights, and then going to bed."

She took a deep breath and closed her eyes.

"Gonna make a conscientious decision to start doing more of this…enjoying life."

"Me too."

She opened her eyes to find him staring at her.

"What?"

"Gia, you are such a beautiful woman."

She chuckled, "And you're a fine ass man. I mean really…you're giving Alonzo a run for his money."

He shook his head. "Was that a compliment coming from you?"

"Yup, but you just had to be with Melanie."

"I told you-"

"Bullshit," she said calmly.

His eyes darted around trying to figure out his next move.

"Well, who am I with right now?"

"You're really gonna pull that line?"

"Gia, you seriously don't see how far my head is up *your* ass? She can come out here right now, and I'll still be right in this spot."

She smirked, looked past him and said, "Hey Melanie!"

He quickly turned and looked.

She burst into laughter.

"See!"

"I just looked, but did I move out of this spot?"

"So you ain't scared, huh? Not even a little bit?"

"Scared of what?"

"What if I do this?" She leaned over and kissed him.

"You scared now?"

"I told you before...I ain't ever scared."

He started kissing her. She pulled off his shirt and ran her hands down his chest to his abdomen. She reached in his shorts and firmly grabbed his penis. He kissed her neck and shoulder. He pulled down her tank straps and sucked her breasts. She leaned back. He got on top of her, and they started making out.

She started panting and pushed him off her. "No, no. This isn't right...I can't."

"Gia. No...please."

"I just can't," she fixed her clothes and ran off. He saw two attendants watching.

"Get out of here!" He put on his shirt and sat at the bonfire with one hand to his head and the other resting in his lap.

CHAPTER 43

Melanie rushed into the airport to find Marla. She searched the bottom floor and the top floor. She looked in every line, but she could not spot Marla anywhere. She looked on the flight board and saw that a flight to Washington, D.C. was coming up. She walked across the airport once more and finally saw Marla coming out of the restroom.

"Marla!" she called. She rushed up to her. Marla turned around and frowned.

"Came to gloat?" Marla asked, "I should kill your ass."

Melanie was taken aback by her comment. "Um, no. I didn't come find you to gloat, and please don't kill me. It was just a huge misunderstanding."

"I know what I saw, and there's no way to explain yourself around it."

"Yes, there is."

"Get out of my face and go crawl back into his bed. I'm done talking to both of y'all asses."

"Marla, I don't want Quinton, and he doesn't want me."

She proceeded to walk away.

"Marla!" she called out, then she blurted aloud, "You've been making him miserable, and he thinks you're about to divorce him."

"Wait," she faced Melanie, "He told you that?"

"Yes...well, not in those exact words, and in the lobby, I may have eavesdropped without him knowing when you two were on the phone."

Marla continued to stare at her with a blank expression.

Melanie went on, "He's been dealing with the death of his mother, and all you've been doing is complaining and accusing him of cheating. He really needs you, and you keep shutting him out."

Marla closed her eyes.

"I know I'm overstepping, but what kind of woman does that to her husband when he's dealing with such a traumatic loss. You're worrying about a kiss? You should be glad that he is not trying to commit suicide."

Marla blew her breath.

Melanie continued, "What kind of wife adds to a man's suffering like this?"

"I just haven't been myself. Okay, bitch?"

"But what-"

"No. You don't get to judge me. Are you saying you would have been a better wife to him?"

"I know I wouldn't have. I didn't like Ms. Carol, remember? He would hate me."

"Obviously, he doesn't."

"He kissed me only because he's hurting, and he's been crying out. But all you've been doing is pushing him further away. I just don't understand that, as his wife, why you would—"

"Damn it, Melanie! I'm pregnant."

"You too?"

Marla frowned, "Who else is pregnant?"

"Kecia."

"Oh," Marla let out a sigh of relief.

"Does Quinton know?"

"No," she said, "I know I've been hell to put up with lately. It's hormones, and jealousy over you and Laila wouldn't go away. Quinton and I started out so wrong, and I thought if he got back up with y'all, he would change his mind about me…that he would leave me for one of y'all or someone else, and I'll be stuck raising this baby alone."

"You know Quinton would never do that," she paused, "to you."

"Hmm…I'm surprised you didn't get the bright idea to get pregnant to trap him into being with you."

"A baby? Ruining this body? Girl, please."

Marla shook her head.

"I'll admit it. I can be a little over the top at times and borderline *cray cray*, but I was going through some things…still am, but I will always hold my head high. And if I don't know anything else, I know you, Marla Gomillion-Harris, have always been confident in your love for Quinton…Because even in middle school, you knew without a doubt that Quinton was yours. And, you've proven that. He was my man one day, and you married him the next. I've never experienced anything like that. I was in disbelief. I just kept saying, 'this bitch married my man'."

"Yeah, I've called myself *cray cray* at times too for doing that. But honestly, it's been a wonderful two years with the exception of the loss of Ms. Carol and my mood swings."

"Well, let it continue to be great. I can assure that

you don't have to worry about me or Laila. That girl is so in love with Alonzo."

"You're telling me. I've never seen him act like that over one woman. I haven't even heard about other women, and you know Quinton tells me everything about his boys."

"Yes, Alonzo is a different man now, and I couldn't be happier for them. Like I am happy for you and Quinton. Now, are you going to come back to the hotel with me to talk to Quinton and celebrate with us?"

She sighed, "I guess."

"Here," Melanie held out her hand, "Let me help you with your bags."

"Melanie Tyler, carrying folks' bags? I have to write this down."

"You're not going to see this too often. Besides, I kissed your man, it's the least I could do," Melanie joked.

"Don't push it. I know I'm pregnant, but I can still kick your ass all up and through these terminals."

Melanie chuckled and shook her head.

"Woo, I'm tired. I tried to call Gia, but she wouldn't pick up."

"She's probably asleep. Quinton may be sleeping right now as well, so if you can't get in, you can stay in one of my rooms until he wakes up."

"I really don't want to be with him tonight," Marla said, "Wait, you've got two rooms?"

Melanie sighed, "It's a long story."

At the hotel, Melanie and Marla made their way to Melanie's room. She helped Marla get settled into her room. Then, she closed the door. With a tote on her right shoulder, she let out a sigh of relief.

"I think I need that drink after all," Melanie said aloud to herself.

"Melanie," a deep voice called.

She groaned. "What now?" She turned around to see Julian and rolled her eyes. "Oh, Julian," she gave him her tote, "I'm staying in your room tonight. Marla needed somewhere to crash until Quinton wakes up."

He ignored her statement. "Did you get my messages?"

"All twenty-eight."

Gia opened her door and peeped her head out, but the two did not see her.

"Melanie, I can't keep up this charade anymore."

"Look, I don't have time for this."

"Unless you want to be assed out tonight without a room, you will make time." She grabbed his arm and pulled him down the hall. They turned the corner and stood in front of the elevators. Gia propped her door slightly open, tiptoed down the hall, and stood at the corner to hear them talking.

"So you're willing to throw away this extremely lucrative deal for Gia?"

"There's something about her. I can't explain it. I just want you to tell her."

"You told her it was a sham?" she whispered.

"But she didn't believe me. You can keep the property. I just want you to tell her the truth."

"I will do no such thing."

"I like her, and I mean *really* like her."

"You don't even know her."

"I know enough."

"Enough to throw away your dream?"

"I don't care about all of that."

She sighed. "This is a complicated situation. Do you know how I would look if it came out that I held a property over your head to get you out here?"

"I'm not concerned with how it will make you look. You shouldn't even be concerned with what these people think. You can keep the property. I'm starting my business with or without your help. I don't have to be at that location. I can secure additional funding to pay for one of the higher priced properties. I've been talking with Quinton and Alonzo. They said they can help me with business planning. They are even considering investing as well. I should have enough money in my savings, so I don't need you or that property."

She frowned.

"You will tell her that I am just posing as your man because of our deal."

"So it's true," Gia came around the corner, "You bribed him," then looked at Julian, "and you played right along with her. You're worse than a cheater. You're just like her."

"Gia," Melanie started.

"I can expect behavior like this from you," then turned to him again, "But you? I thought you were different."

Melanie rolled her eyes.

"Melanie, yo' ass always has one scheme after the other, and Mr. Man of Integrity, you did all of this just to get a property? You'll lay down with dogs, do whatever it takes to get what you want…And you think I want to have a man like that? Well, let's be honest. You were only trying to fuck, but I have something I wanna say to the both of y'all…fuck you."

"As always, you're making a big deal out of nothing."

"Gia, just hear me out."

"No, save it. I don't want to hear anything you got to say," she said, "And Melanie I got half the mind to bust yo' ass out in front of everybody." She marched down the hall.

Melanie looked at Julian as she pressed the elevator button, "Welp, hope you're happy now."

CHAPTER 44

Kecia was lying in Winston's arms in bed as he sat leaning against the headboard. She was in between his legs, and his arms were wrapped around her.

"You just had to have some Sonic ice," he said as he brought his hand up and caressed her face.

"And you just had to jump in Melanie's drama."

"Well, I knew she needed us. Had we not helped, Quinton's wife would be spending the night at the airport."

"Yes, I guess. You have such a big heart...always down to help someone in need. And, I'm right there with you every time I look into those big puppy dog eyes. I can never say no when I look into them."

"Well, speaking of never saying no," he segued, "You give any thought to the question I popped? Because I've got you this time." He gently squeezed her. "There's no way you're falling out of this bed," he joked.

She smiled. "I have, but —"

"When you passed out, that was one of the scariest moments of my life, but I'm glad you and our baby are okay." His face lit up. "I know right now my proposal is probably the last thing on your mind…but that ordeal made me want to be with you even more than before I proposed, and I didn't think that was possible."

Kecia sighed.

"What is it?"

"Quinton…" she cringed, "Winston, I'm sorry."

"And you call me Quinton quite often. Is there something going on that I should know?" he joked.

"No, Winston. I've known Quinton since kindergarten."

"I'm just kidding, but I am serious about marrying you."

"I know, it's just—"

"I mean we have discussed it before. I thought it was something that you and I both wanted. I thought we were moving in that direction."

"We are… it's just that so much has been going on. I just have to think. I'll have a clear head once this wedding is over."

"Are you sure?"

"Yes."

"And you can give me a definite answer?"

"Yes."

"Because now we have our little one to think about."

"I know…we're going to be parents." She smiled, then sighed, "I spent all this time losing weight and bam… about to get right back fat again."

"Well, I saw all of your pictures, and you look sexy in every single one even with your hair in pigtails."

"Don't play."

He laughed. "We're going to be great parents, and I am going to do everything in my power to be the best husband and father a man can be."

"Husband? You're acting like I already said yes."

"You didn't say no." He wrapped his arms around her again and kissed her cheek.

CHAPTER 45

The next morning, Quinton took a shower and pulled on some gray lounge pants. Then, he hopped on the phone with Alonzo and explained what happened with Melanie and Marla.

"Yesterday was pretty rough. After all of that, I think we are going to just chill in our room today…but the big day is tomorrow! Are you ready?" He placed the call on speaker.

"You know it! Laila checked on Kecia, and she is doing good."

"Glad to hear that."

"Just let me know if you need anything."

"I will."

Quinton ended the call. He heard a knock and rushed over to open the door, and it was Marla. He had been waiting on her to finally talk to him. He took her bags and stepped back so she could enter the room. He put her belongings on the bench next to the TV and hugged her.

"Babe, I am truly sorry. Thank you for staying so we can talk it out. I hope we can work through this. Do you want to go out to eat?"

"No, I'm not up to going anywhere. After last night's incident, I don't want to risk running into anyone and pretending everything is ok between us. I just want to see everyone at the wedding."

"I completely understand. I'm just glad you're still here."

"Yeah, well your ass is still in the doghouse. And though I hate to admit it, I am partly to blame since I had been pushing you away."

"But do you still want to be with me?"

"You know I do, but-"

"Marla, I can assure you. I no longer have feelings for Melanie."

"Quinton, I know," Marla said, "I have been a bitch lately and considering all that has taken place, I shouldn't have been treating you that way. I know you have been going through a lot, and I should have been there instead of pushing you away and accusing you of cheating. You had nowhere else to turn. I'm just glad you didn't sleep with anyone, especially that bitch, or we'd really have some problems."

"I wouldn't do that, not to you and if I wasn't drunk and out of my mind, I wouldn't have kissed Melanie."

She sighed, "Well, you make sure you wash those nasty lips and don't be putting them on nobody else."

"Scrubbed three times this morning," he said, "I just don't understand why you didn't trust me after everything I've done in the past two years to show you that I'm all about you. I thought you were getting ready to divorce me, but I should have come to you like a man and asked you."

"That you should have done," she sighed, "But Quinton, I've been going through a few things as well."

They both sat on the foot of the bed.

"But I am your husband. You should have come to me."

"I know, I know," she said, "With the loss of Mama Carol, I just didn't want to put more on you."

"Marla, I can handle it. She raised me to be strong and to take care of my family. Don't ever feel like you can't share anything with me. We are here to work through everything together no matter what it is. So talk to me, what's going on?"

"Well, I've been waiting on the right time to tell you, but there has been nonstop drama here."

"Who you telling," he shook his head.

She was about to speak, but he received a knock on his door.

"Hold that thought."

Please don't be Melanie, he thought.

He opened the door, and it was Taaz.

"Here's your charger." He handed him the black cord. "Everything's good?"

"Yes."

They did a handshake and half-hug.

"Thanks for taking care of your boy."

"Always man."

Quinton closed the door and turned around.

"Is he okay?" She stood up.

"Yes, he'll be fine. I'm just glad you-" He paused and stared at Marla.

"What?"

He lit up.

"What?" she repeated.

"I don't know why I'm just now seeing it. My baby!"

"Quinton, what are you talking about?"

"You're pregnant!"

He rushed over to her, hugged her, got down on his knees and kissed her belly. He wrapped his arms around her and put his head to her belly.

"Our first child," then he quickly looked up, "Am I right? Cuz if you're just getting fat, I know you're about to beat my ass." He joked.

"Get up, boy," she said and he obeyed. "And yes, we're having a baby."

"Now it all makes sense," he held her hands, "How far along are we?"

"Well, before I say it, hear me out first," she sat on the side of the bed, and he sat next to her.

"Marla, what are you saying?"

"I'm saying I want to share something with you without you blowing a gasket or not allowing me to finish."

"Wait...it is mine, isn't it?"

She rolled her eyes. "Yes, of course, it's yours. I have not and will never cheat on you. But please let me explain everything without interruptions, okay?"

He looked at her strangely.

"Okay."

She took a deep breath.

"I'm thirteen weeks."

His eyes grew big. He lifted up her shirt and saw the bulge. His eyes grew even wider.

"You're that far along, and you didn't tell me. So is this why I haven't been able to touch you?"

"Quinton, you said you would let me finish."

He clenched his jaws, "Okay."

"I should have told you this before, and I don't know why I didn't. Maybe it was too painful for me to even talk about but-"

"But what? Come on Marla. Stop beating around the bush and just tell me what's going on because I'm not understanding why you've been hiding a pregnancy from me for almost three months."

"Quinton, please."

"And what's happened that painful for—"

"Quinton, if you don't let me finish, I swear!" Marla exclaimed.

"Okay, okay. You have the floor."

"Seriously this time?"

"Yes. Marla, I'm sorry for interrupting. Go ahead."

She took a deep breath.

"I've had two miscarriages in the past."

"Two?" he asked "With who?"

"My ex, Michael."

"Richmond?"

"Yes. Each time, I never made it pass the first trimester. We weren't really trying both times, but we were excited. And going through that twice was devastating. I began to think maybe I couldn't have kids. Even now, I'm scared, Quinton. I want us to have this baby, and I didn't tell you because I just wanted to make it past the first trimester. I kept thinking that maybe there's hope once I make it past the first, then I can tell you. Because you have already suffered a loss, and I didn't want to take you through yet another."

"So if you had a miscarriage, you wouldn't have told me? Or, you didn't think I would have been the one to rush you to the hospital, not knowing what's going on? Don't you think that would have been an even worse experience for me?"

"I know, I know, Quinton. I guess I was trying to

protect you."

"Marla, it's my job to protect you. It's my job to take on the load, to share happiness and pain with you. My job is to make it bearable or make it go away. Those were my stepchildren that you lost. They were a part of you, which means they are a part of me now."

Marla sniveled.

"And whatever happens with our first child, we can handle it together. But this time, we have Mama watching over us. No matter the outcome, I know she's looking out for our child. But, I have so much faith that this baby is going to live. I feel it."

Marla smiled. "Well, today, we're entering into the second trimester."

"Yes! You see? We're having this baby together."

"I've always wanted to have your children since we were kids. But right now, can we keep this news between us? I don't want the others going overboard."

"Yeah, we would have a house full of gifts next week," Quinton agreed.

"At least right now, they can give all their attention to Kecia."

"So no one else knows?"

"Well, Melanie does."

"What?"

"Don't worry. I took care of her. She is not going to tell a soul."

"I don't think I want to know what you did to silence her."

"You don't," she said as she cracked her knuckles.

He laughed, "Girl, you are something else, but I love you."

He hugged her, and she hit him.

"And I better not ever catch you putting your lips on anyone else because I'll kick your ass and hers."

"You have my word, babe."

CHAPTER 46

Later that night, Melanie sat alone at a table outside in the courtyard. She was staring at the pool. She thought of when she first took Julian to her hometown to show him her family's property.

"Melanie, this place is perfect!" Julian exclaimed.

"Thank you."

"And the asking price is a steal!"

"Yes, I know the owner. She is-"

"She?"

"Yes, women can own mechanic shops."

He smirked. "I know. I was just surprised."

"Well, actually it belonged to her brother, and he left it to her. She rented it to some Mexican guys for a while. Then, they built their own shop, and it has been vacant since. She hasn't thought of selling it, but I can convince her."

"At that price?"

"Yes," she said, "I was thinking you can pave this field and have your antique cars here on display. Then, in the front of the building, you can add on the offices and lobby. You'll have that huge shop and room in the back to put even more vehicles."

"Without preserving her brother's vision? I can have full control of the property? What's the catch?"

"A catch?"

"There's always a catch with you, Melanie. What is it?"

"Nothing."

"60/40 ownership? You get to be Creative Director? Sales Manager? Sell potpourri and handbags in the front office? What?"

"Well, there is one thing, but it's not what you think."

"What is it?"

"In order to secure this property at my guaranteed price, I need for you to pose as my boyfriend on a trip."

"Come again?"

"You heard me."

"You can't be serious right now."

"I am."

"We're discussing business right now, and you throw in childish games?"

"I think it's a very lucrative deal. You accompany me on an all-expense paid trip to Florida, participate in the festivities, and attend my friends' wedding as my significant other, and this place is all yours."

"What if the owner says no?"

"She is not going to say no."

"A trip and my own shop…and I get to pay 40% less than the other properties I visited?" he thought, "Welp, the quicker I do that, the quicker I can get away from you at our current job."

She smirked.

"So is it a deal?"

"Yes, on one condition."

"I think I've been pretty fair."

"I want my own room, or are you all staying at a beach house or condo?"

"Us together under one roof, are you crazy?" she cleared her throat, "I mean no, we're staying at a spacious hotel with rooms and suites."

"Well, my own room, and it's a deal."

"But we have to sleep together."

"That's sexual harassment."

"Ew, don't play with me. I'm not laying one finger on you."

"Well, I'm pretty sure you're going to want us to hug, kiss, and cuddle up in front of people."

"Yes."

"And to get those perks..."

"Perks? Don't flatter yourself."

"Get me my own room."

She rolled her eyes, "Okay."

"Is it that hard for you to find a man that you have to bribe one?"

She frowned. "I can have any man I want, but you're the only one that can foot the bill at this particular event."

"The measures some people take," he shook his head.

"I was planning on showing you this property anyway, but while we were here, the idea just came to me."

"Well, you could've just asked me."

"And you would've said yes?"

"Hell no. This is not the movies. I don't plot and scheme."

"Well, maybe you'll learn a thing or two from me."

"What the hell, Melanie?" Gia interrupted her thoughts. Melanie had dodged Gia the entire day. She ignored her calls and texts. She knew she wanted to discuss the Julian situation without him being around. Besides, it was rare for Gia to contact her.

Gia made her way to the table.

"I know. I can explain."

"Yeah, yeah, yeah…I know you didn't want to look stupid in front of Quinton, and you wanted to show Laila and Alonzo you weren't still salty over everything that went down." She plopped down across from Melanie.

"Well, that's basically it in a nutshell."

"But what I don't understand is how Julian, who's not your man or guy friend, got involved in all of this in the first place?"

"Well, you know how persuasive I can be." She took a deep breath. "He didn't want to be a part of it, but he's trying to get his business off the ground, and I-" Melanie paused as she didn't feel comfortable sharing his private plans with Gia, "I know of a property and a potential investor who would take an interest in his startup, so I did what I do best to get what I wanted out of the deal."

"Really?" Gia shook her head, "Humph…I guess being a ho didn't work."

"Hey, watch it."

"I'm just saying."

"I've never been a ho, but sex was never on the table because he is not into me like that. And, that still perplexes me. He's not into me at all, but he is very much into you."

Gia smirked.

"And I can tell you like him too," Melanie studied

her face, "You do, don't you?"

"No, the he—" Gia paused, "No, I don't."

"Any other time you would have jumped on that."

"Well, contrary to popular belief and all the shit I've talked in the past, I'm loyal. I'm loyal to Kecia, Laila…"

"And me?"

Gia rolled her eyes, and Melanie gleamed in delight.

"I mean I'll never want a dude y'all done had. I know I talked a lot of shit about Laila getting Quinton back when you had him, but I didn't think she would actually do it."

"Yeah, we've all done things we never thought we would do."

"Tell me about it," Gia mumbled under breath. "So you and Julian never messed around at all?"

"No."

"You for real?"

"I think if I were lying, the answer to your first question would have been yes."

"That's true."

"He's a nice guy who is caught up in one of my schemes."

"Hmm, I guess," Gia thought, "Welp, I got what I needed from you…but you need to cut all of that mess out. We are too grown for all those games you be playing. And, Quinton ain't nobody to be studdin'. If I were you, I would've walked up in this hotel by my damn self…with my pixie cut looking fine as hell…with all of Alonzo's college friends trying to get with me. That's how I would've stuck it to Q."

"Yes, that would have been a better idea."

"I'll give you credit. I am noticing a change in you,

and I'm liking this new you, but don't let the old you creep in and fuck shit up. Okay? Fight that shit, girl."

"Thanks, Gia," Melanie smiled.

"Aw, come here girl." Gia held out her arms. Melanie looked around, and Gia said, "Come on."

Then, they hugged.

"I know we've had our ups and downs, but I love your stuck up ass."

"I love you too, crazy girl."

"Now, you sit out here, look pretty, and be all approachable. You better show me about six, seven numbers in the morning." Gia walked towards the hotel door.

CHAPTER 47

Laila was lying in bed as Alonzo packed his bags and placed his belongings by the door. She stared at him and sighed. From dealing with Alexandra to visiting her mother to Kecia fainting at the rehearsal dinner and being rushed to the emergency room, Laila was exhausted. Her boss was her biological father. She couldn't see how she could go back to town and work for him after receiving such shocking news.

She had planned on working there at least five more years to save up some money. Alonzo had already moved most of his things into her house. They had planned on living there until they had enough money saved up to build their dream home, a home they would design together from top to bottom, complete with a well landscaped backyard with lights and koi ponds.

She sighed. *But now I may be out of work*, she thought. *I shouldn't be worrying about this right now.*

The only good news that Laila could look forward to was her impending nuptials and Kecia's baby on the way. She could be an aunt, something that once seemed impossible since she had no siblings.

Maybe I'll even be a godmother.

Laila noticed Alonzo had been staring at her while she was deep in thought. He knew exactly what was on her mind. He sat beside her on the bed and gently rubbed her arm.

"I know a lot has gone on, but with our lives and our friends' lives, this is kind of the new normal."

"But it's one thing after the other. I'm not sure if I can take anymore."

"Baby, I can assure you that our wedding day will be perfect, okay?"

She sighed.

"I have already spoken with the event coordinator and hotel security so they are going to keep Alexandra away from us. I even brought in reinforcements, okay?"

"I just want her to leave us alone."

"If she doesn't, I'll have to get a restraining order or have Gia to beat her ass," he joked.

"Please don't say that. You already know she will."

"Indeed she will."

They heard a knock on the door.

He opened it, and it was his cousins.

"Come on...time to go. You're staying with us," Duke said as they entered.

"Following wedding tradition, how cute," Laila said.

They grabbed his luggage and his garment bag and carried them outside the door.

"But I want to spend the night with you. Forget tradition and any superstition," Alonzo pouted.

"Nope...nope. You are leaving with us right now," Duke said.

Laila laughed.

"But I could spend the night with her," Damien raised his brows.

Alonzo pushed him away. "Boy, get yo' mannish end outta here. You ain't too old for me to pull out my belt."

They laughed as Alonzo followed them out of the door.

He peeped back in the room, "And I'll see you coming down the aisle tomorrow," they kissed.

"Aww, that's enough," Damien pulled his arm.

"Break it up...break it up," Duke said at the same time.

Laila and Alonzo stared at each other as his cousins pulled him away.

Julian received a knock on his door.

He pulled the door open. "Gia." A pleasantly surprised look appeared on his face.

"You know what? You're a fucking asshole."

"An asshole, huh? And you came to my room at 11:23pm just to tell me that?" He bit his bottom lip.

"See your sarcastic, egotistical, arrogant ass gets on my damn nerves," she pushed past him.

He closed his door, and they turned to each other. "Well, at least you've stopped giving me the silent treatment."

"Oh, I'm about to give your no good ass a mouth full. I just don't understand why you would agree to play games with Melanie and pose as someone you're not. That's one thing I can't stand is a fake ass-"

"But I've been nothing but honest with you about everything except that one thing. And then, as I kept trying to get to know you, I came clean."

"Yeah, when you thought you could use that to get

in my panties."

"Gia, you're a beautiful woman, but as I have stressed a thousand times already, I was only trying to get to know you. All I really cared about was getting into your mind."

"Boy please, ain't nobody thinking about you."

He came closer and stood tall.

"This grown ass man begs to differ," Julian said, "If you weren't interested or didn't feel a connection, you wouldn't even come near me. So ponder me this, why are you really in my room right now?"

"Uhh, to let you know that I don't like you. And, I'll be glad when this wedding is over with, so I don't have to ever see your smug little face again."

"Oh really? So basically you *do* like me," Julian said, "But if I'm wrong, please show me otherwise, and I'll be out of your hair forever."

"Uh, uh. I see what you're trying to do. It's not going to work."

"Come on. I'm ready. Throw shots at me. I can take whatever you dish out."

"Oh, I'ma dish it out. I can't wait till your ass is on the first thang smokin' to wherever it is you came from. Because I can't stand you with your slick bald head and big muscles...ol' pretty boy wannabe-"

He grabbed her and kissed her. She looked surprised.

"Damn," she said in almost a whisper.

"Don't stop now, that's turning me on."

"Naw, your smug ass don't stop."

He kissed her again.

"Hey, I'm not a ho. I don't sleep with guys I don't know."

"You know me."

"Well, guys I ain't been knowing that long."

"I feel like we know enough now." He kept kissing her, and she grabbed his penis. She licked her lips.

"Well, after the wedding, I won't ever see you again, and it would be a shame to let all this dick go to waste."

He bit his lip.

"On second thought, naw I'm good," she walked away, and he held her arms.

"Quit playing, girl," he pushed her against the door, held her arms on both sides of her, and kissed her.

"I hate your motherfucking ass." She kissed him hungrily.

"No, you don't," he pecked her lips. Then, the two passionately kissed again as they made their way to the center of the room.

She pushed him on the bed and got in his lap. They stared at each other with pure lust in their eyes. She felt him growing against her and quickly pulsate. She pulled off his shirt to reveal his firm pecks and perfectly chiseled abs.

"Fine ass motherfucker." She kissed him again and nibbled on his bottom lip. She pulled off her dress, revealing her naked body. "Get up."

"Coming to see me without any underwear on. You knew what you were doing."

"Didn't I say get up?" She tried to move, but he held her hips. She pushed his hands away. She got up and pulled off his boxers. "Where your condoms at?"

He pointed to a small black bag on the nightstand beside the bed. She reached in and pulled out one magnum. She tore it open with her mouth. She blew the gold corner piece out of her mouth. Instead of getting up, Julian inched to the head of the bed. She grabbed his dick and slid the condom over his shiny head. Licking her lips as she admired his length, thickness and perfect curve, she stroked him, then straddled him. She slowly slid down on it until he was completely inside of her.

"Ummm," she moaned as she rode him. She leaned on him and positioned her hands on either side of him. She kissed him as she moved her pelvis back and forth, side to side. She sat straight up and got in a squat positon. Then, she rested her hands on his chest and rode him harder and faster, bouncing up and down. They both began to moan loudly.

"Ahhh...Ahh." He eased her up slightly to the head, then moved her body down against his groin and up again, "Ah, Ah...Ahhhh." His right leg began to quiver as he came.

She hopped off of him and eased onto the side of the bed. He knew she was about to leave. He held her hand, "Naw, I'm not done with you."

"Looks like you're out for the count." She sat by him. He eased out of the bed and walked around to her side. He took off his hanging semen filled condom and tossed it in the trash. He picked up a large towel from the chair next to the bed and wiped himself.

"Lay down," he ordered.

"What?"

"Lay...down," he said firmly. She bit her lip to keep herself from smiling and followed his command. He got on top of her and held her arms to her side. He couldn't stop kissing her. He kissed her forehead, lips, and cheeks. He softly blew in her ear and nibbled her lobe. He eased down, placing her breasts in his mouth, paying close attention to her chocolate nipples. He kissed her flat abdomen and teased her navel with his tongue. He slowly kissed her creases and thighs. Then, he stretched her legs wide and admired her bare skin. He nuzzled his face between her legs, kissed her folds, and parted her lips as he slid two fingers in her. He licked her clit, taking his time to savor every bit of her delicate bulb.

For what seemed like an eternity, he devoured her until she grabbed his head, grinded against his mouth, arched her back, growled, and squirted all over his face. She was pleasantly surprised as she wasn't expecting Julian to bring her to such a satisfying climax. Many guys had tried and failed over the years, but Julian delivered.

Damn, he did that, she thought. She grabbed him and drove her tongue in his mouth. He felt around his night stand, grabbed another condom, ripped it open and placed it on his dick as they were still kissing. He slid right in and sexed her as hard as he could.

"What the hell? I'm about to nut again?" He pulled out. Gia pursed her lips as if she was pleased with herself. She hopped up. "What are you doing?"

She slipped on her dress.

"Nuh uh."

"Hold on," she said in a low tone. She switched her hips as she walked towards the balcony and slid back the glass door. A cool breeze hit her as she stepped onto the balcony, and she heard the calming sounds of the ocean waves crashing.

I don't want nobody seeing what I got, she thought. She looked around to see if she could spot anyone, but couldn't see much. Facing Julian, she leaned against the balcony barrier. She seductively pulled up one side of her dress revealing her thighs. She raised her index finger, motioning for him to come hither. He raised his brows and licked his lips. As he stroked himself, he headed over to her.

"You're bad as fuck," he said as he whisked her up and held her against him.

Uh huh. I got that ass cussing now, Gia thought as she bit her bottom lip. She wrapped her legs around his waist and her arms around his neck. After more endless kisses, he slid into her, gripped her bottom, and bounced her on his dick.

She moaned, "Fuck!"

A cool breeze brushed them. She jumped down off him, turned around, and bent over. He traced kisses from the top to the small of her back, then eagerly slid back inside her. He firmly gripped her as he glided in and out.

She rested her hands on the concrete barrier. "Uh, I like that shit…Harder." Julian did just as she said. All of a sudden, they heard voices. A man and a woman stepped onto the balcony next to them, but the concrete column blocked them from seeing one another. The couple were talking and laughing about what had just taken place at dinner. Gia and Julian tried to be quiet as he continued to powerfully thrust in and out, but Gia soon let out a loud moan.

"What was that?" they heard the woman say.

The two tried to keep from laughing aloud and rushed back into the room. As Julian slid the door closed, Gia came up behind him. She gently grabbed his dick while licking and kissing him on his back. She held his hand, led him to his chair, and pushed him down. She noticed her blanket from the bonfire, folded neatly on the back of the chair. She pulled off her dress. She straddled him once more and rode him as hard as she could until they both peaked at the exact same moment.

If Gia never saw Julian again after this trip, she knew one thing for sure, his ass would certainly remember her.

CHAPTER 48

The next day, the ladies were getting ready for the wedding in the first floor bridal room. The room looked like a small living room with tan, pink, and green floral sofas and chairs, classic wooden dressers, two floor length mirrors, and a credenza against the wall. There was also a floral wall divider for the ladies to change clothes.

"Laila, you look so beautiful," Melanie said as Kecia and Gia straightened Laila's dress. They were dressed in their light blue sheath bridesmaid dresses.

"Thank you. Any sign of her?"

"No, Alonzo has hotel security on the job."

"I highly doubt a few banquet attendants are considered security," Gia said, and Kecia hit her. "What? I would be like, 'Bihh, that ain't my job! Bye.'"

Laila sighed. "I just want to look back at this day and have fond memories...you know...like my graduation. That's the last drama free occasion I've sent out invitations for."

"Don't worry," Melanie said.

"And Kecia, you sit and rest."

"I'm fine, Laila."

"Knock knock," they heard a voice say. The ladies looked to see Marla in the doorway. She wore a burgundy baby doll dress with black flats.

Laila's eyes brightened. "Marla, you came!"

Kecia and Melanie gave each other a look.

"Yes, I couldn't miss Alonzo's..." she paused, "...and your big day."

She slowly walked in.

"Well, this is a pleasant surprise."

"Yes, it is," Gia said, "I was wondering why you were blowing up my phone all last night." Gia hugged her.

"Uh...yeah to let you know I'm here," she lied, then glanced at the others, "Hi Kecia and Melanie."

They waved. Marla stood in front of Laila.

"You are certainly a beautiful bride."

"Aw thank you," Laila was surprised at her compliment. Marla awkwardly offered her arms, and they embraced one another.

"I just came in here to tell you that I am happy for you and Alonzo, and I apologize for how I've been behaving towards you. It was uncalled for, and it won't happen again," she said.

Laila didn't know how to respond. She was just glad that Marla was trying to make a genuine effort to get along with her.

Marla continued, "I am pretty sure in the years to come we are going to become the best of friends."

"If Alonzo and Quinton have anything to say about it, we certainly will," Laila smiled, "They'll make sure of it." Marla held her hand and patted it.

"And a quick word of advice...don't punish Alonzo for his past. As a wife, I'm learning that myself…look forward and give no thought to what's behind, okay?"

"Okay, that's excellent marital advice."

She smiled again, "Well, I am about to find a good seat towards the front so see you ladies out there."

"That was sweet," Melanie said. Gia and Laila looked at her strangely.

As Marla walked out, Laila brought her attention back to Kecia. "Are you staying hydrated?" she asked, but before Kecia could answer, she pointed towards the credenza full of drinks. "Gia, get her one of those Dasanis."

"I told you I'm fine."

Gia ignored Kecia and handed her a bottle.

"This is your day. The attention should be on you," she said, untwisting the cap.

"No, our attention is on you right now."

"And our baby," Gia added.

"So come on…drink."

Kecia grumbled and took a swig of water. "Y'all gon' have me racing down the aisle to piss."

"Just exit stage right, and you'll be fine," Melanie said.

"But I'm feeling okay now, and I hate that you canceled our performance."

"It was for the best. You can sing to us on our one-year anniversary."

"Okay, sounds like a plan," Kecia smiled, "Just look at you."

"Yep, our baby is all grown up," Gia said, all three of them started straightening her dress again. Her dress was beautiful and simple. A chiffon dress with thin straps, sweetheart neckline, ruching, and flared out at the bottom. Melanie placed Laila's veil on her head.

"I'm just happy to have each of you here with me."

"Where's Aliza?" Melanie looked around.

"She's down the hall with Alonzo's mom. She wanted to get a photo of Ms. Alice helping with his tie."

"Aw, how precious," Melanie beamed.

"She has the ring?" Kecia asked.

"Yes."

"Now take a deep breath," Melanie said, "You are going to do just fine, okay?"

Laila obeyed, "Okay."

"So here's your something borrowed," Melanie said as she placed a pearl clip in Laila's hair.

"And your something blue," Kecia said. She handed her a bouquet with blue satin ribbon covering the stems.

"And the new new," Gia said as she placed a diamond bracelet around her wrist and clasped it.

"They are all so beautiful. Thanks ladies."

"Selfie time," Gia said as she pulled out her phone. They all posed for the pic.

"One more," they all stuck out their tongues and made goofy faces. "Are you ready to become Alonzo's wife?"

Laila exhaled hard. "Yes, I am."

Soon, everyone was seated outside in rows of white folding chairs in a beautifully decorated grassy area. There was a white runner down the aisle with fuchsia flower petals covering much of it. Fuchsia, light gray, sky blue and white were the colors of choice. Beautiful palm trees surrounded their selected wedding spot. The bridesmaids walked down the aisle and were escorted to the proper spot by their perspective groomsman. The guys wore gray tuxedos with white button down shirts, sky blue ties, and fuchsia pocket handkerchiefs. Alonzo wore a custom gray tuxedo with a light blue lapel and bow tie. He looked dapper as always.

As Laila appeared down the aisle, everyone stood. Gia stared at Alonzo, then nudged Kecia. "Look at him trying to be hard," Gia said.

One tear fell from Alonzo's right eye. He quickly rubbed it.

Kecia and Gia said, "Umm huh."

"Shh…that's so sweet," Melanie said.

Aliza came down the aisle. Laila's heart kept racing.

Laila, calm down. Focus on Alonzo…look at him. He is just so imperfectly perfect for me. I just want us to work. We have come so far. I've imagined this day all my life. Becoming a wife with my girls by my side.

She looked at Quinton, smiled at him, then looked back at Alonzo.

All of my family are here, and I wouldn't trade either of them for anything in the world.

As Laila asked beforehand, Alonzo stood in place until she reached the arch. She saw the breathtaking backdrop of the ocean and felt calm.

Throughout the wedding ceremony, Kecia kept her eyes on Laila and Alonzo, but noticed Taaz staring at her. She searched the crowd, spotted Winston, and smiled at him.

I love you, Winston mouthed to her.

She mouthed, *I love you too.*

Taaz read her lips and followed her gaze. His jaws tensed as he shifted the weight in his legs. Then, he looked at Alonzo and Laila.

"Does anyone here have just cause as to why these two should not be married? Speak now or forever hold your peace."

Laila's heart began to flutter so intensely that she could fill it in her throat. Her hands were shaking, and Alonzo held them tightly. "Everything is fine." He softly assured her.

They looked into the crowd, then back at the preacher.

"Well, then..."

"I have something to say." A familiar voice called out.

Alonzo and Laila quickly turned their heads to discover a woman standing, wearing a plunging neckline black dress, purple scarf over her head, and mirror shades. She took her shades off.

"Alexandra."

She squeezed past the people on her row.

"Alonzo, you're supposed to be with me."

"How did she get in?" Aliza asked the bridesmaids. They shrugged.

"This bitch," Gia said, "She's just like the killer in a horror movie...won't stay dead for nothing."

Just like Laila's dream, Alonzo let go of her hands and walked slowly toward Alexandra. Laila was disappointed. Her face became red hot.

"That's it," Gia said to Melanie, "Hold my bouquet." She marched past Alonzo, down the aisle. The guys went after her, but she was too fast for them. When she reached Alexandra, she drew her fist back and punched her. Alexandra's head tilted to the side, and she rubbed her jaw. She pulled off her scarf and let it fall to the ground. Then, she swung her hand, slapped Gia, and grabbed her hair. Guests that were sitting near the center aisle scrambled away.

Gia pushed Alexandra into some chairs that collapsed. She immediately got up and rushed back at her.

"I swear black folks can't go nowhere without fighting. Damn," Taaz said.

Quinton and Taaz tried to pull Gia back. The other two groomsmen, Lawrence and Al pulled Alexandra back. The angry ladies both elbowed the guys and stomped their toes, broke away, and came at one another again. Laila looked on in disbelief. Winston quickly got up and held Kecia back, keeping her from going down the aisle.

Alonzo wedged himself between Gia and Alexandra.

"Gia, chill out," Alonzo said to her, then looked at his ex, "Damn, this is my wedding, Alexandra! You can't just show up and try to ruin my life...I do not want you anymore. I've moved on, Alley...damn, what is it going to take for you to leave us alone?"

"Maybe the answer is me." Everyone looked down the aisle past Alexandra, and it was Alonzo's ex-girlfriend, Gallena. She wore gray slacks and a black blouse. The crowd gasped.

Laila's eyes watered. Her worst fears had come true. Alonzo's past was catching up to him at their wedding, and they all wanted him. She shook her head, then rushed to her left and hurried into the building. Melanie followed her.

Kecia brushed Winston off, "I'm fine." She rushed down the aisle and stood next to Gia.

Alexandra looked back at Gallena. "You want some of this too? Get in line."

"Alexandra, this has to stop."

"Looks like it won't. You have me and even Gallena here fighting for you."

"I'm not here for Alonzo. I'm here for you," Gallena said.

She turned around and looked at Gallena.

"Alexandra, I should have never fought my feelings for you."

Everyone that had attended high school with them said, "Huh?"

"Well, you did."

"I should have went on the road with you that last time, but I was scared, and I left you alone. I don't blame you for coming here trying to mess up what Alonzo's got going with lil' quiet bushy haired Laila. I didn't give you much of a choice. But, who would have known that Alonzo would bring me and you together...a girl I couldn't stand, hated, and fought day in and day out."

Gia said, "Hold up! I'm confused. After all of this, the bitch is gay?"

"Bi maybe."

A mischievous grin appeared across Gia's face. "Ooo...wait till I tell Jaquan and Shantavious."

"She sholl did give them a hard time in high school."

"I should put that bitch in a chokehold now that she ain't looking."

Kecia held her arm.

"Now, how did Gallena know where to find us?" Quinton asked Alonzo.

"Don't worry I called her."

"You what?" Taaz and Quinton asked. Quinton gazed over at Marla, who remained seated in the front. She shook her head. She mouthed, *I'm sorry,* for saying that she hoped Alexandra and Gallena would show up. She moved her hand across her lips as if she was going to keep her lips sealed from now on.

"Don't worry, it's handled," Alonzo assured his confused friends.

Alexandra's voice softened. "Gallena, I don't understand. Why are you really here?"

"Well, Alonzo told me to come and get my girl, and that's exactly what I'm doing."

"What are you saying?"

"I'm saying I want to make us work," she said, "The whole nine yards this time."

"I –I…"

She came closer and held Alexandra's hands. "Don't tell me you'd prefer Alonzo over me when you've spent many nights with me, not even thinking about him. I got him all the way out of your mind. I was the one visiting you, and you would come home to be with me, not Alonzo."

"Damn, Alonzo. She's just shredding the fuck out of your manhood," Gia said. She could feel Julian's eyes on her, but she never looked his way.

Taaz bit his lip and stared at the two ladies. "I need them to reenact exactly how she got you out of her mind."

Alexandra closed her eyes.

"So who do you really want Alonzo or me?"

"I want A-"

"Aw damn," Alonzo said in disappointment.

"You… you Gallena. It's always been you."

She grabbed Gallena's waist, pulled her close, and

kissed her. Taaz started clapping, and everyone looked at him.

Quinton's mouth dropped. "I so was not expecting that," he said.

"Damn, this just made me a happy man," Taaz said snapping shots with his phone, "I sholl needed this."

Alonzo nodded to Security, and two security guards came up the aisle. Each guy grabbed Alexandra's arm and pulled her away from Gallena's embrace. "I apologize. We were on the lookout, but she got past us."

"Alonzo, I'm sorry. Tell Laila that I apologize," Alexandra called out as they dragged her away.

"Are you sure you want to deal with all of that crazy again?" Alonzo came up to Gallena and hugged her.

"I wouldn't have it any other way," she responded, "You deserve to be happy, and Laila is your happiness."

He hugged her again.

"I'm happy you came. I really didn't want to get the law involved."

"Right, glad you didn't."

"Well, you got your hands full with that one."

"Trust me. I know exactly how to handle her," Gallena said. Alonzo raised his brows and smiled.

"Aw shoot, can I see?" Taaz asked.

She looked around and recognized a few faces.

"Hey Taaz, Chuck, Quinton, Gia, Kecia. Wish I could have gotten here earlier to prevent all of this, but she is out of your hair now. See y'all at our next reunion."

She walked away.

Alonzo looked towards the front. "Oh no, where's Laila?" He rushed down the aisle.

"Damn, she probably thought all of Alonzo's women were trying to break up the wedding," Gia said to Kecia.

"Yeah, maybe that's it, and not you going all Floyd Mayweather in the middle of the aisle," Kecia smirked.

CHAPTER 49

Kecia and Gia rushed and followed Alonzo into the building to find Laila uncontrollably crying and hyperventilating with Melanie consoling her in the banquet prep room.

"Everything is going to be okay," Melanie said as she fanned her.

Alonzo walked up to them. "Baby, I handled the situation."

"You call that handling it?" Melanie shook her head.

Alonzo continued talking to Laila. "We can finish the ceremony. They are both gone."

He tried to touch her, but she stepped back. "What? No! I can't go back out there. The whole moment has been ruined. I don't want to look back and think on my wedding and picture Alexandra and Gallena standing down that aisle."

"What are you saying? You don't want to marry me?"

"Is this going to be our lives? Huh?"

"Laila, no," he took a deep breath, "Trust me. I promise it won't be. You don't have to—"

"No! As your wife, am I going to have to

constantly fend off women to convince them that you're mine?"

"You have to listen to me. Alexandra was just con—"

She interrupted, "Because if that's the case, I want no part of it."

He kept trying to talk.

"No, you don't hear me. I don't want any part of this. I'm done."

"Laila, I'm not letting you go," he attempted to grab her.

"Take your hands off of me," she jerked away.

"Laila—"

"Let her go, Alonzo," Melanie said.

"Come on, man," Quinton said. He pulled his hands away from Laila. She marched off, and the girls followed.

"Just let her cool off. Okay? Everything's going to be fine."

Alonzo walked around the room and paced with his hands cupping the back of his head. Winston entered and followed Kecia.

"Kecia," he called.

Melanie turned around and stopped Kecia and Gia. Winston came up and put his hand around Kecia's waist. Melanie looked around the room.

"I'll see about Laila. Winston, you make sure Kecia gets some rest. Quinton and Alonzo, take a breather, and Gia, you go man the crowd," Melanie ordered.

"Why I always gotta man the crowd?" Gia pouted.

"Cuz you been don' attacked they asses," Taaz joked.

"Shut up boy," she said and grabbed his tie, "You're coming with me." They left out of the side door.

Alonzo was still in a daze. His mom came through with his sister behind him.

"Boy, what the hell is wrong with you?"

"Mom, I know what you're going to say. I had nothing to do with this."

"You're sure?" Aliza asked.

His mother placed her hand on her hip. "For that girl to go through all this trouble, you had to have been giving her something. If not you, then your little peeter weeter, some hope, or something."

"I hadn't seen her in years, then she popped up here. Ma, you remember how crazy she was."

"Both of 'em," Aliza added.

Alice glared at him. "Well, I just made sure that security hauled them *both* out of this hotel. And now, you better fix this." Alice and Aliza both walked down the hall towards the hotel lobby.

Quinton walked over to Alonzo as Taaz reentered.

"So you actually invited Gallena?"

Alonzo didn't respond.

Taaz shook his head. "Boy, you wild!"

Quinton asked Alonzo, "And, you didn't foresee any of this happening?"

"I didn't foresee my wildest dreams coming true," Taaz grinned.

Quinton was curious. "Yeah, how did that happen? They hated each other."

Alonzo sighed and finally spoke. "It's a long story, but somehow the girls squashed their feud. We all started messing around, and eventually they left me out."

"Are you serious?" Taaz asked, "How you not gon' tell us that, man?!"

"You might not want to tell Laila about that part of your past."

"Pretty sure she has an idea."

Taaz asked, "Let me make sure I heard you right, Lonzo. So the three of you fu-"

Alonzo let out a frustrated groan. "Yes!"

"My ni—"

"Taaz, this is not the time, man," Quinton said.

Alonzo finally addressed Quinton's original question. "Since Alexandra wasn't letting off, I thought of the one person who could put her in her place. The one person that Alexandra was feeling just about as much as me, maybe even more."

Taaz sat in a chair. "Man, out of all the ways this day could have gone…"

"I sure as hell wasn't expecting this," Quinton finished.

"Man, forget them. I just want Laila. She's supposed to be my wife right now, and my past fucked me."

He walked out.

CHAPTER 50

Later that evening, Kecia and Winston were in their hotel room. Kecia rubbed her feet as Winston paced the room. Her bridesmaid dress was laying across a chair. She had on a blue robe, and he was still wearing his white button down shirt and black dress pants.

"What kind of spectacle was that out there today?" He pointed towards the door.

"It's what I call a typical Saturday."

"So this happens regularly? This cannot be healthy."

"You'll get used to it."

"I mean it's like a hood movie or something," he shook his head, "I have worked too hard to build a life for myself and my family to be involved in some ghetto, *Love and Hip Hop* type drama."

"Well, don't get involved."

"Kecia, you're pregnant with our baby, and you were just taken to the emergency room. You don't need to be under any stress, especially of this magnitude."

She rolled her eyes.

"At first, I was all for helping out and being there for your friends, but since I have landed, there has been nothing but drama...one thing after another with person after person."

She glared at him. "And you are saying all of this to say what exactly?"

"I don't think you should be around them."

She stood up. "Wait a minute. Am I hearing this correctly? Are you telling me I need to let go of my friends?"

He sighed, "Don't you see what they're doing to you?"

"I've been around most of them for nearly three decades, and I am doing just fine. This doesn't even sound like you," she paced too. "You're going to say some bullshit like this after you've proposed to me."

"And because of your friends, you continue to put off giving me an answer."

She folded her arms and stood still. "If I gave you an answer right now, it sholl wouldn't be what you were hoping for."

"Kecia, then why have we been dating? I thought the whole point of it all was to get married and have children. We've gotten one part down so far...I just want you to be stress free during the pregnancy, and I want you to be my wife. Is that too much to ask?"

"Yes, if it's at the expense of my friends and family," she exhaled, "If you want to be my husband and not my baby daddy, then it's a package deal. You get me, my mom and dad, the whole family. You get Gia, Laila, Melanie, Alonzo, Quinton, Marla," she took a deep breath, "and Taaz...you get them all if you want to be with me."

He sighed.

"I'll let you think more on that during your flight home tomorrow."

"Wait, you're not coming with me?"

"No, I have to be here for my very much still single friend," Kecia's phone buzzed, and she picked it up from the nightstand. It was a message from Taaz. *Kecia, I need to talk to you.*

She put the phone down.

"Okay, I understand, and please forgive me for what I said. I guess it's just me being an overprotective dad already. This is all pretty new to me." He came close to her.

"Well, just remember the baby is in here," she pointed to her belly, then to her face, "not right here."

"Okay," he sighed. "I love you."

Kecia turned her face away. "Aw, you're still upset at what I said. Well, I am going to spend the rest of our lives making it up to you." He pulled her face to his and kissed her lips.

"Again, I haven't said yes yet."

"But you still haven't said no." He smiled. She shook her head. He kissed her again.

A while later, Quinton walked down the hall and found Alonzo sitting on the floor, with his back resting against Laila's door. He wasn't wearing his jacket and had untied his bowtie. He had an open bottle of wine next to him. Alonzo looked up to see him.

"Quinton, I tried everything to get in her room. She really isn't coming back down."

"Come with me." Quinton helped him up and pulled him to his feet. Alonzo draped his arm across

Quinton's shoulders. He looked sad and defeated. "We've had enough drama for today. She's had enough drama to last a lifetime. Let's get some sleep and approach this with fresh eyes in the morning, okay?"

"If I can't have Laila, I just want to go home."

"Okay, we'll get you there."

CHAPTER 51

The next morning, Kecia and Gia were walking together down the hall.

"Gia, how do we always end up in some mess?"

"Girl, we ain't living right," she replied, "I've been meaning to ask you. Did you ever accept Winston's proposal?"

"Not yet."

"Are you?"

"I don't know, Gia," Kecia said, "Can we worry about me later and focus on Laila?"

"Okay, okay," Gia said, "How do we know she's even still here?"

"You know that girl ain't gone nowhere. She has either cleaned the ice cream out of their lil' store downstairs or is guzzling some wine."

"With the air blasting and under the covers," they said simultaneously.

They knocked on her door.

"Laila," Gia called, "I know you're in there."

"Go away," they heard her say in a hoarse voice.

"I hope she's not in there sloppy drunk."

"Laila, open up," Kecia called, "It's Kecia and

Gia."

"If Kecia wasn't pregnant, we'd knocked this door down right now."

"Hmm...speak for yourself."

People passed by and looked at them.

"Laila, if you don't open the door. I'ma bust into these white people's room next door, go out on their balcony, climb on the ledge, and get on your damn balcony. I've been seeing that shit on TV for years, and I've always wanted to try it. Looks like now is the perfect time."

"You know she's crazy enough to do it," Kecia cosigned.

"Laila, either way I'ma get in your room. You hear me?"

Then, Gia started knocking on the next door, "Hey, can y'all let me in y'all room for a sec?" she knocked again, "Hey, I'm tryna see something real quick."

"Gia, wait," Kecia whispered. They heard the locks moving.

The door slowly opened and revealed Laila with her hair all over head and wearing a big charcoal gray t-shirt and pink shorts.

"Damn," they said.

"Y'all really stayed behind?"

"Yes, we didn't want you here by yourself."

"Yeah, this was supposed to be my honeymoon."

"And, we didn't want you to be alone so we stayed behind to have a girls' trip."

"Really? That's sweet of you. Where's Melanie?"

"Oh, she had to leave."

"That figures," Laila smirked.

"Yeah, we're going out to eat."

"Aw, I like your dresses," she admired their white sundresses. Gia's with purple flowers, and Kecia's with blue flowers.

"Oh, we got you one. We don't want you looking all raggedy with us."

Kecia hit her. Gia handed her the bag.

"That's so sweet of you girls."

"So you hop in the shower, and I'ma go in my room and get my tools."

"Okay," she made her way to the bathroom.

"Kecia, stay with her and make sure she doesn't run off."

Kecia rolled her eyes. "Get the makeup too. It looks like she's been crying all night."

As Gia styled her hair, Laila stared at herself in the mirror. "Can't I just stay here forever? I gotta deal with the whole 'my boss is my daddy' drama. Ew...what if I would have slept with his son, Brent, ew! But he is like a brother so I couldn't, but now he really is my brother. But then, what if my mother slept with a third man, and it's not even my boss that's my biological father. I would've made a whole scene for nothing, and I would be left finding the mystery man."

"Laila, breathe."

"We will figure all of that out when we get home."

"But then, I'm wondering if he's known all this time that I'm his biological child. If he knew, why didn't he bother to come to his own daughter's wedding? Cuz I gave him an invitation."

"I thought you said his wife was sick."

"Well then there's that. Maybe it was a good thing because they would have seen my ghetto fabulous wedding that didn't happen and worse...I would have to face him or maybe I would have marched down the aisle and slapped him for what he did or didn't know about his possible daughter."

"Laila."

"I know...I know. Breathe," Laila exhaled, "Can one day go right?"

Kecia sighed. "Well, I don't know about that. But today, it's our job to fill you with food and liquor and dance away all our troubles."

"Well, you make sure you stick to iced tea and drink plenty of water."

"And I'll take the long island iced tea," Gia added.

Kecia leaned over to Gia. "Sounded like you were taking some long ass *D* last night and the night before."

Gia's mouth dropped, and she smacked Kecia with her towel.

Laila lowered her shoulders. "Alonzo is probably angry with me that I left him high and dry."

"Yeah, girl."

"But we told you what went down."

"I know. The whole moment...my moment was ruined, but I didn't stop to realize that it was Alonzo's day that was also ruined," she scratched her face, "He really wasn't cheating on me or entertaining them, and I didn't believe him."

"Tried to tell you."

"Yeah, girl. I don't know how you gon' get him back."

Laila sighed. "He was outside my door all evening, pouring his heart out to me, and I didn't even bother to open the door or let him know that I believed it wasn't his fault."

Holding her curling wand, Gia paused, "Well, some of it was his fault."

"Yeah, he should have been more forceful in getting rid of her," Kecia said as she flipped through Laila's *Essence Magazine*.

"And end up in jail?" Gia asked, "Alexandra would have loved that shit. No wedding for sure then."

Laila folded her arms. "Well, he shouldn't have looked so good or ever turned on that charm or ever shared that nice juicy d—"

"Uhh Laila!"

"I'm sorry. What if I messed up us ever being together by running?"

"Laila, clear your mind and be still," Gia smacked her shoulder as she finished curling the last section of hair.

"Well, with all that alcohol that you're about to fill her up with, I'm pretty sure her mind will be all the way clear," Kecia put the magazine down on the bed and stood by Gia, "Now, move out the way so I can do her makeup."

They finished fixing her up, and she was beautiful in her white sundress with pink flowers and curls pinned up with a few hanging in the front.

"We're going to the Lighthouse restaurant. It's like a five to ten-minute walk along the shore."

"Ok, I guess...I have nothing better to do."

CHAPTER 52

Laila lagged behind her friends as they happily talked about their lives. She kept looking down at the sand and kicking it. Kecia and Gia abruptly stopped, and she ran into them. They stepped aside, and Laila noticed that a wedding was in progress. She admired the beautiful decorations and recognized some familiar faces. She peered down the aisle to see Alonzo standing there waiting for her. He wore a white linen button down shirt with the sleeves folded up his arm, blue suspenders, light blue pants, and white shoes. Laila noticed Aliza and Melanie get up from the back row. They were holding a bouquet in their hands and wore the same dresses as Kecia and Gia.

She was speechless as she looked at her friends who were smiling ear to ear.

"Your wedding awaits."

"And it's bitch free this time."

Laila's eyes grew wide. "You tricked me."

Gia folded her arms, "Am I good or what?

Melanie and Aliza approached her. Laila hugged Aliza.

"Sis, please say you'll marry my brother today."

"I—" she paused, "Melanie, you stayed!"

"Of course, I have to make sure my best girl gets the wedding of her dreams with this redo."

"Yes, yesterday was just a rehearsal," Aliza smiled.

"This is your big day today, that is if you still want to be with him."

"Want him? Of course I still want him"

Aliza gave Alonzo a thumbs up. Kecia and Gia took bouquets out of their totes and gave the bags to the attendant who was standing near them. The ladies walked down the aisle to their spots. Laila admired beautiful white draped sheer fabric on the center aisle chairs and pink, blue, orange, and purple flowers lining the white runner. Quinton and the groomsmen, wearing white and blue linens, stood proudly.

Looking for Love by Mult-y began to play as Laila made her way to the aisle. She smiled. She remembered battling with Alonzo over this song when they picked the playlist for the wedding. She did not want the song because it was a staple at all black weddings, and she wanted her playlist to be different, but Alonzo pushed for it. He really wanted her to walk down the aisle to that particular song. She made a deal with him that at their renewal ceremony, then he could have his song pick. *Well, it technically is our next ceremony.* She smiled to herself.

Alonzo walked to meet her just as he did at Quinton and Melanie's wedding rehearsal, but this time he did not stop at the first row. He continued past all of the guests and met Laila just past the last row. He held her hand and bowed with the other hand behind his back. He kissed her hand and presented her with a pink and white lily. He placed it in her hair. He had tears in his eyes. "You don't know how happy I am that you are with me."

They walked down the aisle, and Laila noticed that most of their guests were still there...the people who mattered the most.

Laila smiled as he led her to the pastor. They stood before him under a beautiful wooden pergola. Alonzo leaned over and whispered, "I am truly sorry for everything. I-"

Laila put her forefinger to his lips. "Shh..." She smiled as she gently held his chin and wiped a tear away. "I forgive you, and I apologize as well. I couldn't ask for a better man to spend the rest of my life with. I love you with every part of my being, and I know that you feel the same way, which means so much to me."

Tears continued to pour down his face as they turned to Pastor Douglas. Quinton handed Alonzo a handkerchief, he quickly wiped his face.

"Who gives this woman to be wedded to this man?"

Kecia, Gia, and Melanie stepped out of their line and said, "We do."

Everyone giggled. Alonzo held Laila's hand as she held the bouquet in the other.

"Well ok. Dearly beloved, we are gathered once again but now on this beautiful beach to witness and celebrate Alonzo Tyrell Davis and Laila MeAnn McKee uniting as one. Now, let me be honest. I almost didn't come back today, but God had planned otherwise. I had a dream of a great storm, and there were two palm trees standing side by side. As the water rushed onto the land, the winds came with great force. The palm trees began to lean. At one point, one palm lost sight of the other. When the storm calmed, the winds ceased and the water receded. Both palms were still there right next to one another. They were bent, but not broken. Even in the midst of the storm, they remained. And, the sun came out and together they arose standing tall once again. And, God showed me that you are those two palms so I want to say no matter what comes against you, get into God's Word and pray together. With God as your center, no man or woman can come between you two. You can make it through anything and do all things through Christ, who strengthens you both. Okay?"

"Okay."

"I apologize everyone. The Lord just laid that upon my heart to tell this young couple."

"That's alright," Gia said.

"Okay, Mother Gia," Kecia quietly picked at Gia.

"But marriage is a beautiful institution created by God and should never be taken into lightly."

Kecia looked up and noticed Taaz staring at her. She hid herself behind Gia to block his view of her.

"I'm almost afraid to say this again," the pastor joked, "but is there anyone here today that has just cause as to why this couple should not be united in holy matrimony? Speak now or forever hold your peace."

There was silence.

"Is there anyone here today?"

The whole crowd said, "No." Then, everyone laughed.

"Well okay, moving forward," Laila and Alonzo recited their vows and exchanged rings. "By the power vested in me, I am happy to finally pronounce you as man and wife. You may kiss your bride."

Alonzo cupped the back of Laila's head with one hand and held her chin with the other. They passionately kissed each other for a long time. Members of the crowd clapped, laughed, *ooed*, and blushed. *You and I* by Avant featuring KeKe Wyatt began to play.

As Alonzo picked Laila up and carried her down the aisle, she wrapped her arms around him. He planted a kiss on her as he walked.

Melanie, Kecia, and Gia grabbed and hugged one another.

"We finally got her down that aisle."

"Thank the Lord, chile."

"Bout ran my blood pressure up."

Then, Aliza met Quinton, Melanie met Taaz, Gia met Al, and Kecia met Lawrence.

Alonzo and Laila went straight onto the dance floor in the sand and shared their first dance as husband and wife.

CHAPTER 53

Later that night, Melanie, Kecia, and Gia met in the lobby.

"You both received Laila's message to meet her on the beach at 8:30?" Melanie asked.

"Yeah, we got her message."

"I thought she'd be laying up legs spread."

Kecia groaned. "Uh, what has Alonzo done now?"

"Man, they hadn't even been married a whole day yet." Gia shook her head.

Melanie took a deep breath. "Well, let's be prepared to put out whatever fire his ass has started up."

"His ass? Might be *her* ass."

They walked through the courtyard and down the white steps. They looked over to see Laila grinning at them by a bonfire. They all started smiling.

"Our bonfire!" Gia exclaimed as they walked over to her.

"Hi ladies."

"Why, Mrs. Davis." Melanie was impressed.

"What are you doing? Shouldn't you be on your

honeymoon?" Kecia asked.

"No, not until after I spend time with my girls," Laila poured wine in empty glasses and handed them to Gia and Melanie. She opened a smaller bottle, and poured the liquid into a glass for Kecia.

"You know any occasion with me is not complete without a glass of wine and grape juice for you, Kecia."

"Oh, how thoughtful," Kecia smirked.

"So much has happened, and all three of you have been with me every step of the way. I couldn't have made it through any of this without you. And, out of all the occurrences, we didn't get to do what we had originally planned. And for you to pull off this wonderful day as if you have been planning for months is amazing. I love you ladies so much, and I cannot wait to be right by your side on each of your wedding days."

"Girl, don't have us out here getting all teary eyed."

They hugged her. Then, they all sat around each other.

"Now all we need is some fireworks, and it'll be just like *Waiting to Exhale*."

"So what now?"

"Just enjoy one another's company and take in this peaceful night."

They sat in silence as they sipped. They looked restless as if they didn't know what to do now that there was no more drama. They look around and sighed. Then, Kecia interrupted the silence.

"Are we ever going to expose this bitch for bringing a fake boyfriend to the wedding?" Kecia asked.

Melanie's eyes grew wide, and she pursed her lips, then sneered at Kecia.

"Fake boyfriend?" Laila asked.

"See, I wasn't even gonna say anything to anybody," Gia held up her hands, "But Kecia."

Melanie gulped her glass of wine, grabbed Laila's bottle, and poured a full glass. All eyes were on her. "Yes, yes. Julian was never my man. We just work together, and I got him to pose as my boyfriend to save face. I hadn't seen Quinton since all of that drama went down with my failed wedding attempt, and I wanted to show him and everyone else that I'm doing perfectly fine without him—which I am by the way—but nothing says that and 'screw you' better than a fine man on my arms."

Laila drank. "I can't say that I'm surprised. It sounds like something you would do."

"I resent that," she said.

"Well, turns out he is actually Gia's man now. They were fucking for like five hours straight last night."

"Dang, Kecia, you just spilling all kinds of tea."

"Well, the whole floor could hear y'all. Surprised y'all didn't get no complaints."

"He sholl didn't get any complaints from me," Gia mumbled and took a sip, "But anyway he is not my man. I sent him on his merry little way."

"Well, Julian is hot," Melanie said, "So Gia, how was he? Was he your best?"

"Bitch, I ain't gon' tell you."

"Well bitch, it's not like I can steal him from you. He is definitely not interested in me."

"That's true, but anyway you can't steal what's not mine because I am not planning on seeing him anymore. So, don't plan any schemes for me and him to bump into each other, or I'll kick your ass."

"Whatever."

"Girl, Julian is sexy as hell. If you don't get with him, you are crazy," Laila said.

Melanie agreed. "Right, he's got the looks, the intellect, a great job, no kids, his own place..."

"And he loves putting up with yo' ass already," Kecia added.

"Yeah, what would you say?" Laila asked.

They said simultaneously, "Gurrrrl, you should get with that."

They burst out laughing as Gia smirked, trying not to smile.

"Don't use my words against me."

"I'm just saying, everybody needs somebody to lay up against at night," Laila mimicked Gia, "I know I finally got mine."

They laughed and clanged glasses.

"Well, I ain't ready for all that, which brings me back to Melanie. If you bring him anywhere near me when we get home, I'm for real about kicking yo' ass."

"Like you kicked Alexandra's ass?" Laila joked, "And thanks by the way."

"I can't believe she thought she was going to beat you after all the times you've fought."

"Right, the bitch won't roll over and admit defeat."

"But her and Gallena?" Laila asked, "I never saw that coming, and y'all said they were kissing?"

"Girl, those tongues were going at it," Kecia said.

"Taaz bout busted a nut looking at them," Gia said as she poured more wine in her glass.

They started laughing.

"'Bout like another time he busted—" Gia and Kecia glared at each other. Gia smirked, then drank her wine like she was sipping tea. Laila and Melanie weren't paying attention to them.

"Wait...Shantavious and Jaquan are going to have some words for her," Laila said.

"Right as much as she picked on them in high school for freely being themselves," Melanie said.

"Don't worry. I already texted them and sent pictures."

"So messy."

"It's all playing out on Facebook and in the comments on her YouTube channel."

"Wait a minute, the bitch has a YouTube channel?" Melanie asked.

"Yasss girl."

"Wow, but they all need to just let that old high school mess go."

Kecia smirked, "Have you let Quinton go?"

"Yes, I have."

"I heard Marla almost beat the yellow off your behind when she caught you two kissing," Gia said.

Laila's eyes grew wide, and she almost spit out her wine. "Wait, you kissed Quinton? How did I miss this?"

"In my defense, Quinton was drunk, and I was helping him back to his room. But, I got Marla to come back to him."

"No, you hitched a ride with me and my man to go get her from the airport."

"Lawd, y'all are taking me too fast," Laila said.

"Yes, but through Quinton's desperate alcohol infused kiss, I felt nothing, and I realized what I did in bringing Julian was not necessary. I don't have to prove anything to anyone or force anyone to be with me. I shouldn't want someone to regret they are not with me. It takes less energy to just move on, be my authentic self, and not care what anyone else is doing. Now, let me see Alexandra's YouTube comments."

They laughed as Gia handed her phone to Melanie.

Kecia smirked again. "So much for that."

"You're enjoying your grape juice?"

"I am," Kecia said. She knew they were going to eventually get to her proposal and cheating, so she tried to distract them with a toast. "Here's to Alonzo and Laila. May you have a lifetime of love, happiness, great sex, and no more drama."

They clanged glasses again.

"I'll drink to that," Laila said.

CHAPTER 54

The next day, Laila and Alonzo were standing outside seeing everyone off. They kissed Alice, and Alonzo closed her car door. They waved goodbye as Aliza drove off. Then, Marla and Quinton walked up to them. Marla smiled and hugged Alonzo. As she hugged Laila, the guys grinned at one another.

Marla spoke. "Congrats you two. Laila, you've got something on your hands with this one, but like me and this other one, you're going to love being married."

Laila smiled.

"I'ma let you in on a little secret. Those two are the ones that's really married, we're just the side chicks."

"What?" Alonzo asked.

"Hell naw," Quinton said.

The ladies laughed.

"We are definitely going to become the best of friends because there's no tearing these two apart."

"Exactly so see you at holiday gatherings, family functions, and all the other get-togethers."

"I'll have a seat saved for you right next to me cuz

you know Alonzo's always late for everything."

"Hey, I was on time for both my weddings."

Laila playfully hit his shoulder.

"That's because I didn't let you be late," Quinton said.

"Exactly."

Laila looked at Marla's belly, "Oh yeah, I guess congratulations are in order for you two as well."

"Yes," then Marla hit Quinton, "See I knew Alonzo was going to be the first one you told."

"Well, of course, our baby's godparents must know."

"See...you mess up everything," she said, "What if I wanted to surprise them with the news at the baby shower, gender reveal, the baby's christening, or something?"

"You know that ain't your style."

"Well, I am honored," Laila said, "Thank y'all!"

"Psst..." Alonzo said, "I better be the godfather."

"Yep, the closest you'll ever get to being Quinton's baby daddy."

"Get your girl, man." Alonzo said.

"I'ma just say it's hormones."

"Those out-of-control hormones."

"Yeah, I can't put her over my knee this time," Quinton said, gently squeezing Marla's arm. "Gotta wait a few months."

"I wish you would," she said, "See y'all."

Laila smiled. "Bye Marla."

Quinton helped Marla into the SUV.

"Gotta wait on Taaz, and then we'll be on our way."

"Okay." She smiled as he kissed her cheek.

As Quinton walked back towards the hotel, Kecia had just finished hugging Laila and was headed to her ride, which was waiting near the porte-cochère.

Laila and Alonzo began talking to Melanie. Taaz walked past them without a word. His phone buzzed, and he looked at the screen. It read, *Nyema Bae*. He pressed decline, then he placed his phone in his back pocket. Quinton called his name.

"Hold on for a minute," he said.

Taaz went directly to Kecia's ride and walked to the back, left side window where Kecia was sitting.

"Kecia." He tried to get in, but the doors were locked.

She let down the window.

"So you not gon' say bye to me?"

"Bye Taaz."

She looked over towards the hotel and saw Melanie hugging Laila and Alonzo.

"I've been thinking, and I really need to talk to you."

"Taaz, I'm going to be late for my flight. I can't."

"No, this can't wait."

"Not now, Taaz. I just can't with you right now."

"Kecia, look at me," he pleaded, but she stared at the back of her driver's head. Taaz blew his breath, "Kecia, is there any way that baby could be mine?"

"Driver, please go."

"Kecia."

"Driver!"

"No wait, Kecia!"

The driver pulled off, and he stared at the SUV.

"Q, is he alright?" Alonzo asked Quinton.

"Yeah, I got him," he replied, then called out to him. "Taaz, we gotta go, man."

Taaz slowly made his way to the SUV and got in. Their driver drove off.

Gia read her text from Kecia as she stepped outside. *Had to get away from Taaz…Be back to get you in a few.*

Gia began texting, *You do know we bout to all be sitting up at the airport and probably on the same flight if he coming home, right?*

She placed her phone in her tote and approached Laila and Alonzo.

Alonzo grinned. "First one in, last one out."

"Always have to save the best for last," Laila smiled.

"Our ol' ride or die boxing champ," Alonzo said as he started boxer shuffling.

"Umm huh," she smirked, then looked at Laila and held out her hand.

Laila was confused. "Gia, what are you doing?"

"I said I would shake the hand of the woman that got Alonzo's hoish ass to settle down."

"Really, G?" Alonzo shook his head.

"Well, I'm a woman of my word so…" She continued to offer her hand.

Laila rolled her eyes and shook her hand.

"You really got this fool to settle down. You did that shit, and you know what?"

Laila smirked, "What?"

"That makes you one of the baddest bitches to ever walk the face of this planet."

Alonzo examined her face. "Are you drunk?"

"Hey, I'm hung over from last night. Turns out I can't hang with those bougie bitches anymore."

Laila shrugged. "Well, I tried to warn you."

Kecia's ride pulled up under the porte-cochère.

The driver got out and placed Gia's luggage in the back.

"Well, you caught the bouquet. Now you're next," Alonzo said, "Then, I can shake your man's hand for good luck cuz he's gonna need it."

"Haha...very funny," she said, "Naw, Kecia's probably next whenever she finally says yes. It didn't work out the first two times I was engaged."

"The first two times?"

"Yes, two."

"Wait, when were you...we'll talk about this later."

"I'm gonna take my time before I get engaged again cuz I don't want to see a replay of this."

"Well, you know what they say," Alonzo licked his lips, "The third time's the charm." He grinned.

Gia glared at him. "Bye y'all."

"Bye Gia. Be safe."

The driver opened Gia's door, and she got in the SUV. Alonzo wrapped his arms around Laila and kissed her on her cheek as they watched the vehicle pull away.

"Ready for our next adventure, baby?"

"Yes, I am."

They kissed. He held her hand and led her back to the hotel.

ACKNOWLEDGEMENTS

First, I would like to thank God for His favor, for His love, and for who He is. I thank Him for blessing me with each of my talents. I trust Him to show me the purpose that He has for me, and I pray that I will fulfill it and make Him well pleased.

I would like to thank my sons, my mother, father, siblings and the rest of the family, including my church family as well as friends and colleagues. I truly appreciate your continued support. You have all made sacrifices for me and words cannot express how honored I am to have each of you in my life. Much love to you all.

Last but certainly not least, thank you for purchasing this book. I hope you enjoyed reading it just as much as I enjoyed writing it. I look forward to bringing you even more stories in the very near future.

Love,

Dominique

ABOUT THE AUTHOR

Dominique Lewis is a Mississippi author and copywriter. She has been writing stories, lyrics, and poems since she was 11. Now, it is her desire to release all that she has created throughout the years and help others to pursue their dreams. Ignoring many of the traditional rules of novel writing, Dominique stays true to her creative writing style, penning dialogue-driven stories with colorful dramatic characters and frequently switching scenes to make readers feel as if they are watching a movie!

She holds a bachelor's degree in Interdisciplinary Studies from Mississippi State University and an MBA from Belhaven University. She is the proud mother of two sons, Jayden and Triston. In her spare time, her interests are: singing, entertainment, traveling, dining, music, hair, and fashion.

Dominique is currently working on growing her media/publishing company, DNL Media and releasing more content and books like the children's book, *The Power Boyz* that she co-wrote with her sons.

"No matter what you do in life, be sure to place God first at all times, and He will lead you to where you should be."

Connect with me online!

Follow @luvdominiquenicole on Instagram or Like my page on Facebook to get the latest info on upcoming releases:

https://www.facebook.com/dominiquenicolelewis/